Maggie's Farm

Maggie's Farm

Larry Neitzert

Copyright © 2009 by Larry Neitzert.

ISBN: Hardcover   978-1-4415-4349-3
             Softcover   978-1-4415-4348-6

All rights reserved. No part of this book may be reproduced or transmitted in any form or by any means, electronic or mechanical, including photocopying, recording, or by any information storage and retrieval system, without permission in writing from the copyright owner.

This is a work of fiction. Names, characters, places and incidents either are the product of the author's imagination or are used fictitiously, and any resemblance to any actual persons, living or dead, events, or locales is entirely coincidental.

This book was printed in the United States of America.

To order additional copies of this book, contact:
Xlibris Corporation
1-888-795-4274
www.Xlibris.com
Orders@Xlibris.com

Dedicated to Chester and Ruth Neitzert. They taught integrity, pride, and work—not with words, but with the lives they led. The things I do well, I do because of their example and love.

"I ain't gonna work on Maggie's farm no more."

From *Maggie's Farm*—copyright 1965—Bob Dylan

PREFACE

The beginning of a first novel is an act of courage, adventure—and foolishness. This foolishness would not have been completed without the encouragement of many friends and acquaintances.

Colleagues and friends have consistently urged me onward when I sheepishly confided—"I'm writing a novel." Each in their own way heartened me, instead of greeting me with the expected snicker or disinterest. There are too many to say thank you to—so I extend a blanket gratitude to all who prodded and encouraged.

There are three individuals that I must mention. First is Rosanne Fifarek, a teaching colleague. It was she who I first sent the first four chapters and confided my dream. Her response of "Larry you should proceed with the greatest of haste," and her later reading of the finished manuscript are valued. Besides her stellar career as a high school English teacher, she set the sails for the publication of *Maggie's Farm*.

A second individual is Mary Kay Simon, my sister-in-law. She read the manuscript three times, including the final proof read. Her red pen created carnage with each reading—and improved the story. Her corrections and suggestions each time strengthened my resolve to write.

Ron Levitsky, a fellow teacher and author, gave valuable suggestions at the beginning. He has been "an encourager" as rejection slips mounted. Sandwiched among the polite reject letters from agents are his letters and emails—"keep writing."

This dream would not have bloomed without the encouragement of my wife, Jo Marie, who good-naturedly tolerates my sins and foibles and lets me journey—part of the day—to "Larry-land." To my four children—they are my masterpiece.

CHAPTER 1

The blue skirt slid up the secretary's leg as she repositioned herself at her desk. She returned to the electric typewriter with a machine gun rhythm that was producing pages of university documents. Now the skirt was several inches above the knee, and the dark top of a nylon stocking was visible. Across the reception area Robert Hartman sat staring at the nylon leg. The manila folder that he had nervously been tapping on his leg, rested quietly.

It was the second week in September and Bob was in the Dean of Students office at Michigan State University anxiously awaiting his future, but he could not help staring at the flesh colored nylon leg before him. Seductively sandwiched between the blue skirt and pale tan was a delicious dark synthetic brown. It was this small dark patch that encouraged the eye to stare and the mind to fantasize what might lie beyond.

The secretary stopped typing and looked up at him. "Are you OK?" She pulled the wandering skirt down to cover the top of her stocking. "You look like you don't feel well."

"I'm fine. I'm just a little nervous about seeing the Dean. I was supposed to see him at eleven," Bob said.

"Dr. Jenning is running behind schedule today. He should be with you in a couple of minutes." She returned to typing.

"Hell," Bob thought as he turned his view to the clock on the opposite wall. "Here I am expelled from Michigan State and trying to be readmitted, and I'm caught looking up the skirt of the Dean's secretary." The embarrassment fit nicely with the badge of nervousness that he wore, but the secretary was young and attractive with a misplaced skirt. The view was an itch that demanded to be scratched.

Finally, overcoming the temptation, he stared at the clock on the wall and realized that he had only been here for fifteen minutes. The sports jacket felt heavy and the tie choked his breathing as he wondered if perspiration was soaking through the white shirt. He was not looking forward to meeting the Dean, but it was the Dean who would determine if he could return for his senior year. He had cut his hair, shaved off his beard, and for the first time in over two years wore a tie and jacket.

Bob was surprised in June when a dismissal letter arrived from East Lansing. He did not think one poor term would cause his enrollment to be terminated because he still maintained over a 3.0 grade point average. "Flunking-out" did not bother him. He had been questioning himself as to why he was at school and had considered dropping out of college several times over the last year. But his parents were determined that he graduate and were terribly upset with the letter from the Dean of Students. After working for the summer and with the selective service looming on the horizon, Bob changed his mind about college. Especially motivating was the prospect of being drafted in the fall if he was not enrolled in school.

At the end of summer when he had decided that he wanted to return to State, he began to practice what he would say. He was uncertain of the questions that the Dean might ask, and what his responses should be. The phone rang and the secretary answered after the first ring.

"Yes Dr. Jenning, Robert Hartman is waiting to see you. I'll send him in." She turned to him and said, "You may go in now."

Bob walked down a short hall to the first door on the left with a sign above it—"Dr. Phillip S. Jenning, Dean of Students". He felt sick to his stomach. He had the urge to turn and leave, but he knocked quietly on the door and stepped into a large office where a middle-aged man with a green tweed jacket and red bow tie sat behind a desk.

"Dr. Jenning?"

"What can I do for you, Mr. Hartman?" Dr. Jenning asked as he stood and shook Bob's hand.

"I would like to apply for readmission and take classes this fall. I received a dismissal letter in June because of academic reasons, and yet my current grade point is a 3.36."

"That seems odd. Sit down please. Let me look at your folder."

"I have some letters of reference from professors in my department."

"Just hang on to them for a moment, please. Let me see what's in your folder, so I can better understand the situation."

Sitting down, the Dean took a file folder from the top of several similar folders on his desk. Pushing his wire rimmed glasses up on his forehead, he examined the contents of the folder.

Bob sat down and began to tap the folder on his knee, but then stopped. He put the folder in his lap, clasped his hands, and sat still. Although the room was air conditioned, he felt queasiness in his stomach and his shirt still stuck to his skin. He looked around the room and repositioned himself several times in the chair. Behind the Dean was a table under a window that looked out onto the campus. The table was filled with more work to be done, all neatly arranged in piles of different levels. On the right wall were framed photographs of different Michigan State athletic teams, and on the left wall was a bookcase filled with economic and political science books. The desk was organized with work stacked neatly to one side. There was a desk blotter and the accompanying pen and pencil set which sat at the front of the desk. On each side of the desk was an autographed baseball on a pedestal. The left ball carried "Al Kaline" in black script and the right ball had several autographs covering it. Both balls bore the marks of having been in an actual game. Finally, Dr. Jenning looked up.

"I see now why you were dismissed, even with your high GPA. You failed all of your courses from Spring Term. It's University policy that when full time students receive a zero point for a term, their enrollment is terminated."

"I didn't know that."

"Most students don't know about that section of the academic progress standards, but then most full time students don't fail every class," Dr. Jenning said as he took his glasses from his forehead and laid them on the desk. "Most of the time I deal with students whose GPA has fallen below a 2.0. But this is academic policy and does happen occasionally when an upperclassman receives a 0.0. Now how in the devil did you fail all of your classes in a single term?"

"I don't know. I just had a bad term."

"No, a 1.0 is a bad term—a zero point is a disaster! But you had excellent grades until last Spring Term. Was there a death in your family?"

"No."

"Did you have a serious illness, or were you hospitalized for something?"

"No."

"Well, I'm having a hard time understanding how your grades dropped so dramatically, Mr. Hartman. My experience tells me that when this type of performance comes across my desk there was usually a personal or family disaster in the student's life or—," Dr. Jennings paused and leaned forward on his desk. "There was too much partying. Did you join a fraternity last year?"

"No, I didn't join a fraternity," Bob replied as he fidgeted in his seat. The uncomfortable shirt and tie that had irritated him earlier did not seem as bothersome now as the unrelenting stare of the Dean.

"Well what happened then? You have an excellent transcript until last winter. I still can't understand how you could bottom out so badly in just one term." The office rang with stillness as Dr. Jennings continued to stare at him as if he were an insect at an entomological exhibit. Bob shifted his weight in the chair again and adjusted his tie. Again it seemed to be cutting off his air supply.

Finally he said, "I didn't take any of my final exams."

"I thought that there was some foolishness like that. And why wouldn't you take your final exams?"

"I don't know. I guess I was disillusioned and trying to find myself."

"I don't want your guesses, Mr. Hartman. I am going to need a better explanation than 'disillusionment' if I am going to consider you for re-admission."

"I guess—ah, well I mean," Bob squirmed feeling Dr. Jenning's stare pin him even tighter to the entomological board of his chair. "Well sir, I wasn't sure if I had selected the right major and just stop going to class."

Bob paused and realized that this was the big play of the game—touchdown or tackled behind the line for a loss! In high school he had been the star running back on the football team. Would he be a star here in the Dean's office? He began his story of fiction and non-fiction. He talked for several minutes about how he was uncertain about his major and disillusioned with society. He was "trying to find himself" and had not applied himself to his studies, but after thinking over the summer, he wanted to return and graduate from Michigan State University.

"I know I screwed up, but I really do want to finish here at State and get the degree that I started on three years ago. I still don't know what I want to do for a career, but I do believe that a degree in mathematics is the best choice for me."

The Dean silently listened to the story. Bob could not tell if he was having a successful run; in high school when he came through the line with the ball there was usually a lone halfback that took the first fake or was too slow to catch him—touchdown. Dr. Jenning still remained between him and the goal line, and it appeared that he was not taking the fake as Bob weaved his story.

"And while you were finding yourself, how much beer drinking and card playing were you doing? And how many times did you sleep most of the day simply because you were too lazy to go to class or because you had been up all night? And how many parties did you attend off campus while you were disillusioned with society?"

Dr. Jennings stood directly between him and the end zone. The goal line seemed a long way off, and he sensed he was about to be tackled.

"I did some."

That short statement covered a hitchhiking trip to Chicago, canoe trips on the Red Cedar and Au Sable Rivers, countless hours playing volleyball and basketball, parties off campus most weekends, and most important reaching the age of twenty-one—the legal age for admission to bars.

"How do your parents feel about this?" Dr. Jennings asked, and after another pause. "And why now the sudden change of heart. How do I know that you'll not take your finals in December this time—as you did the last spring?"

"They were upset," Bob said. "But they really want me to finish school. I will be the first college graduate from my family."

He remembered how his mother had sat and cried about the shame to the family—what would the relatives and neighbors think, and how could he be so thoughtless to throw away this opportunity? She was convinced that Satan had his hand in this and that prayer was the answer. His dad just shook his head and went to the barn, slamming the door behind him with the same vengeance as when the cattle were in the road or a piece of equipment had broken down.

"I imagine they were upset. I see from your application that you come from a farming background and that you were very active in 4-H."

"That's correct, sir."

"My experience has been that young men and women who are raised on a farm are not afraid to work and usually don't come here and waste the opportunity—no, the privilege—of an education at this great University."

Bob sat with the necktie around his neck that felt more like a noose. He sensed approaching disaster. His coat and tie, shaved face, short hair, and words of contrition would not halt the approaching train wreck. Dr. Jenning talked about work, perseverance, and the value of a college education. "I see from your file that you had some success as an athlete in high school—all-state in football, I believe. Why didn't you go out for the football team here?"

"I did try out my freshman year, but after the first week I knew that it wasn't for me. Most of the players were on scholarship, and I was just a walk on. Besides, Lawsonville is a small rural school and I was all-state in class D. Everyone else seemed to come from class A schools, and they were just bigger, faster, and hit harder than what I was use to. I decided to focus on school and not play football." Remembering the folder in his hand, he took two pieces of paper out and extended it forward.

"Would you like to read these letters of recommendation from former professors that talk about my academic ability?"

"Those won't be necessary. I don't doubt your ability. I only question your level of commitment." Again the Dean lectured him.

Bob sat there politely listening and answering, "Yes, Sir."—"I know, Sir."—and "I agree with you, Sir." For all of his agreement, he heard none of Dr. Jenning's monologue because he was already seeing the arrival of his induction notice in the mail. Dr. Jenning paused and looked at him across his desk. He put his glasses back on and picked up a pen and a piece of paper.

"I'm going to go out on a limb for you and give you another chance, Mr. Hartman," he said. "I have known other students who have made similar poor decisions. Some learned from their mistakes and some didn't. Those who didn't learn from their mistakes ended up back here in my office, or they left the University permanently. I do believe that you have the potential to make something of your life and make a contribution to society—as we all should do."

"Thank you, Sir."

"Here are the conditions: you are to repeat all of the classes that you failed and earn a 3.0 or better in them. You're to take one other class that applies to your major and pass that class, and you are on academic probation for the fall. If you meet all of these conditions for Fall Term, then in the Winter Term you should be right on track to graduate in June. And you will not be on academic probation. But if you do not meet each of these conditions for Fall Term, not even the President of the University will help you. Do you understand?"

"Yes, Sir—and thank you. You won't be sorry that you gave me another chance, Sir."

"Now take this form out to Miss Crampton, and she'll complete the necessary paper work," Dr. Jenning said as he scribbled his signature on a form that he took from the file folder.

Bob accepted the documents and walked from the room trying not to skip or shout. He gently closed the door afraid that an unconscious slam would elicit another lecture on opportunity and responsibility, or more critically, cause the withdrawal of the sacred missive he now possessed.

He walked down the hall elated at his success, turned into the secretary's office, and handed her the paper work. He sat in the same chair where he had so nervously waited thirty minutes ago. Now he relaxed as Miss Crampton prepared the documents for readmission. While she typed, he stared at her nylon leg and wished that the blue skirt would again wander upward, and then he could fully enjoy the dark top of the stocking and hope for an even better view. But it stayed tastefully lying a few inches above her knee.

Placing the completed form in his manila folder, Bob set out for the Administration Building where his admission would be complete once he paid the fees. It felt good to be returning to State and to know that his future for the next nine months would be the familiar routine of college life. At the end of the school year he would have to deal with the problem of Vietnam and his future, but for now a II-S student deferment would keep the draft away from him. There were classes, beer, girls, and the predictability of life in East Lansing.

He walked across the Commons and by the library. The sights were familiar—students walking shaded paths, sitting in groups, or alone in their solitude. Occasionally he saw someone that he recognized, but with the University the size that it was, most faces were unknown to him. He easily spotted the freshmen, and he smiled as he thought back three years when he had arrived here.

Then he walked these same paths with a feeling of excitement and fear. Dressed in new clothes that his mother had bought, he carried a book bag crammed with all of his text books, notebooks, and a new slide rule that he needed but did not know how to use. He had more new clothes than he had ever owned and was impressed with his stylish attire—until he arrived on campus and saw what his roommate and others on campus were wearing. He really was a farm boy from Lawsonville, Michigan!

There were more students in his dormitory than in his entire high school, and when he ventured beyond the dorm, his anxiety increased. Could he find the rooms where classes were? Would he be able to do the work? Would people laugh at him? Maybe he should have stayed at home and gone to a local junior college instead of this huge sprawling complex where he was only a number and needed a map to find anything. Would he survive East Lansing?

CHAPTER 2

He had survived at Michigan State.

Bob had learned the complexities of the University and declared a major in mathematics after his freshman year. Now he needed to complete the terms of probation, enjoy his final year at State, and graduate in June.

He sat on a bench in the shade under Beaumont Tower and took his jacket and tie off and laid them next to him. Dr. Jenning's office had been air conditioned and only his anxiety had made him sweat, but now the heat of early September was having its effect. He looked back on the Commons and counted the squirrels that foraged on the grass beside the sidewalks and bike paths as students walked by; neither paid attention to the other. He counted six squirrels in his view and thought that the last time he had gone hunting. He had walked all day in the woods and had seen only two squirrels and had shot only one.

Actually the Commons was better known as "old campus," but it was his roommate freshman year who had insisted on calling the area the Commons. It was two acres of mature shade trees that had been there since the nineteenth century circled by a drive. On the north side sat the Union and on the south side was the Library; along the edge were various dormitories and academic buildings. At one point this area had comprised all of the Michigan Agriculture College. As the College became a University, it spread like spilled ink across the Red Cedar River and south away from the town of East Lansing. In 1967 it was still oozing southward.

The University continued its sprawl across the Red Cedar River with modern buildings, athletic complexes, and new traffic patterns, but the Commons maintained its nineteenth century appearance. Here bike paths and sidewalks crisscrossed under maples, oaks, sycamores, and beeches that carried bronze tags that gave the scientific name, characteristics, and uses—even the scenery was used to teach. With the squirrel census completed, Bob turned his attention to gazing at people who were crossing the Commons;

his attention focused more on the females than the males. He divided the females into students or secretaries by their clothes; students wore shorts and secretaries wore heels and skirts. Finally he saw a familiar face walking towards him—Jim Ellis who last year lived below him in an apartment. Bob called to him, and Jim came over to the bench.

"Farmer Bob," Jim said. "Why are you here so early?"

"I had some business with the Dean."

"Oh, that business from last spring—I told you if you hang around with Elwood and me, you'd have problems. You'll be a derelict just like us—'gettin high—gettin by.' Did you get everything straightened out?"

"Yes, I'm back in school—on probation."

"Well, that's better than taking an all expense paid vacation to Vietnam—courtesy of Uncle Sam—who loves you so much."

"What are you taking this fall?" Bob asked.

"I took two classes this summer and actually passed them. I'm signed up for fifteen credits—three of those are a repeat of a philosophy class that I never wrote the paper for Spring Term. My parents have their fingers crossed and hope that I will graduate in another year and a half," Jim said as he sat down beside Bob. "Have you seen some type of demonstration, or maybe someone standing on the steps of one of the buildings giving a speech? There's some type of Black Power demonstration and the frat boys are to be there and raise hell. It should be interesting—Black Power meets Idiot Power."

"No, I haven't seen anything. It may be on another part of campus." Both relaxed and watched students pass. After a moment Jim turned to Bob.

"Are you living with Harry again, or did you move back into the dormitory?"

"I'm going to room with him one more year. Are you guys speaking these days?"

"Oh ya, we're fine. He gets pissed because he thinks I'm stoned too much, and then when he gets too 'preachy-teachy,' I get on his 'Make the World Safe for Democracy' attitude. He wants to be Gandhi and save the world and doesn't realize that it's all just a load of crap."

"Anything political sure does fire him up, and with the expansion of the Vietnam War that he hates, he certainly has something to focus on."

"You should have seen it this summer. He and Woody got into it in July. Good thing I was sober and got between them, or I think Woody would have kicked his ass."

"What was that all about?"

"Harry had been out East to some conference or demonstration, God only knows what 'save the world' stuff he had been listening to. Anyway, he came back and was going on and on about 'capitalism' and 'the military-industrial complex' and then he said something about the people dying in Vietnam. Woody heard it that people who die there are stupid—and you know how Woody feels about Vietnam. But Harry meant that it was stupid that anyone had to go there. I saw right away his point, but Woody missed it."

"Jesus, he was pissed. He came unglued and I thought that there was going to be a fight. They both backed off when I pointed out the misunderstanding. But they haven't really haven't spoken to each other since July."

"This should be an interesting year," Bob laughed. "I'm living with a guy who doesn't want to speak to my beer-drinking buddy down stairs. One guy I live with and the other I spend most of my time with. What am I suppose to do, be the referee between the two?"

"They'll be OK—just avoid the topic of politics," Jim replied. "If you don't have anything for dinner, I made some chili this morning before coming over to campus, and there's always beer. 'Come on down,' as Bob Barker says. We'll have a welcome back supper for you."

"OK."

"Well, I am going to see if I can find that demonstration. Maybe it'll be next week when classes have begun," Jim said. "I need to stop at the book store and buy books too."

Bob watched Jim become one of the many students that were traveling along the sidewalks and bike paths. He thought about the argument from the summer between Harry and Woody. Both were older than he was, both were friends from last year, and both stood at opposite ends on many points. But he considered each a friend.

Harry Greenbergh was two years older than he was and had graduated from MSU. He and Bob had been roommates in the dormitory on campus, and last year they had moved into an apartment. The first week Bob had met his neighbors in the apartment below them—Elwood Rademaker and Jim Ellis. Bob immediately became friends with the two and although Harry was polite, he never built the friendship that Bob did with Woody and Jim. Woody did not attend college and had served in the military. He had been part of the early commitment of combat troops to Vietnam in 1965 and had served a little over a year there. After his military obligation, he returned to the Lansing area to work and share an apartment with an old friend from high school—Jim Ellis. Bob had not seen either of them yet this fall, but he did call Harry and make arrangements to live with him when he decided to return to school. If he had not been able to re-enter the University, he had decided that he would live with Harry in his old apartment until he was drafted. Bob had dropped his possessions off that morning while Harry was at work. The apartment was neat and organized, as usual, and Bob made sure that he placed his things in his bedroom and closed the door. If he had left anything lying around, Harry would quickly, but quietly, pick it up and put it in its correct place.

There was still plenty of time until the Administration office re-opened so he took his checkbook from his sports jacket and subtracted the last few entries. There had been a check for rent to Harry and a small check for cash. As he subtracted the last two entries he realized that he had over a thousand dollars in his checking account. After he paid his registration and tuition fees to the University and purchased books, he still should have more than enough money for the entire year. In addition he had three thousand dollars in a saving account back in Lawsonville—a thousand dollars of which he had added this last summer from a construction job on a new express highway that was being built there.

So far he had been able to pay for his education at Michigan State from the money he had saved during high school, summer jobs, and working during the school year. He had always been able to find some part time work in the cafeteria or grill of the dormitory. He had even worked one year at the Library. It was necessary that he cover the expense of his education because there was little income from his parents' dairy farm, and there were four other siblings at home.

Bob entered the current balance into the register and put the check book into his shirt pocket. He was certain that he would have enough money to complete his senior year, and it would not be necessary for him to work part time. Perhaps, he thought he might get a small job on campus anyway, just to earn a few dollars. The University always provided part-time work for those who were interested, and it seemed unnatural for him not to work.

He left Beaumont Tower and walked in the shade of the Commons. There was little direct sunshine, as ancient trees were so tall that their canopy provided an open and airy cover for faculty and students who traversed these paths. He walked by the Museum and wondered what does one put in a museum at an agriculture college? Some day he would have to stop and see what was actually in there. He sat down on a bench near the Administration Building and again checked his watch—twenty minutes until it would re-open.

A student walked by in a Reserve Officer Training Corp uniform. Bob could not tell if he was in his first year or last year of ROTC. Although he had been required to attend two ROTC meetings as a freshman, he had decided not to join. At that time he did not think much about the military, but then he had never even heard of Vietnam in the fall of 1964.

His roommate freshman year, Harry Greenbergh, had been a member of ROTC at that time and spent hours polishing buttons and shining shoes and boots. The next year Harry dropped out of ROTC before he had to make a final commitment to the army. Harry had become unsure about the new American commitment to Vietnam and sure of his lack of commitment to ROTC. Harry was the first person that Bob knew who began to raise questions about the military, the draft, and the war in Southeast Asia. Until he had roomed with him, Bob thought very little about politics or military obligation. Now in his last year of school, he thought constantly of what lay ahead for him after graduation day.

From his vantage point he saw the various signs that announced Rush Week—Rush Week would be the second week of classes when freshmen would be encouraged to join the various fraternities and sororities. The one that caught his eye was the largest and just off to his right. "BROTHERHOOD, INTEGRITY, LEADERSHIP—Are You Man Enough For SIGMA SIGMA SIGMA?" It was brazen in color and larger than all of the other signs.

He smiled as he thought back to his freshman year. He had not been man enough!

CHAPTER 3

"And Flo, she doesn't know that the boy she loves is a Romeo."

Bob sat in the warm September sun, but his mind was back three years earlier to a September evening as he attended his first fraternity rush party. The Motown sound filled the apartment as freshmen and sophomores drank beer and mingled with fraternity brothers from Sigma Sigma Sigma. A few would be asked to join the Tri-Sigs, but most would be passed over.

It was Bob's third week at MSU, and everything was still new and perplexing. He could now locate his classes but was still in awe as he maneuvered around a campus that spread over acres and acres. In his high school, he had three minutes between classes, now there were twenty minutes between classes—sometimes that wasn't enough time. And the people—everywhere were students and professors. Along with all of the strange and different faces were activities that had not been available at home—concerts, lectures, movies, and sporting events. Last week was the beginning of Rush Week where students had an opportunity to see if they wanted to be a part of a fraternity or sorority. He knew nothing about the Greek life, but everyone on his dorm floor had gone—so he went.

He had attended a few of the formal meetings at the fraternity houses and had gone twice to Sigma Sigma Sigma fraternity. Then he had been invited to the Saturday social party outside of East Lansing. A fraternity member had informed him that the Saturday party would not be in the fraternity house and would be the most fun. The houses were never supposed to serve alcohol, just as there was to be none in the dormitories on campus. East Lansing was a dry town by city ordinance; thus, numerous drinking establishments for thirsty students were located a few yards beyond the city limits. Then there were the numerous student apartment complexes and houses that were rented each year by students. These generally were "party centers" each weekend and especially during Rush Week. Tonight he was packed in a student apartment with a beer in his hand.

Bob had been picked up by a Tri-Sig named Roger who shook his hand vigorously and said, "You're going to have a great time tonight. The Tri-Sigs are a great bunch of guys. I've got two more perspective pledges to pick up on East Campus before we head to the party."

Driving an old Dodge full of freshmen, Roger droned on about the benefits of fraternity life, and that there was only one House to join if they decided to go Greek—Tri-Sigs. He himself had been a shy freshman from Ohio three years ago, but Sigma Sigma Sigma had really made a difference to his success he had enjoyed here.

"My buddy Dirk has it all set up for the party tonight. He promised his girl friend he would get a date for her roommate who is a lardo, if we could use her apartment for the evening while she and Chunky went to a movie," he laughed. "He had to promise that there would be no alcohol this evening. No beer at a Tri-Sig party—like that is ever going to happen." He chuckled as he pulled into the parking lot of the apartment complex.

"Maybe one of you guys will be the lucky one and have to go out with old Chunky. She has a great personality—too bad that her ass is as wide as a house."

The six nervous freshmen with their English Leather cologne unloaded and followed Roger into a ground level apartment filled with students holding beer bottles in one hand and cigarettes in another. Motown created a beat for the evening conversation which was echoed by the clank of beer bottles being dropped in a garbage can in the kitchen. A bottle was put into Bob's hand as Mary Wells sang from the stereo.

"Nothing you could say would tear me away from my guy."

In the living room couples were dancing, so Bob tried not to look awkward and nervous as he leaned against the wall and took a deep swig. He stifled a gag. This was the only the second time that he had drunk beer, and he was afraid that someone, especially one of the coeds, would laugh at him if he coughed. He was nervous enough being here and was concerned that someone would learn that he came from a small town in southern Michigan and had been raised on a dairy farm. His father was a farmer—not an executive at Ford or General Motors.

He finished the beer and got another one from the kitchen. Someone offered him a cigarette, which he took. He walked back through the living room as the Temptin' Temptations took over the stereo and the dancers crowded the living room. He took his previous spot against the wall and surveyed the crowd through the dim light and cigarette smoke. Inhaling, he tried to tell who was a prospective pledge and who was a fraternity member. He also gazed at the numerous coeds and tried to summon enough courage to talk to one.

His throat and lungs burned from the cigarette, and he fought back a cough. Finally in desperation, he swallowed some beer from his glass, allowing a half cough to escape. He wiped his lips with the back of his hand and quickly glanced around to see if anyone had noticed his cough, but everyone was too self-absorbed to notice a choking freshman. He emptied his bottle, put the cigarette out, and went to the kitchen for his third beer. Along the way he met several fraternity members who introduced themselves, and after vigorously shaking his hand and telling him how glad they were he was there, they moved on to someone else. It was difficult to hear over the music and he promptly forgot the names of those he met.

He was back to his familiar spot and decided to give up on the cigarettes. They burned his throat and mouth, but the beer had had a pleasant effect. It gave him an uncontrollable urge to grin, and his body wanted to gyrate to the beat of the music. He danced a couple of times, but when the music stopped his partner moved on—or he did. The lightheadedness felt good as he was again leaning against the wall and there was a tingling sensation in his fingers.

Someone was tugging at his sleeve. "Robert, Robert. What are you doing here?" He turned and saw Jennifer McKnight from his hometown. Jenny was a freshman at State and had been a neighbor on a farm that joined the Hartman dairy farm. They had attended country school for three years and then had gone to school in Lawsonville when the one-room school house had closed.

"I might pledge Tri-Sigs, Jenny. What are you doing here?"

"A girl in my dorm is pinned to a Tri-Sig, and the fraternity wanted some girls to come to this party. It sounded like it would be fun, so I came along," she said. "Are you serious about pledging?"

"I might."

"Good for you. I don't think my parents would let me pledge a sorority. Maybe next year I'll be able to join," Jenny said. "I was so ready to leave home and come to school this fall. It was so boring at home. Here there's so much to do, and the people are so interesting—not a bunch of dumb farmers, like at home." He leaned close to her to hear because the music was so loud. Amazingly, her perfume smelled fresh and enticing considering how the cigarette smoke permeated everything.

"Have you heard anything from Tommy since he joined the Marines?" Bob asked. "I saw him just once last summer when he was home from Camp Pendleton before he shipped overseas."

"No, but my folks have. He's doing fine, and he really loves the Marines. But he would never write me—I'm just his little baby sister who worries too much—that is what he told me before he left. I wish he was here."

"So do I. Would you like a beer?"

"No, I don't drink. I don't like the taste of it. I think that I'll go to the kitchen and get a coke and see what's happening out there. I'm supposed to catch a ride back to the dorm with someone named Jane." She turned and took a step toward the kitchen and hesitated and then looked back and said. "If you're ever over to west campus call me sometime. Maybe we can get together?"

As she walked away he could not help but notice how well she seemed to fit into this fraternity scene. Until now he would have thought of her as "Cow Eyes Jenny" or "String Bean Jenny" who would be dressed in jeans, sweatshirt and braids. Now she walked across the room in a plaid skirt and matching sweater, knee socks, penny loafers, and long brown hair flowing over her shoulders. He had never seen her when her hair was not in a pony tail or braided—now she filled these clothes out differently than in high school. He thought that he would call her next week, and they could go to a show on campus or maybe have a coke and talk. She was one coed that he didn't feel shy and nervous around, and she certainly looked different now. He would not be ashamed to seen with her, as she was now quite a fox.

Bob left the living room looking for a bathroom. Not only was the beer having an effect on his brain, it was also affecting his kidneys. He turned down a hall where the bathroom was located and stood in a line with other anxious freshmen waiting their turn.

"Open the God-damn door," the first person said pounding on the door. "Are you peeing with it or are you playing with it?"

He turned to the others in line and said, "Jesus Christ, I've got to piss!" Each in the line carried the same pained look on his face as the guy in front of him rocked back and forth. Suddenly someone who was two in front of him leaned over and sprayed vomit on the opposite wall.

"Jesus Christ, man!"

"Oh no!"

"Man, you got it on my shoes."

The orderly line quickly disappeared as people left their positions. A second burst covered the wall again as gravity pulled the first projectile to the floor. Chaos reigned as all left their position in the line.

Bob quickly returned to the living room where dancing and drinking still continued. He saw the patio window across the room that led outside, where earlier a drunken fraternity brother had fallen into the screen, and it had been pitched aside. His only comment as he was rescued from a web of screen cloth and aluminum frame was: "Hey—I didn't spill any beer!"

Edging his way along the wall to avoid the dancers, he stepped through the gap and into the September night. Bob walked to the edge of the patio, relieved himself and listened to the sounds that surrounded him. The music that had so invigorated him earlier now seemed too loud. It was a warm night and as the noise of the party lessened at his back, he became more aware of the sounds and smells that wrapped this East Lansing apartment. The evening was noisy here just as it was back home. City people talked about the silence of rural living, but he always was amazed at how noisy the farm was—especially in the evening when things were supposed to be quiet. In his mind he could hear the wind that blew from the west across open fields to the Hartman farm. There was the movement of the trees by the house and the sounds from the barns—a door not latched, loose shingles on the roof, or tarps covering equipment that had not been properly secured. And there was always the sound of livestock, unless the wind drowned out their comments and complaints.

Drifting away from the revelry inside, inhaling the heady odor of September, he felt the coolness of the night air which seemed to clear some of the alcohol and tobacco from his body. There was the acrid smell of burnt leaves, and a full moon illuminated everything. Inside the music still roared as he again thought about the farm back in Lawsonville. It was fall and he knew the harvest of corn and beans would be in full operation.

"Hey, Bill, I've been looking for you," a voice said from behind. "You need another beer."

Bob turned around to see a tall blond fraternity brother walking toward him with a cup of beer in one hand and a bottle of beer in the other. He wore khaki trousers and penny loafers, and on his sweater was a fraternity pin. "Here, take this beer and join in the fun."

"It's Bob."

"Oh, I'm sorry. It's Bob then. I'm Marty Summerfield, President of Sigma, Sigma, Sigma." He vigorously shook Bob's hand.

"I hope that you are having a good time," Marty said. "Everything OK? Have you had a chance to meet some of the fraternity members?"

"Yah—it's a great party," replied Bob. "Everyone seems real nice and friendly."

"Well, that's what we're about here at the Tri Sigs," said Marty. "Our motto is one for all and all for one. Brotherhood is real here at Sigma Sigma Sigma—not some phony word like the other fraternities on campus."

Marty took a deep drink from his cup and then continued, "Say, Bill, if you got a minute, I want to talk to you about something that is really important—something that could have far reaching effects for you in the future." He paused again and looked Bob in the eye. "What do you think about pledging Tri Sigs? We would like you to join this fall's pledge class."

"I don't know—I haven't really thought too much about it," replied Bob, shifting his weight from one foot to the other, and then back again.

"Let me tell you something, Bill. See this pin here. When you walk across campus and a coed sees a Tri Sig pin on you—she knows what it means. And what it means is that you are above and ahead of the rest of the guys here at State. You'll never have any problem getting women, if you're a Tri Sig. And we always have good looking women at our parties—not a bunch of dogs like you will find at other frat parties." Marty paused and looked at Bob. "It could be a real advantage for you to be a Tri Sig."

"I don't know—I don't know if my parents will let me pledge a fraternity my freshman year. My dad is pretty strict about college," said Bob as he switched his bottle from one hand to the other. His parents were a quick avoidance to a question that he had not considered. He knew that his parents would know nothing about fraternities.

"Well, we sure would like to have you at Tri Sigs," Marty said. "Look, we know what type of person you are. We have a brother who works in the Dean's office. We know that you were valedictorian of your class and that you had strong scores on your ACTs, and were a hell of an athlete. All-state in football wasn't it? In another year you will be Honors College and perhaps some of the academic honoraries. Who knows how high you will go, and Sigma Sigma Sigma can help you climb to those heights," said Marty. He paused and looked at Bob. "I won't bullshit you. With the credentials that you have, we could use someone like yourself here."

"I don't know. I sure would like to make Honors College, but I don't know how well I'll do. Michigan State is a lot different than my high school," Bob replied and gave a half-hearted laugh. "You have more confidence in me than I do."

"Ah shit, you'll do fine," Marty said. "Just like you can help us, we can help you."

"What do you mean?"

"Listen—let me tell you a little secret. I'm headed for medical school somewhere next fall," Marty added. "Do you know about the OC 200?"

"No."

"Well, it's organic chemistry and every pre-med has to pass this class to graduate. This class is a real ball buster. It is taught by Professor Duggan. We call him Old Dumbdick. He's a tough son-of-a-bitch, and he takes pride in the number of students that he can fail."

"When I took the class two years ago, he had me by the short hairs. I had gassed the midterm and was just barely passing the lab work. I was lost going into the final exam. But I had pledged Tri Sigs and one of the brothers here at the fraternity got a hold of the final exam. Well, I aced the final and ended up with a 3.0 in the class!"

Marty threw back his head and drained the last drop of beer from his cup. He paused a minute and looked at Bob. Bob began to shuffle from one foot to the other and again nervously tapped the edge of his bottle. There was a moment of silence.

"That's what I mean, Bill—you help us and we help you. If you are a Tri-Sig you will always have someone cover your back if you're in a jam. Even if you don't get into a jam, this fraternity can give you a lot of assistance to be successful here at State. Brotherhood is real at Sigma Sigma Sigma—not like at some of the other fraternities on campus," said Marty. He waited for Bob to reply and when there was none, he added.

"Well, I don't want to bore you with a lot of my personal history. Really do give serious thought about pledging Sigma Sigma Sigma. We don't extend the invitation to everyone. There are a lot of dinks floating around on campus, and you don't want to be a part of them, do you?"

"No—I guess not. I'll think about your offer," said Bob. "Tri-Sigs seem like a lot of fun, and they're a great bunch of guys."

"Damn straight they are, Bill," Marty looked down at his cup. "Christ, the old cup of wisdom is empty. I guess that I'd better get some more hooch. Think about it and meet some of the other brothers. Have some fun this evening."

Marty turned around and walked across the patio stepping through where once was a screen and disappeared into the Supremes. Bob watched him leave, turned his gaze to the moon. Again, he smelled the lingering trace of burnt leaves in the air and felt the cool dampness on his face, but now he had a headache and a queasy feeling in his stomach. The earlier tingling sensation in his arms and legs was replaced with an unpleasant clamminess, and the beer that had made him feel so wonderful now gave him an urge to vomit. He thought of what his roommate had said the first week of school.

"You can always tell the rookies—they have a couple of drinks and they toss their cookies."

Bob did not want to be known as a rookie so he sat down on a bench and leaned his head against the building, worried that he might not be able to control his stomach. He watched as someone came on the patio and relieved himself, and then returned to the party. Two more came out and went to the same spot for the same duty, and one slipped and fell in the common urinal. The other one helped his partner up and both were laughing and singing: "Baby love, oh my Baby love" as they stumbled back into the dancing crowd. He closed his eyes for just a minute.

"Come on Bill. God-damn it, let's get going. Everyone has left and I have to get you back to the dorm."

Bob woke up as someone shook him. For a second he did not know where he was, then he recognized Roger, the fraternity brother who had brought him to the party. There was no music coming from the apartment, but a dull headache provided a beat for his brain. They walked into the vacant apartment and stood in the room that had once been filled with dancing and drinking freshmen. The room did not look like it had when he arrived several hours earlier. In one corner was a broken chair and something that looked like vomit next to it. Everywhere there were beer bottles and cigarette butts; some of the beer bottles were lying on their side and a few of the cigarette butts were actually in ash trays. The stereo was quiet as a Budweiser bottle rotated slowly on the turntable.

"Wait here while I get my jacket," said Roger. Then Bob heard a soft sob from the kitchen. Although he could not see into the kitchen, he could hear the painful sobs in a female voice.

"But Dirk, you promised—no beer and no girls. Look at our apartment now! It's trashed."

"Honey, it isn't that bad. We'll be over in the morning and clean the place. That screen can just be bent back into place, and it'll work fine."

The sobbing voice was covered by the crash of beer bottles into a trash can and profanity from another female voice. The owners of the apartment had returned from the movie to the destruction by the Tri-Sigs.

As he was remembering the ride back to the dorm with Roger, the bells in Beaumont Tower chimed and Bob came back to the present. He looked at his watch and saw that it was one o'clock. Grabbing his jacket he walked to the Administration Building to pay his registration fees. He smiled as he thought back to the Tri-Sig Rush party.

He wondered which pledge had gone on a date with Chunky. It had not been he.

CHAPTER 4

"Are you back in?"

"Yes," Bob replied as he sat on the couch reading the latest *The New Republic*.

"How much begging and crawling did you have to do?"

"Not much—just a few lies and a promise to take my final exams. I'm on probation for fall term."

"Well that is better than Lyndon Johnson sending you to Vietnam to crawl in the rice paddies," said the tall redhead who had just entered the apartment with two different newspapers under his arm. "It is good to see you again, Roomie."

"You're stuck with me for another year, Harry. Do you think that you can finally teach me to be neat and tidy like you?"

"No, but someone has to live with the slobs of the world, and I guess that it has to be me."

"Screw you!" Bob laughed as he threw the pillow from the couch.

Harry deftly caught the pillow with one hand while holding the newspapers in the other. Smiling he put the pillow into a waiting chair and turned to the kitchen table where he sat the newspapers on top of other papers. He squared the pile of papers and then picked up the day's mail that Bob had brought from the mailbox downstairs.

This would be his fourth year rooming with Harry Greenbergh. Bob watched as Harry neatly used a letter opener to open the mail. He had been uncertain about his new roommate when he arrived in East Lansing in the fall of 1964. Harry was a junior from New York City who spoke with a distinct Eastern accent. In spite of their apparent differences, they had formed a friendship and Harry had become a mentor. Bob remembered the first day he had met Harry in their dorm room. Harry had just returned from an ROTC meeting and was still dressed in his uniform. Although he no longer was a member of ROTC, Harry still maintained a crisp clean appearance. As usual, his shirt and pants were pressed, his shoes were polished, his red hair tied in a pony tail, and he never went a day without shaving. He was a study in military precision and discipline and would now have been a second lieutenant in the United States Army somewhere if his politics had not changed.

"How was your summer?" Bob asked. "Still working at the book store?"

"Yes. It was slow this summer, but now that school has started, I should get forty hours a week. They made me an assistant manager in August, so I'll get a pay raise," Harry said as he laid the mail on top of the newspapers and again squared the pile. Walking into the living room, he sat in a chair across from Bob.

"The exciting news for the summer is that we now have a draft counseling center, and I'll be working there at least three nights a week. The University will not allow us to be on campus, but a church in East Lansing has given us a free room. It'll be open every evening after five."

"Did you hear anything from the FBI this summer? Is that who will contact you, or will they send you something in the mail?"

"Like a magazine sweepstakes?—You have just won an all expense paid trip to your nearest federal prison, courtesy of Robert McNamara," Harry laughed then smiled at his embarrassed roommate.

"You know what I mean."

"Yes, I know what you mean. I'm just giving you a hard time since I haven't seen you all summer. No, I haven't heard from anybody, and the way that it will probably happen is that the FBI will contact me to come to their office for an interview, and then they'll turn the information they gather over to the federal district attorney. At some point he'll make a decision to prosecute or not." Harry stretched back and kicked his shoes off.

"At least that is the way that I'm told it will happen. If you run or hide they will issue a warrant for your arrest," he said. "But like I told you last spring, I'm not going to Canada, and I am not going underground. The Justice Department will have no trouble finding me, and I'm going to have my day in court."

Harry had been drafted last winter, and Bob had not been surprised when he refused induction. After he quit ROTC, Harry had begun to question more openly American presence in Southeast Asia. He eventually joined the SDS on campus and became involved with the fledgling draft resistance movement. Last February he had refused induction into the army. When Bob went home for the summer, Harry had been trying, with others, to have draft counseling on campus, which the University refused to allow. Apparently they had a change or mind, either caused by the persistence of Harry Greenbergh or the ever increasing student unhappiness with the events in Southeast Asia.

Harry had graduated in 1966 with a duo major in political science and philosophy, but had continued to work at a local book store—the same job he had the last two years of college. The University had provided him with an education and Washington provided him with a career. He was now in full time opposition to the Vietnam War. Like an old time traveling pastor, he lived on nothing and focused only on "saving souls." Instead of bringing them to Jesus, he tried to take them from General Westmoreland.

"What are we doing for supper?" Bob asked. "If I am cooking, you know it will be PB&J, and I don't think that you have fixed anything."

"No, I worked all day."

"They've got chili and beer downstairs, and we are invited."

"No, I don't think I'll go."

"I understand that you had a little falling out this summer with the Woody and Jim in the Sin Den down below us," Bob said with a smile.

"Oh that's patched up, I hope. There was just a misunderstanding between Woody and me," Harry said. "Jim is the one who gives me a pain in the ass. I get tired of him being high all of the time and his sarcasm. And I am really tired of his constant quotes. Does he think that he is the only one on the planet that reads? I wonder what he would do if he wasn't 4-F and his parents were not paying for him to attend school?"

"Well, what are we going to do for dinner?"

"Aw hell, I guess we can go down there. But I am not staying long. I do have to work tomorrow and I have to be there at six in the morning," he said. "I hope that we don't catch any disease while we are there."

"You can always get a shot. Besides the chili has been cooking all day and should be sterile. And bacteria can't live in alcohol, so the beer should be safe."

"That's real funny. Maybe you can stand it, but I don't know how they live in that chaos and dirt. They are animals down there."

Elwood Rademaker and Jim Ellison lived in the apartment directly below them. While Harry tolerated them, Bob liked them both, and some of his problems from last spring were caused by spending too much time with them. He knew that he would have to change that habit this fall if he was to graduate. Woody and Jim's apartment was the infamous Sin Den, known to all in the complex and the management; it was visited about once a month by the complex manager or the local police because of the parties or noise. Since this apartment complex was outside of East Lansing, alcohol was legal for those who were over twenty-one, as were both Woody and Jim, although many who congregated there on weekends were not. But they paid their rent each month and were able to avoid eviction—a paid rent receipt being the main criteria for a successful stay in this complex. As for the police, Woody always talked his way out of each complaint with a promise to turn the stereo down and to send all under-age drinkers home.

Woody Rademaker was five years older than Bob and a Vietnam vet. He worked as a mechanic and enjoyed the life near campus because it provided ready access to girls, beer, and parties—all of which he enjoyed immensely. Woody's roommate was Jim Ellison. Jim had gone to Duke University on a full academic scholarship and done well the first year, but then had stopped attending classes and flunked out. He had attended a couple of junior colleges and now was enrolled at Michigan State University. He attended classes sporadically and at different times had been on academic probation. He received money from his parents for all of his expenses at school, and because he had accidentally injured an eye in youth, he did not have to worry about the draft. There was nothing that he seemed to want to do except read and get high.

Harry and Bob walked into the apartment without knocking. They could smell the chili, but there was also the typical evening smell of marijuana. Woody was lying on the floor watching cartoons, and Jim was sitting at the table reading the *New York Times*. He looked and greeted them.

"The boys from Mount Olympus have arrived. Are you here for enlightenment or food? If you want enlightenment, you will have to consult Woody the Buddha who is engrossed in Road Runner cartoons at the moment. I can provide the chili."

"We'll settle for chili and beer."

Jim went to the kitchen and got two beers from the refrigerator while Harry and Bob sat down at the table. Harry began to read the paper Jim had laid down.

"Say Harry, the *New York Times*—is that 'all the news that's fit' or is it 'all the news that shits'?" Two beer cans flew across the room and were caught. Harry shook his head in disgust and opened his beer.

Retrieving two bowls from the cupboard, Jim filled them with hot chili from a pot that had overflowed on the stove, mingling with the remains of other cooking disasters. The sink was filled with dirty dishes; the wastepaper basket was overflowing; and the counter tops were cluttered with kitchen items, books, and clothing. In one corner sat a beer keg that was probably empty—but maybe not.

"Don't you guys ever clean the kitchen? How do you stand to live in such a mess?" Harry asked.

"No, we like it this way. We are growing bacteria for the university," Jim said grinning. "I think that somewhere here is a strain that will cure 'save the world' liberals. Shall I put you at the head of the list to be vaccinated?"

Disgusted, Harry took the bowl and went into the other room. Bob followed, careful not to spill any of the contents of the hot bowl. Like the kitchen, the living room was a study in mess. Magazines, newspapers, and clothing were scattered everywhere, and along one wall was a board and brick book shelf filled with books. Among this disarray was Woody—stretched out on the floor watching Elmer Fudd chase Bugs Bunny across the screen. Woody was enthralled with the antics and laughed at each punch line with glee.

"Could we watch the evening news on CBS? I want to see what is happening in the world," Harry asked as he threw a jacket and magazines on the floor so he could find a spot to sit on the sofa.

"Aw shit—that stuff is stupid and boring," Woody replied, but he changed the channel to *Walter Cronkite and the Evening News*.

"The pundits of video land to enlighten and entertain," Jim said. "Cronkite does more than Milton can to justify God's ways to man. Cronkite, Cronkite, the stuff to drink, for the fellows whom it hurts to think." Harry watched the news while Woody sat up and leaned against the bookcase.

"Well, Bobby is back. How was your summer?" Woody asked.

"It was fine. And were you able to stay out of jail while I was gone?"

"No problem. You know you're the one that causes all of the trouble. You're so damn good-looking the women can't keep their hands off of you, and I just seem to get drug into your fights," Woody said.

"Somehow I think it's the other way around."

"You mean I am the good-looking one?" Woody asked with a smile.

"No—you start the fights and I get drug into them."

Last year had been a disaster, both for trouble and fun. Twice Woody had been given what he called "free rides in the police taxis"—although they were far from free when the fines were paid the next day. Once in the spring Bob had just missed sharing a "free taxi ride" because he jumped a fence and sprinted into the woods.

When Bob turned twenty-one in late winter, he began going to the bars with his new friend Woody, who was always ready for action on the weekends and sometimes during the week. Woody became an "older brother" who was introducing his "younger brother" to the bar scene in the Lansing area. Bob was having a wonderful time and by Spring Term rarely attended classes, either because he was too hung-over, or he had not been there for several meetings and found it easier to just skip class and catch up on the work he had missed. Then there would be a new bar to attend or a drinking party in the Sin Den. He fell further and further behind in his course work.

Fights and trouble seemed to follow Woody as his life focused on beer and women, both of which were found in bars or the numerous weekend parties around campus. Although small, he was quick and absolutely fearless. Bob had seen him win several fights against much larger opponents, and, if he did not win, that fact would not stop him the next time the opportunity appeared. He was very loyal to friends and would without question support a companion. Fighting was just an activity that he engaged in—like playing pool or cards.

Regardless of the injuries or the hangovers, he always went to work the next day and would be ready to party that evening.

While Harry was engrossed in Walter Cronkite, Bob and Woody talked about what each had done during the summer. Bob had worked and banked a thousand dollars; Woody had several one night quickies, lost no teeth, and stayed out of jail—both had been successful. Jim lit a joint and offered it to everyone, but all refused.

"More for me to enjoy, comrades."

Suddenly Harry swore and everyone turned to watch the TV. On an airstrip with a Vietnamese sun beating down were body bags laid in a row—each precisely spaced—a study in geometry and engineering precision. The viewer could see the dark bag with the closed zipper running the entire length, but he could not see the dead American inside waiting to finally return to his home and family. Walter Cronkite gave the daily figures for dead and missing. Again the number of Viet Cong and North Vietnamese killed greatly exceeded the number of Americans sacrificed. There were no sanitized and orderly pictures of Vietnamese dead shown.

"Those dumb son-of-a-bitches," Harry exclaimed. Quickly, he glanced at Woody who again was lost in the TV—but not cartoon fantasy.

"I mean those idiots who sent those Americans there—not the soldiers who died there."

"Hey, Bob you're the math major here—how is that every day we'll kill five, ten, fifteen, twenty times as many of the enemy as Americans die and have been doing that since the beginning of the war and still we're not winning. I can't figure it out. The government wouldn't lie or doctor the counting, would they?" Jim asked as he inhaled and held the smoke in his lungs. Then he exhaled and said. "I'm an English Lit major, but maybe you can explain it, Harry."

"They're lying son-of-a-bitches. There's your explanation, and we need to do something about it. I don't see how smoking your brains out helps the situation."

"It sure helps me." Jim said with a huge grin. "Do you think Bobby McNamara gives a shit about what I do?"

"Someone should," Harry said softly as smoke seeped through the room. Harry stood and drank the last of his beer. He politely wiped his bowl and spoon with a napkin and took everything to the kitchen. Returning, he picked up his things from the couch and said.

"Thanks for the chili—it was very good. I'm going back upstairs. Bob, if you need to get up early in the morning you had better set you own alarm. I have to be up by five to get to the bookstore on time."

Harry left and Jim rolled another joint. Bob and Woody talked some more, finally Woody said. "Let's go to Emma's and see what's shaking. Perhaps we can find some young ladies. They'll surely want to welcome Bobby back to Lansing."

"I don't know if I should go. I usually end up in trouble with you."

"Aw come on, it'll be fun. Old Jim-bo can go with us too."

"Count me out," Jim said. "I'm too stoned to go. Two roads diverged in a yellow wood. And I took the Mara-hoo-na road."

"Do you remember the last time we were at Emma's and I got sucker punched trying to keep you out of a fight," Bob said. "I'd just as soon start this term out without a hang-over or black eye."

"If you would have let me kick his ass like I wanted there wouldn't have been any problem. Just because I can't walk, doesn't mean that I can't fight. Besides it's Thursday, and you'll have a couple of days to sober up."

They left the apartment complex and headed to a small town outside of East Lansing where Emma's was located. This was one of Woody's favorite bars, and he had begun taking Bob there last spring. Even though he had been thrown out of the bar several times, Woody and his money were always welcomed back. There would be no college students there; most of the patron s were working class, and Friday and Saturday there was usually a local country band. The bands drew what Woody liked best—divorced or single women.

Bob stared at the countryside in the dusk as Woody sang a Conrad Twiddy tune with the radio. A trip to Emma's fit well as an ending to a perfect day.

CHAPTER 5

The drive south from East Lansing was slow as Bob listened to what Woody had done during the summer. They first drove through the farm lands of Michigan State and then into farm lands of Ingham County. The route was familiar from the spring and the countryside looked like the miles of roads that surrounded the Hartman farm back in Lawsonville. This country road, in comparison to East Lansing streets, had fewer pedestrians, cars, stop lights—and cops. It would be an easier drive home. They pulled into the parking lot at Emma's and Woody was almost out of the car before it had stopped.

"I think we'll be lucky tonight, Bobby," Woody said. He was like a little boy coming down the stairs the first thing Christmas morning. They walked into Patsy Cline crooning from the jukebox. *"I go out walking, after midnight."* There would be no Bob Dylan here, but lots of Loretta Lynn and George Jones.

The familiar smell of fried food came from the grill behind the bar. Later in the evening, cigarette smoke would cover the order of French fries, hamburger, and onions, but right now the grill food was winning. Emma's was different from the many bars near the campus that were populated with college students—those with legal and altered identification. Besides the difference in music on the jukebox, the patrons were different—here were truck drivers, factory workers, farmers, and other laborers. Here people majored in manual labor and low wages, not sociology and business administration. Here also could always be found those who did not labor except at stories and holding a bar stool in place. Woody first brought him a month before he turned twenty-one; he had never been asked for identification. He had been readily accepted because he was with Woody and did not act or talk like a college student. Also, he knew when to laugh at the jokes about politicians and wives.

The stools at the side bar were already housed with patrons. The rest of the bar was filled with tables that had been there for years; it would be impossible to calculate the amount of beer that had been wiped off of these tables or the number of stories that they had heard. A pool table, jukebox, and a small dance area claimed the back. Woody would be there later if he found some one to bump and grind with.

Opposite the bar was a room that was dark where a live band could perform on the stage at the end of the room. Long tables with benches were located here, and waitresses made a steady procession bringing pitchers of beer when a band played. Once on one of these tables, Bob had stood singing "All Shook Up" and when asked to sit down, he immediately went into "Jailhouse Rock." A bouncer escorted him from Emma's amid a flurry of profanities—at least that was what he was told the next day as he sorted through his embarrassment and headache trying to remember the events of the previous night. Woody had protested Bob's ejection and had also been thrown out. Bob was surprised that Woody had gone without a fight, until he remembered that he had been thrown out the week before after an impromptu striptease for a bachelorette party. With several young girls cheering, he had made it only to his shirt before he was ejected from Emma's with a promise from Gene, the owner, that he would be barred for life if he tried that again.

"A brewski—or do you want a shot?" Woody asked.

"I'll stick with beer. The whiskey gets me in trouble and someone has to be able to crawl to the car and drive."

"OK. A beer for the lady."

Bob sat at a table in a corner while Patsy Cline began "Sweet Dreams of You" in the background. Woody returned and sat down. "Lucille will be over in a minute with a pitcher."

"When did you start drinking today, Woody?" Bob asked.

"Oh it was slow at the shop and the boss was gone, so we started after lunch. I knew that you were coming to East Lansing today and I wanted to get a head start on the celebration."

"Bullshit! You didn't know if I was even coming back this year."

"I was just hoping for the best, Bobby—just hoping for the best."

Just then Lucille sat a pitcher of beer and two glasses on the table. She was in her late twenties or early thirties and waited tables five nights a week at Emma's. Lucille always worked on the weekends, and with her long blonde hair in a pony tail, tight blouse, and usually a short skirt, she not only had to carry drinks to the tables, but had to brush off countless advances and comments. She had a quick reply for an unsavory comment and always dodged the groping hands. If anyone got out of control, Gene the bartender would ask him to leave—with help if necessary.

"They can say or think what they want, honey," she had said last spring. "—just as long as they tip well. And if they drive a Corvette, they might be able to handle the merchandize." Bob put a couple of dollars on the table to pay for the pitcher.

"Woody already took care of it, Bobby," Lucille said. She stood next to him and put her hand on his shoulder. "It is good to see you back. We missed you this summer. Are you back at State?"

"Yes, this is my final year, if I can stay out of trouble with Woody."

"He's a good one to get you into trouble."

"Aren't you glad to see me too, Lucille," Woody said as he reached out to pat her on the bottom. Lucille deftly brushed his hand aside with her right hand, then stepped toward and him and patted him on the cheek with her left hand.

"I'm always glad to see you Woody—especially from a long way off," she said over her shoulder as she headed back to the bar. "Don't touch the merchandize, Woody, unless you drive a Corvette or Cadillac."

"God, what a woman," Woody said as he watched her walk to the bar. "I swear that those black slacks are air-brushed on her tonight. I sure would like to get into her before the worms do."

"No chance of that Woody."

"Well, there are other ladies here tonight. Let's go get a couple of them, Bobby."

"I'm fine. They're all yours—give a whistle if there're too many for you."

"There are never too many for the old Woodpecker." Woody poured two glasses of beer and headed toward the back with a full glass.

Bob took a long drink and sat his glass back on the table. He had drunk several beers at the apartment and this one was making him feel light-headed and mellow. Good thing that he did not have class tomorrow, he thought, because he would probably not be feeling well in the morning. He was taking his second drink when he realized that he had been sitting at the same table last spring when Woody and he had met Ginger and Earl. The next day he had a terrible headache.

It was exam week and Bob had one more final exam to take, but since he had not taken any so far, he didn't plan on showing up for that one either. Woody had taken a day off of work, and they began drinking beer at noon and driving on country roads south of Lansing. It was a beautiful day and one six pack had turned into a case. Around nine they ended up in Emma's, which had a full crowd. Bob used the restroom as soon as they entered. When he came out, Woody was sitting at this table with two strangers—Earl and Ginger. Woody motioned him over and he sat in a vacant chair next to Ginger. Woody and Earl were telling stories about being in the military. Earl was veteran of the Korean War, and when he learned that Woody had served in Vietnam, he insisted on buying them a pitcher. While the two talked and laughed, Ginger quietly smoked a cigarette and occasionally sipped from a gin and tonic. Bob sat and drank his beer while stories of officers, sergeants, and drunken leaves were exchanged. Ginger turned to him.

"And what do you do, honey?"

"I attend Michigan State University."

"Oh, what do you study there?"

"I'm a math major."

"Wow, you must be pretty smart. I couldn't do arithmetic. I cut and perm hair. I went to beauty school—and Earl is a truck driver. He drives for Winston Freight and is usually gone during the week." She turned her head slightly and patted a hairdo that was piled high on her head and held tight with spray.

"Honey, do a girl a favor and give me a light."

Bob took the lighter from the table and lit the cigarette as Ginger leaned close to him and held the hand with the lighter. She had long manicured bright red finger nails and on each finger was a ring. She inhaled deeply and then relaxed and exhaled a column of smoke to the ceiling.

"Thank you, sweetie." She laid her hand on his knee and held it there while she inhaled again.

"You're kind of cute."

Bob looked at her, and she smiled at him. She was older than he or Woody, but younger than her husband. She wore a lot of make up, and the blouse she was wearing was tight and low cut.

"Would you like to dance, honey?" Her hand rubbed his thigh above the knee but was moving upward.

"I don't dance," Bob said and quickly stood up. "I need to use the restroom."

When he returned, Woody and Earl were still in conversation and there were new drinks for everyone. Bob slid a chair in between the two veterans and across from Ginger. Ginger was now between her husband and Woody. She lit another cigarette and smiled at Bob. Ignoring Bob, Earl continued on with his conversation with Woody.

"Those God-damn hippies over on campus ought to be shot. If I had my way everyone one them would be in the army. Put those smart-asses in boot camp for a couple of days, and then we'd see how much demonstrating they would do."

"They're just using their Constitutional right to protest and question the policies of the government," Bob said avoiding looking at Ginger. "They are just using the First Amendment privileges."

"They don't have any rights. They're traitors—along with that whore Jane Fonda. If they won't fight for the country and protect us against the damn commies that are trying to take over the world, then they need to get out of this country. Let them go live in Cuba or China and see how they like it there."

"Maybe it isn't so bad there."

"Jesus Christ, have you got shit for brains. It's communism," Earl said turning his full attention to Bob. "Nobody wants to live like that. The communist take over the country and force you to do everything their way. You don't have any freedom, and they tell you who you got to marry and what you got to think."

Woody and Ginger got up to dance while Earl was fully engrossed in explaining to Bob the evils of communism and how the communists need to be stopped in Vietnam or else they would expand and control the entire world. Usually Bob avoided this argument, but he had been drinking all day and could not resist challenging Earl's arguments. Earl's speech was becoming more slurred, but he ordered another pitcher of beer and poured another glass for Bob. Bob tried to pay for this new round, but Earl had the money to Lucille before he could reach his billfold. Earl got up to use the restroom and fell backwards into the adjacent table. Laughing he apologized to the couple sitting there and continued on past his wife and Woody who were dancing by the jukebox.

On his return Earl continued on about current affairs with truck driving stories added and always comments about those unpatriotic people who did not support President Johnson and the war in Southeast Asia. Bob listened politely but was getting bored and was having trouble concentrating through all of the beer. When Earl began to talk about the Detroit riots and "Martin Luther Coon," Bob left the table. He was ready to go home.

He could not find Woody who had the keys to the car. He stumbled as he looked in the restroom and then he went outside. Sometimes Woody would pass out in the car, but he was not there. He went back inside and still could not find him. Woody would not leave without saying something to him. Perplexed, he walked back to the darken side room that was used for live music but was now vacant. He stumbled and bumped into a chair as he entered and let his eyes adjust to the dark as he rubbed his shin. Two exit lights at the end were the only illumination, and showed there was no one present. He turned to leave when he saw movement on a table by the stage. He took a step forward and then realized what was happening. Returning to the bar, Bob ordered a Coke and sat on a barstool. He had enough beer for the evening and his mouth was dry. It might be a few minutes before Woody was ready to go.

In the mirror Bob saw Ginger come out of the back room and sit down at the table with Earl who was asleep with his head on the table. She signaled and Lucille brought another gin and tonic to the table. Ginger's hair was in perfect shape but there were a couple of buttons unbuttoned on her blouse.

As Lucille sat the drink on the table, Woody emerged from the dark back room with a grin and walked over and slapped Bob on the back.

"Ready to go, Bobby?"

"You are amazing—just simply God-damn amazing!"

"Well, while you and Earl were saving the world I just thought that Ginger and I might work out our own problem." Bob watched the grin in the mirror grow even larger and knew that tomorrow there would be a story to be told. There was always a story and Woody had a thousand of them to tell. As he sat at the "Ginger and Earl" table thinking about Woody's grin, he was brought back to Emma's in the present with the sound of glass crashing and breaking at the back of the bar.

Bob looked toward the sound and saw Woody lying on the floor with a bar chair turned on its side. Bob rushed to help up his friend who also needed the assistance of the table to steady himself.

"Keep your God-damn hands off of her, buddy," a large man standing on the other side of the table said, "or you'll be picking your teeth out of your ass."

Woody was in trouble—as usual.

CHAPTER 6

Bob helped Woody stand.

"Tell your buddy to keep his hands at home, or there'll be more trouble than he knows what to do with," the man said who was standing. "I'll knock his God-damn teeth down his throat if he touches my wife again."

There were several people at the table and three were women, so Bob was not sure which "lady" was whose. Lucille was busy wiping up a spilled pitcher and resetting the overturned chairs upright. The patrons all appeared drunk and the man standing with a red face and clenched hands was slurring his words. He was two inches taller than Woody and fifty pounds heavier, neither of which would have stopped Woody if challenged to a fight.

"Lucille, let me buy a couple of pitchers for this table," said Bob as he led Woody to the other side of the bar.

"Aw, I didn't mean anything," Woody slurred. "She had been rubbing my leg and you know that she wanted some of the old Woodpecker. Let's do a shot of Jack Daniels."

"No, someone has to drive," Bob said.

"Aw shit! I can still drive. Just point me in the direction and put the wheel in my hand. You know that I am a driving son-of-a-bitch."

"Yah, I know. Driving in the ditches is where you're a driving son-of-a-bitch. I've been on a few of those trips with you."

"Well, it ain't my fault," Woody laughed. "Someone put those ditches in my way—they weren't supposed to be there." He almost fell off of his chair but caught himself and readjusted into the seat.

"Oops," he said and laughed. "Someone is moving the floor. God, I got to piss. Now you watch everything, Bobby, and if you get too many women to handle, you give me a whistle."

Woody headed for the restroom. He stumbled again but caught himself and weaved to the bathroom. Bob knew that there would be an argument about who would drive when they left this evening. As drunk as he was, Woody would be at work tomorrow, ready to do this all over again the next evening. Woody seemed to care for nothing but women and drinking, and Bob suspected that the reason that he lived near Michigan State was the party atmosphere of students. He asked Woody one time why he didn't use his GI benefits and get a college degree.

"Books ain't for me," Woody replied. "Just let me work on cars and get my hands dirty. You college boys buy the books; all us old grease monkeys need is a wrench and hammer."

Everything had returned to normal. Bob looked over his shoulder and saw that the table across the room was back drinking and laughing; someone was putting money in the juke box. Lucille came over to the table.

"You guys OK—do you need another beer?" She wiped the table with her bar rag. "If Woody gets into another fight here, Gene might not let you guys in at all. I know he likes Woody, but last month there was a heck of a fight when Woody took on two guys in the parking lot. Gene called the cops. Good thing that everyone left before the police arrived. The funny thing is that the next night all three were in here drinking together and everyone was best buddies."

"That doesn't surprise me at all," Bob said. "You'd better give me a coke because someone has to drive home."

"One coke—watch it, honey. Like I said, Gene likes Woody but one more fight, and he'll kick him out of here permanently." She walked over to the bar and then returned with a coke.

Bob sipped the coke waiting for Woody to return and felt good. He was back at school and with his friends—the beer from this evening was also helping his mellow feeling. Tomorrow he would buy books, finish moving into the apartment, and just wander around campus for a while. There would certainly be a party somewhere this weekend and then classes would begin on Monday.

While he waited for Woody to return, he thought about the first time he was in Emma's last spring—it looked exactly now as it had then. It had probably been the same for several years with only the records on the jukebox changing during the preceding years. A new record began on the juke box and Sergeant Barry Sadler was singing the "Ballad of the Green Beret."

"Fighting soldiers from the sky, Fearless men who jump and die. Men who mean just what they say. The brave men of the Green Beret."

Bob's mind left the bar and Woody and went back to spring time over a year ago to the Methodist Church just a mile from home. There he was a pallbearer for his friend, Thomas McKnight. He had never been a pallbearer; he had never attended a funeral for someone so young; and he had never attended a military funeral.

The McKnights farmed the land next to the Hartman's, and he and Tommy were the oldest sons. The families had been neighbors for years and the two boys had grown up together playing and working. Tommy was one year older and always big and strong for his age while Bob was smaller but would become tall and solid by the time he was in high school. He had quickness and speed and Tommy had the strength. When they both were at Lawsonville High School, they were two farm boys who anchored the football team that was conference champions three consecutive years. Both had played on defense, but it was on offense that the two were stars; Bob was the running back and Tommy the offensive guard. Bob received all of the accolades, but he knew that Tommy was the one who caused his success. Tommy never seemed to mind his role and enjoyed reading the Friday night accomplishments of his boyhood pal.

"I'll knock 'em on their ass, you just get to the goal line." He would smile a wide grin that usually accompanied a black eye or bruise. These farm boys led the Lawsonville High School to two undefeated football seasons. Bob's senior year the team suffered its first defeat in three years, but he was still voted all state for the second consecutive year. Tommy, who attended every game Bob's senior year, had been working on the farm at home when Bob was accepted to Michigan State University. A week after Bob's acceptance Tommy joined the Marines.

Bob saw Tommy only one time after graduation. Tommy was home on leave, and they spent the day wandering the fields and woods that surrounded their farms. The next day Tommy left for the West Coast and later shipped to Vietnam. He occasionally heard about his friend when he saw Jenny, Tommy's sister, on campus, but there were no letters. In the spring of his sophomore year his mother called with the news that the McKnight family had just been notified Tommy had been killed in Vietnam. He was wanted home for the funeral.

The services were held in the Methodist Church that the Hartmans attended. The McKnights were not church goers, but that never really mattered since if you were in the neighborhood you were considered a member. Besides a local family was in need, and without hesitation everyone reached out to do his part. Bob's part was to be a pallbearer, and he did his duty. And that was what people there did—they worked; they served; and they never questioned.

After the funeral he stood in a cemetery where both his grandparents and many relatives were buried and listened. The entire family looked strange not dressed in jeans, and Jenny McKnight looked even more out of place dressed as a college coed. The McKnights did not shed a tear and quietly watched the coffin being lowered into the grave, after which a flag was presented to Mrs. McKnight from "a grateful nation." At that moment, Bob felt a nail go through his heart—a nail that was ice cold. It startled him so that he looked away from the grave and out over the cemetery, surrounded by the open farm fields of southern Michigan. It was spring and a warm breeze blew from the southwest across daffodils and crocus that dotted the graveyard. Some of the fields had been worked and were ready for planting; others laid with the remains of winter waiting for the plow. The hardwoods were not in full leaf yet, but dogwood was blooming and everything was in early bud. It was warm; it was spring; it was the time of year that he always enjoyed; yet there was a chill inside of him.

Mr. and Mrs. McKnight politely shook hands and exchanged hugs with people who offered their condolences, and then there was a dinner in the basement of the church. As the McKnight family was leaving for dinner in the basement of the church, Tommy's sister, Jenny, walked over to him and hugged him. He put his arms around her trying to comfort her, but there was nothing he could say. Jenny put her head on his shoulder and squeezed. After a few moments she turned loose and stood looking at him as she held his hand. Finally, she dropped his hand and joined the rest her family in the church for a meal put on by the church ladies. For the rest of the spring and into the summer, he tried to think of something that he could say to Jenny, but he never could find the words. He could not even bring himself to go see the McKnights, but in June when he came home, he wrote a letter to them. He felt it was a coward's way out of saying something to Mr. and Mrs. McKnight, but he just couldn't bring himself to go to the farm and meet them face to face. It was that blank stare on Jenny's face that haunted him that summer. The vacant stare that appeared to reveal nothing, but masked a deep pain stayed with him. It reminded Bob of a pet dog he had when he was ten.

Old Floyd was a collie and had crossed the road to chase a woodchuck. When Bob called him back, he ran across the road and was hit by a car traveling on the gravel road in front of their house. The car never stopped. Bob watched Floyd roll two or three times and end up in the ditch. Floyd walked out of the ditch and wobbled around; he collapsed just as Bob ran to him. He had a dazed looked that Bob remembered when he saw Jenny at the cemetery. Bob ran to get his father who could always fix anything.

"He is hurting badly, Bobby. He looks OK on the outside but he is busted up pretty bad on the inside. He isn't going to get better; we should put him down. You wouldn't want old Floyd to suffer, would you, son?"

Sam Hartman carried Floyd to the corn field behind the barn. Bob sat on the ground and petted Floyd's head while his father got the 22 rifle from the barn. Floyd was not panting and licking as he always did, rather he rested quietly in Bob's lap. Bob put his head down next to Floyd and laid his cheek on fur that had the usual burrs tangled in it. He did not want his father to see him cry as the tears just flowed on to collie fur. He was too old for crying, but he could not stop the tears. They buried Floyd in the earth—just as they had later done with Tommy.

"*Put silver wings on my son's chest. Make him one of America's best. He'll be a man they'll test one day. Have him win the Green Beret.*"

As Sergeant Sadler finished the song, Bob thought of Jenny clinging to him in the cemetery, and he sensed that she needed him to do something. He had seen her a few times, but they had only spoken briefly and never about Tommy or that day. His mother had said that she was having a difficult time at State and appeared to be taking Tommy's death hard. Although she continued attending classes and did well academically, she had moved into an apartment in East Lansing and did not socialize with other students as she had done before Tommy was killed. Mrs. Hartman suggested that he see Jenny and talk with her since they had been neighbors and classmates. He did not know what to do or say, so he did nothing.

In the fall after Tommy's death, when Bob returned to campus, for the first time he began to have doubts about the American presence in Vietnam. Of course, his friend and roommate, Harry, who by then actively opposed the war, only added tinder to his small spark of doubt. He wanted to believe that Tommy had died for something noble and important and not just for political decisions in Washington. He wanted some significance for the McKnights and especially for Jenny—they deserved something more than a piece of red, white, and blue cloth.

Bob finished the last of the coke but was still light headed from all of the beer earlier. He was ready to go. All he had to do was to find Woody who still had not returned from the restroom. He looked around the bar for his friend.

"Shit!" he muttered under his breath. Woody was sitting at the table with the people he had irritated earlier.

As he neared the table he saw that his fears were unfounded and that the individual who earlier had promised Woody new dental work was now his best friend—a very drunk friend. It was difficult to tell who was more drunk—Woody or the "dentist." Woody's hands were now under the table resting on the thigh of a lady sitting next to him.

Bob dragged him up and to the door, much to the protest of Woody's new friends. They all testified what a wonderful guy Woody was and couldn't he stay for one more drink—they would be happy to buy. Woody fell over a chair, and Bob carried him out to the car as he repeated over and over what a "great guy" Bob was and "he could drive home."

On the ride back to the apartment Woody snored in the passenger seat, his head was slumped down. He slurred several times: "It's great to have you back, Bobby." Bob drove slowly and held a steady course in his lane. It was two in the morning and there was no traffic, but he did not want to be stopped by a sheriff deputy who would insist he take a ride to the jail in Mason. He put Tommy and Jenny out of his mind because he needed to use all of his powers of concentration to drive.

CHAPTER 7

It was dusk with an October moon rising that would eventually cast its light on the farm yard and surrounding fields. The full moon complimented the warm evening. Later coolness would race onto the farm to mingle with the sounds and smells of ruminating cattle and resting people.

Bob had returned home for the weekend and now walked down the lane from the barn to the woodlot. There generations of Holsteins spent their time between milkings, and where he had played among the trees and the abandoned farm machinery. Sometimes he played alone, and sometimes with friends—but it was always without adults. The cattle kept the ground mowed as oaks, maples, and sycamores provided a covering for a Tom Sawyer world where pirates and knights roamed, wagon trains moved westward through Indian territory, and World War II was continually fought. This had been a refuge from farm chores and where Tommy and he had waged constant battles against cousins, neighbors, or make-believe villains since early elementary school. But by high school, he was too busy with other activities to spend much time here. It had been three years since he had even ventured back to the woods.

He was home for the weekend to celebrate his mother's birthday on Sunday. Everything was going well at Michigan State because this time he was attending all classes and completing assignments. Tonight there was a home high school football game, but he chose not to attend. He did not want to answer endless questions from local people about "How is it going?" or "What are you doing at State?" Instead of reliving past glories at the field, he chose to return to the woods where he had enjoyed spectacular victories over gunslingers, Confederate soldiers, Gestapo agents, and ne'er do wells—none of which made the local papers like his previous football wins.

A breeze from the west caused the corn to emit a dry rustle and a clean fragrance. Around the barn there was the smell of Holsteins or diesel fuel, but along the lane there were none of those barn smells. In another month the corn would be harvested, and then the wind would have a clear shot across the field to drive snow and cold against anyone who walked this lane. As dusk approached, the last of warm fall day was hurrying westward.

He walked out of the lane and into the wood lot. His intentions were to wander through the woods to the old farm and then complete the circle by returning home on the road. It was a small open area surrounded by the pastured woods that four hours earlier would have been filled with Holsteins with full udders. Here also were old trucks, tractors, and other discarded farm equipment. There were even a couple of old horse drawn implements sandwiched in with discarded stoves, refrigerators, and other household appliances; the area was a museum of technology and the changing nature of American farming. Bob's father and grandfather would have been required to pay the Lawsonville Dump to discard broken and obsolete equipment. It could be abandoned here on land that would not raise crops—for free.

Bob stood by a cedar tree at the end of the lane and surveyed the scattered junk—some of which he had helped bring here, but most landed here before he and Tommy had made the woods their kingdom. Their realm had to be shared with domestic and woodland animals, but the boys were still the rulers. Crushing some needles in his hand he smelt its pungent odor, and noticed someone sitting on an old Oliver tractor across the lot looking into the woods. He recognized Jennifer Mc Knight's pigtails immediately. He was surprised to see her here. Not because she'd never been here—she had always quietly tagged along as Tommy and he adventured in the woods, but because she was now an English Literature major at Michigan State and this did not seem like the place for a Spartan coed to spend her time.

He remembered how he had promised himself that he would talk with Jenny sometime after Tommy's funeral, but now he was just curious why she would be back here. He moved toward her, careful not to step on a dead stick. Quietly he skirted an old hay rake and stepped across the tongue of a hay wagon that had four flat tires. Without a sound he walked up behind her as she peered into woods where the moon light did not penetrate.

"Hey!" he said as he grabbed Jenny's leg resting on the clutch pedal.

Jenny screamed and would have fallen off the seat if Bob had not held tight to her ankle and steadied her.

"Darn you, Robert," Jenny said when she caught her breath, and then nimbly jumped off the tractor and stood besides him.

"What are you doing?" he asked.

"Nothing—I was just thinking"

"Staring into the woods?"

"Oh—I have a paper to write for Monday."

"On what—Oliver tractors, old combines, or just about junk farming equipment?"

"No," she laughed. "The paper is for an English class, and it's about sexual tension in *Hamlet*."

"Can't you do research in East Lansing on that topic?" he asked with a grin.

"Oh, you guys all think the same. No, I write better at home."

"I'm walking back to the Old Farm. I haven't been there for some time. Would you like to tag along?"

"Sure," she replied, and they both headed for a trail that would lead through the woods to the Old Schmidt Farm. It was dark in the trees, but the trail was wide and the cattle kept any shrubs from growing. He had walked this trail so many times he could do it blind folded.

Through the Hartman woods was an open field and on the opposite side was the abandoned Schmidt farm. Sam Hartman had rented the land from an old couple who no longer were able to farm it, and when the childless couple died, he purchased the eighty acres and the building. The land was contiguous to the Hartman's and good farm land, but the out-buildings and house were so run down, they were of little use. The homestead sat a quarter of mile off a dirt road, so Sam blocked the drive with timbers so that the local teenagers would not have a place "to neck and party." Bob and Tommy's kingdom of the woods had included the Schmidt Farm where there was always something to explore. There had been epic battles waged there with apples or corn cobs, which were in good supply, and in the summer they would spend the nights in the old farm house. Hotdogs were cooked outside, ghost stories were told, and then their courage would be tested as they slept the night in a "haunted house." Jenny had accompanied them on most of these adventures. Bob had not been to the Schmidt Farm since going to college, and he was curious as to how it now looked.

They emerged from the woods and walked a short distance across an alfalfa field to the farm. The rising moon was now above the woods, but the warmth of the day lingered. The breeze had died, and quiet wrapped the woods and fields as Jenny and Bob approached a fence that separated the vacant farm from the surrounding field.

Bob grabbed the top of the fence post and with one quick step on the wire, swung himself over the fence. He turned and offered his hand to Jenny.

"Here, let me help you."

"You think I've never climbed a fence?" Jenny laughed, but she took his hand. She did not climb as confidently as he, and as she swung her leg over the top strand of wire, she caught the heel of her shoe and fell.

"City slicker," said Bob as he easily caught her.

To stop her fall she put one arm around his neck and then pulled herself to him, completing the action that a rusty stand of barbed wire had begun. She hung on to him, and he remembered that moment in the cemetery when she hugged him and held on to him so tightly. As then, he did not know what to do.

He was certain that she had not hurt herself from the fall, and yet she clung to him. He placed his arms around her and then she pulled herself closer. They stood there as two statues. Still uncertain he looked back toward the woods and held her.

Bob's hands were around her waist and resting on her hips. Her head with its brown pig tails rested just below his chin and her breasts flattened across his chest as she pulled herself into him. It surprised him that she had breasts. She had always been a tall, skinny, shy girl. There had been names and teasing about her looks and awkwardness when they went to school in Lawsonville, until Tommy heard about it and then a few bruises eliminated the name-calling. She had never been very popular in high school, but had excelled in the classroom. Each summer Bob's mother pointed out her name in the local paper as being on the Dean's list at Michigan State. Now his hands rested on hips that were soft and as Jenny moved close to him, those hands instinctively wanted to slide down on her bottom.

"My God," he thought. "This is Jenny—she's like a sister!" But she was not his sister, and she did not feel like that skinny, long-legged tag-along from years before. The fragrance of her hair filled his nostrils; it was the sweet aroma of iris blooming in the spring.

"We had better go," she said as she loosened her arms from around him and began walking toward the barn.

Everything was lit with moon light. Although the buildings were never used, the weeds were mowed, and nature's illumination softened the scars and hid the age of the buildings. It looked like a working farm—minus the people and animals.

They walked past the barn with the door lying on the ground and sat on the edge of a concrete tank once used to water horses and livestock. They reminisced about things from their childhood and talked about life in East Lansing. She laughed easily with him about old times, but there did seem to be a distant hurt that he could not understand. Twice she leaned, resting her head on his shoulder without saying anything. Each time he wanted to put his arm around her but as he hesitated she pulled away. He avoided the topic of Tommy's death because he did not know what to say.

Finally she said, "I'd better go home. Will you walk me home, Robert?"

"Sure," he replied. "There might be bears or pirates lurking."

"A damsel in distress," she laughed. "Are you my knight in shining armor?"

"The armor is not very shining, I'm afraid. But I can protect you from bears and lions that may appear along the way."

"More shining than you think." She took his hand as they left the old horse tank.

Leaving the Schmidt homestead, they crossed the piled timbers that blocked the entrance from the road. Holding hands, they walked along the deserted gravel road. The only house on this road was the McKnight farm, which was half a mile from the Schmidt Farm. Suddenly Bob grabbed Jenny and pulled her to him and yelled. "Watch out, bears—a damsel coming through!" Then turning loose he picked up a stone and threw it into the brush along side of the road.

"There was a big bear by that tree. I think it was Yogi Bear," he whispered to a startled Jenny, then he exclaimed in a louder voice. "Watch out Yogi. This damsel knows Prince Hamlet."

Jenny was laughing so hard that she stumbled backward, but caught her balance before she landed on her butt. Bob picked up several small stones and stuffed them into his pocket. "More projectiles to protect this damsel—if other creatures should appear."

They continued up the road with Bob acting out his charade, throwing rocks at Leo the Lion and Yogi the Bear. Jenny giggled each time, which only encouraged him more. When they reached the driveway to the McKnight farm the back porch light was on. Jenny said good night. She took a couple of steps and then returned to him. She reached up with both hands and pulled his face toward him and gently kissed him on the cheek.

"Thank you, Robert," she said and then quickly ran to the house.

He walked home in the moon light. It was an easy trek that he had made countless times before, but never as confused as he was now. He wished that he had said something about Tommy other than telling tales about when they were in school. He needed to tell Jenny how he felt about Tommy's death, and how he still thought about his childhood friend, but he did not know how to approach it and felt more comfortable avoiding the topic. He sensed a distance in Jenny that was undoubtedly centered on the death of her older brother. Beyond the question of Tommy was a new view of his old classmate. He had known her all of his life, as the shy skinny sister of his best friend, now he could not forget the feel of her breasts touching his chest or her hips as she pressed against him after tripping on the barb wire. His hands remembered the feel of her hips as he held her and her fragrance remained in his brain. This was Jennifer McKnight, but a different Jenny than he had known in high school. The road, washed in moon-light and surrounded by the sounds of early fall, easily took him home, but it did not lead him to any understanding.

The next morning Bob woke early, ate breakfast, and went to the barn. His father had already done the milking and was gathering ladders and tools for roofing the hog barn. When Bob got home for the weekend, his father asked him to help shingle it. The Hartmans had not raised pigs for several years; the old hog barn was still used as storage and in need of repair. His father who believed in "waste not, want not" had the younger Hartman children paint it in August, now he and Bob would shingle it. The old ones had to be removed, a few boards replaced, and then a new layer put in place.

The morning which had started out cool, quickly warmed as they began to replace boards. They worked at an easy pace with very little conversation. Each time Bob bent a nail or dropped his hammer from the roof and had to retrieve it, his father laughed and said: "Better buy that boy some books and send him to school—he can't roof."

"I know Dad—too lazy to work and too stupid to learn anything useful," Bob replied with a grin. They continued to work on in silence, each enjoying the company of the other. After lunch his Dad ran some errands in town, and Bob returned to roofing, finishing four hours later. He felt sore and tired, and his hands were definitely not used to the manual labor.

"I didn't think that you would get done today. I thought that I would have to finish that roof after you went back to school," his father commented. His dad very seldom gave compliments, but there was a note of satisfaction in his voice.

That evening after supper he washed, shaved, and changed clothes, then walked outside toward the barn. Most of his friends expected him to turn up at a nearby gravel pit where on such a warm evening there would be drinking and smoking. He had gone a few times last summer. There were always the same ones drunk or stoned, the same ones nursing a beer all evening, and the same ones who just stood and looked on in smugness. This evening he wanted to go back to where he had been last night. Jenny probably would not be at the Schmidt farm, but he still hoped that she would return this evening and they could talk some more. He walked down the lane and entered the wood lot. It was dusk and the air was still so again cedar smell welcomed him to his old haunt where he had found Jenny last night.

He was disappointed when she was not there. He crossed the clearing in the wood lot and took the path to the hay field. When he climbed the fence he paused and remembered how Jenny had felt after she tripped on the top strand and he had caught her. He passed the Schmidt's barn and stopped near the horse tank. He stood there in the fading light, listening to the absence of sound and lost in a mixture of past and present.

Suddenly he felt a sting on his neck, and, when he grabbed the spot where the bee had stung him, he felt an object go by his head. Instinctively, he bent down as a third object passed his head. On the ground at his feet, he saw his bee—a small hard apple. He heard a girlish giggle and looked up to see a brown pony tail duck around behind the old house. He was under attack!

He knew he was engaged in a "war" that he had fought several times in the past with Tommy and other neighbor boys. The ammunition in these battles were corn cobs, apples, or tomatoes—never rocks. Strict rules of conduct were followed—for the first few minutes. Sometime these engagements branched out into the woods, but the farmstead was the major focal point of conflict. The numerous buildings provided places to hide and from which to attack as sometimes as many as ten boys engaged in combat. Tommy and Bob were usually on opposite sides with Bob always winning the early battles until the contest turned to a wrestling match, then a stronger and bigger Tommy triumphed. Even though most of these battles ended in profanity, name calling, and occasionally crying, there was never any report to adults or long term grudges held.

Bob recognized his opponent and knew he was engaged with a veteran of many of these childhood battles—Jennifer McKnight. Bob ducked behind a tree and then sprinted to the old feed lot where he gathered a handful of corn cobs.

He attacked as she ran from building to building. Although she moved quickly, and it was becoming dark, it was easy to locate her because she continued to giggle. She threw apples at him but they were wide of their mark, and they came without any velocity. Bob, on the other hand, had several open shots that should have been sure "kill shots." He threw wide each time.

Jenny ducked into the old milking parlor of the barn and went out the back side. This was a play that he had used several times in the past to trick newcomers. Rookies would track him through the parlor and then they would be ambushed as they exited the barn. Instead of following her, he went around the building and lightly vaulted onto the roof of an old chicken shed. He quietly walked to the opposite edge, being very careful to place his feet only on the underlying supporting rafters and not making any noise on the tin roof. As he suspected, Jenny was underneath him lying in ambush. In previous battles "fire from heaven" would reign down on an unsuspecting opponent. Instead, with a yell, he jumped on her.

He quickly pinned her and sat smiling down at his prey. Laughingly she tried to escape as she thrashed from side to side, but his strength and weight were no match for her, and he held her firmly on the ground. She stopped moving and looked at him and smiled. Without thinking he bent down and kissed her lips. She welcomed his kiss and as he turned loose of her arms, she put her arms around his neck pulling him close to her. He rolled to the side and she willingly followed. They kissed for several minutes, and then they lay in the grass with Jenny snuggled on his shoulder.

The night was quiet and the moon was again full. The evening cooled as she lay next to Bob with her arm across his chest. They talked quietly with long pauses, and they wrapped their arms around each other. A Michigan moon blanketed them in softness.

The conversation was of nothing significant, punctuated with silence as the evening changed to night. Jenny drew even closer to him and rested her leg across his. She turned her head and kissed him and as he returned her kiss, without thinking, he ran his hand up her side and rested it on her breast.

"Don't!" and she pushed him away.

"I'm—I'm sorry—I didn't mean it," Bob said.

"I know—I just can't"

"That's not what I want or meant.—It was stupid. I'm—I'm sorry"

"It's OK, Robert." She lay there for a moment, then sat up. Bob held her arm lightly.

"I'd better go home." Jenny said.

"Please don't go. It's my fault. I wouldn't do anything to hurt you or to make you feel uncomfortable—I'm an idiot."

"No, you're not," she said as she pulled free from him and then took his hand and kissed it and placed it next to her cheek. "If you're an idiot, then you're a wonderful idiot. It's not you Robert—it's me." She paused and looked away still holding his hand on her cheek. He lay on the ground and did not know what to say or do.

"I really need to go," she said.

"I'll walk you home."

"No, I really would rather go myself," she said as she placed his hand on his chest. "This has been fun, and you really didn't do anything wrong."

"I feel like a jerk, and I still think that I was out of line. I didn't mean to make you feel uncomfortable or like I was trying something—I just wasn't thinking."

"I know and it's OK. It isn't you—it's me. I just can't." She bent down and gently kissed him on the lips. When she lifted her head, he saw a small tear as she looked down on him. Quickly she got up and without looking back ran around the shed, disappearing into the night.

As Bob lay there for a few minutes, for the first time he noticed the coldness of the night. He shuddered, sat up, and wrapped his arms around his knees he had pulled to his chest. He tried to replay the events of the evening in his mind and to label all of the feelings that he now felt. It was too difficult and confusing so he stood up and made his way home.

As he walked the path in moonlight, he again tried to understand what had occurred. The events of the corn cob apple fight he understood and he was beginning to accept this new view of Jenny as a woman and not a skinny tag-along, But there was something distant and troubling about her.

As he kicked clumps of sod along the familiar gravel road left there by the county road grader, he worried that she might misunderstand about tonight.

CHAPTER 8

"What is the difference between a tablespoon and a teaspoon?"

Harry was in a cluttered kitchen with an open cookbook on the table. Baking ingredients and tools were spread around the usually tidy kitchen, and two cabinet doors stood open.

"The tablespoon is the larger one," Bob replied. "What are you making now?"

"I'm trying to bake a cake."

"Why are you doing that—do you know someone with a birthday?"

"No—I just wanted to try it. Things aren't going well, and if it turns out to be a disaster, I'll send it to President Johnson."

"You could always send it to the Sin Den downstairs. Jim will eat anything sweet or crunchy after he has been smoking. Add a pound of sugar and some dried leaves and he will munch on it all evening," Bob said.

Since he hadn't worked, Harry had been in the apartment all afternoon cooking. There were chocolate chip cookies on the table, some type of meal was simmering on top of the stove, and now the task of cake baking was being undertaken. Bob preferred to read *Mad Magazine* and *Time* while Harry cooked. They were supposed to share the cooking duties, alternating weeks, but Bob cooked by opening a can or ordering a pizza. This offended Harry's idea of the good life.

The year before moving into the apartment, Harry had become very involved with organic living and extremely choosy about the food that he bought and ate. He began doing more and more of the cooking and this carried over to this year. Even after a year of study and practice most of these endeavors were disasters. Food was overcooked, or undercooked, or ingredients were added incorrectly. Still Bob willingly ate these experiments because he did not want to cook.

Harry had graduated with honors, and when it came to talking politics, he had an almost unlimited grasp of ideas and practicalities. Yet half cups and

55

quarter cups drove him wild with frustration. Bob, on the other hand, raised by a mother who canned and froze everything, could never understand how someone could become so confused and be as inept as Harry. There had been many times when Bob had to prepare a meal for his four siblings because his father was still in the fields and his mother had some type of errand that required her to be away from the home. He did not enjoy cooking, but he could do it. Harry enjoyed it, but was baffled by it and never could measure correctly and would not follow the directions of a recipe.

"Let's eat," said Harry. "Another meal fit for a king."

They sat at a small table in the kitchen. The kitchen and living room were one room with two bedrooms to one side, separated by a single bathroom. They had lived here for over a year, and as opposite as they were, they got along well together. Bob took a bite of meat loaf and uttered a small cough but continued to chew. Harry took a mouthful and then stopped with a perplexed look on his face.

"Shit!" he said. "This is too salty."

"Not if you like it pickled," Bob said and burst out laughing. He scratched his head in goofy sarcastic manner and said, "Here is another fine mess you've got us in. Pickled meatloaf is my all time favorite. Could we have this every evening—please—please."

Harry said nothing. He pushed the offending meatloaf aside and ate the rest of the meal as Bob made humorous comments. It was not that bad, but the opportunity to harass his friend was delicious. Harry had experienced the ribbing before about his culinary skills, and he suffered the complaints and sarcastic compliments good-naturedly. When they had finished eating, Bob cleared the table and prepared to wash the dishes.

"Leave the dishes. I have to clean up the mess in the kitchen. I hope that I can clean better than I can cook."

"You are a man of many talents, Chef Harry," Bob said. "Can I borrow your car this evening?"

"You criticize my cooking and now you want to borrow my car, a royal coach fit for a king?" Harry returned the sarcasm. "You couldn't be going bar hopping with Woody the Wonderful because he always drives. If you were going on campus for a meeting or to study, you'd walk. Therefore, you must have a date and want to impress her with such a fine vehicle."

"Your royal chariot is a 1959 Buick held together with tape and wire that starts and runs by prayer. And if it gets me on campus and back it will be a miracle out of scripture. And you are the royal ass and not the royal king."

"You do have Betty the Buick accurately described," Harry laughed. "My guess is that you have a date with Jenny. I have never seen you date anyone more than three times, and never call a young lady more than twice—unless you were drunk."

"Jenny and I are seeing a movie on campus this evening."

Bob knew that Harry would loan him his car as he had done ever since he drove Betty Buick from New York City two years ago. Several parts of Betty were wired together and the rust spots had been sprayed with Rustoleum, giving it a patch-work quilt effect. The tares in the upholstery were covered with tape and a board had been wedged under the front seat to keep it from dropping through the rust. Betty would never leave the Lansing area, but she would make it to campus for a movie.

Harry had met Jenny a week ago and almost immediately a mutual admiration society had been formed. The three of them had pizza one evening, and Jenny asked all of the right questions that pushed Harry's buttons. She was impressed by how knowledgeable and informed he was on current topics, and that he had regularly attended plays on and off of Broadway with his parents for years. Harry also approved of her. "Where the heck did you find her? She is too smart and too pretty for a hillbilly like you," Harry said the next morning. "You had better date her or I will." As expected Harry loaned Betty.

It was Jenny who had called him on Wednesday the week after the chance meeting at the Schmidt Farm. They had chatted on the phone for over an hour about nothing, and then she had asked if he wanted to go to the library the next evening and study. He had accepted and since then had seen her every weekend and studied with her once or twice during the week. It was now the last of October, and they were going to see *Singing in the Rain*.

He really did not need to spend the time studying because he was repeating classes that he had taken last spring. Halfway through the term he had scored very high on every test and quiz. But he enjoyed an opportunity to be with her and the library was where she spent most of her evenings studying—afterward they would have coffee and talk, and then he would walk her back to her apartment. She lived alone in a one bedroom apartment a few blocks from Grand River.

She had wanted to see this movie and he agreed, although he never enjoyed musicals and was not much of a fan of old movies. But he could not resist an opportunity to spend time with her.

After picking her up, he drove onto campus and parked. The theatre was only half full and they sat alone to one side. When the movie began, she placed her hand on his arm and then intertwined her fingers with his as Gene Kelly sang on the screen. She touched his arm or laid her head on his shoulder, and then she sat up straight as she became more engrossed in the movie. Bob, instead of watching Kelly and Debbie Reynolds, found himself staring at his old neighbor and childhood playmate. Her brown hair was in two braided pig tails just like she wore it when she was in elementary school. When Jenny looked at him and smiled, he quickly turned away in embarrassment and watched Donald O'Connor sing "Make 'em Laugh" as he performed his crazy antics on the screen.

When the movie was finished they walked to the exit and saw rain falling outside. They turned and grinned at each other. They stood near the entrance for several minutes chatting while everyone left with their umbrellas. They had none but the hall was about to be locked. Bob tuned to Jenny and opening the door said: "Shall we proceed into 'Singing in the Rain'?"

Jenny laughed and walked into the rain that fell straight down. There was no wind and the weather had been unseasonably warm, even though it was October in Michigan. They ran along the street trying to reach the car that was some distance before they became too soaked. But after a few yards, Jenny pulled up out of breath and grabbed his arm.

"I can't run like you," she gasped.

"That's no problem. I like the rain. I won't have to shower in the morning." He kissed her on the cheek and then took her hand and they walked along the sidewalk while the rain continued. A fall collection of maple and oak leaves hurried in the gutters and formed dams at the drain grates so that pools of water formed. Bob began to walk with one foot splashing in the gutter and other on the sidewalk. He was so wet that it really did not matter, so he dropped her hand and jumped with both feet into the water with its collection of leaves and debris from the campus. Jenny laughed, and the more he splashed, the louder her laugh became.

It was late in the evening and since it was not a weekend, there was no traffic on the street. He turned and looked back at her. She too was soaked by the rain and, her brown hair was now matted and a mess. One pig tail still remained and hung over her shoulder to the front, but the other one had become undone and spread over the right side of her face. She brushed hair out her eyes and stopped to catch her breath. Water dripped from her forehead and nose, mascara ran down her cheeks.

"God, she's more beautiful than I've ever seen," Bob thought.

Needing little encouragement, he took three quick steps, leaped, and grabbing the light post with his left arm, swung himself entirely around the post and landed back where he started breaking out in a chorus of "Singing in the Rain." He continued on down the street swinging on each post with similar agility and increasing the volume of his song. Jenny followed, her body shaking with laughter so at times she had to stop. Her response only increased his song and dance routine as they walked in the rain until they came to the sidewalk that took them to Beaumont Tower and from there to their car.

When they reached Beaumont Tower, no one was there and the lights around the base of the bell tower lit the concrete where drops of October rain splashed in standing puddles of water. Both were now so soaked that there was no need to try and avoid the rain. Jenny stood on a concrete bench and sang.

"Singing in the rain, I'm singing in the rain"

"What a glorious feeling, I'm happy again," answered Bob as he jumped on an opposite bench. As he returned to his Gene Kelly impersonation, he leaped off the bench and began hopping toward Jenny opposite him. In a similar manner she left her perch on the bench and splashed in the rain toward him. When they met in the middle he grabbed her and kissed her as the Tower chimed twelve. They stood under the bell tower in the light and rain, impervious to the soaked clothes that clung to their bodies.

"We'd better go," Jenny said as the rain lessened a little. By the time they reached Betty the rain had stopped. It did not matter because their clothes were completely soaked and their feet made a sloshing sound in their shoes.

"Do you have anything that I can sit on? I'm so drenched that I don't want to ruin the seat," Jenny said.

"You can't hurt this old piece of junk. A little water on the inside will probably be good for Betty the Buick."

"Well, I don't want to have Harry mad at me," Jenny said as she slid into the passenger side.

"That would be impossible," Bob said as he turned the key. The starter whirred a few times and then engaged. "He thinks that you're the Queen of Sheba, and he says that he can't figure out any reason that you would have anything do with this Michigan farmer."

"He is very nice," Jenny blushed. "But did you tell him that I'm just a farm girl from the same town as you."

"It doesn't matter to him. To him you're perfect."

"I still think he is nice." Jenny laid her head on his shoulder as they drove through the deserted streets of East Lansing to her apartment.

It was late as Bob drove home. He chuckled knowing that Harry, who had to be to work at eight in the morning, would have to sit on a wet seat. He, on the other hand, did not have a class until afternoon and would enjoy the comforts of the bed as his friend enjoyed a wet posterior.

He thought of how much he enjoyed the evening, especially his companion. Musicals were boring, but bearable with Jenny. The last couple of weeks he had spent with Jenny since she called him were intoxicating, and he found himself wanting to spend more and more time with her. For the first time tonight she seemed to enjoy herself without reservation. Each time he felt the presence of a dark line that separated him and Jenny. This line puzzled and frustrated. Many times she would push him away both physically and emotionally, and yet each time she would draw herself back to him. If he did not call or see her for a couple of days, she called and asked what he was doing and then suggested that they do something together. He truly enjoyed her company but this "go away closer" behavior was frustrating him. There was an inexplicable sadness about her that he was certain was caused by Tommy's death. They both avoided talking about his death in Vietnam, and Bob did not know how to approach the subject or bridge this gap between them. Nevertheless, halfway through the term things were going well. He attended all of his classes, his grades were very high, and he hardly ever spent time with Woody or Jim. Jenny now was his focus.

He would graduate in June and then a decision about a career and military obligation would need to be made. Until then he was enjoying himself—and time with Jenny.

CHAPTER 9

"Crank it!"

Bob held the choke of the carburetor closed on the pickup, and this time the motor fired. The ether had done the job. He quickly worked the throttle linkage a couple of times as the motor raced and then settled down to run smoothly. He put the air filter back in place, screwed on the cover, and closed the hood. He climbed into the cab as Jim slid from behind the wheel. Bob gunned the accelerator a couple of more times, and the 1954 Ford pickup ran smoothly now that ether had prodded its cold and stubborn motor. Bob had driven the old farm truck to East Lansing after Thanksgiving vacation at the suggestion of his father. With two weeks of school and one week of exams, the truck would take him home for Christmas vacation.

"Old Jezebel is running fine," Bob said as he put it into gear and drove out of the apartment complex. "Harry said that we should be early at the Teach-In if we want to get a seat."

"I can hardly wait to hear what 'Make the World Safe for Democracy' Harry has to say." Jim looked at a flyer advertising the Teach-In. "I had Belfast for a class, and he is pretty neat. Dr. Refior is an ass, and this ROTC guy may find the Viet Cong friendlier than the students."

"Well Jim, you may be dazzled by what you hear at the Teach-In tonight. You might even convert and join the anti-war movement with Harry—or maybe you will enlist in the army and kill gooks."

"Perhaps the Pope will be Jewish, marijuana will be legalized, and Rachel Welch will call and want to screw me."

"As a matter of fact she did call the other day. But Woody took her out, and she came back with a big smile on her face. It looks like you missed your chance, Jimbo." Bob turned Jezebel into the parking lot.

"You ought to leave the humor to this one-eyed pothead, Farmer Bob—sarcastic humor does not fit you," Jim mumbled. "I hope this piece of junk starts when we leave. It is too damn cold to walk home,"

"It always starts and runs. Sometimes it's ornery about it and requires a little swearing. I will leave the swearing to you. We can always drive your car."

"You got me there," Jim laughed. "Since I don't have one—we won't have to debate the essence of my car that does not exist."

They walked the two blocks to where the Teach-In was to occur. It was six-thirty. A cold December wind blew from the west and Bob zipped his jacket tighter. The wind bit at him now, but in a couple of months this same wind would feel mild when Michigan was wrapped in deepfreeze of February's snow and chill.

They were thirty minutes early but the room was already filled with noisy students and faculty. They chose to stand against the wall to the side while some students sat on the floor in front of the stage. There were several anti-war posters and signs displayed around the room. Harry came in from the back, squeezing by several people as he made his way through the hall. He took an indirect route when he saw Bob and Jim.

"This should be an interesting night. This is way more than we expected."

"Give 'em hell, Woodrow Wilson," Jim said with a grin.

Harry just shook his head and moved to his position on the platform at the front of the room. A few minutes later the other members of the panel took their place on the dais, and at seven o'clock the moderator asked the audience to quiet. After several tries, the moderator finally gained control and welcomed everyone to the Teach-In. After a short comment about courtesy, respect for divergent ideas, and the university being a repository of intellectual curiosity and freedom, he introduced the panel members.

"Each member of the panel will have ten minutes to present his ideas concerning the war in Vietnam. Afterward they will have two minutes for rebuttal to any comments from other panel members. We will do two rounds of rebuttal, and then each will have five minutes for a closing statement. We will not take any questions or comments from the audience. Again let me state the absolute necessity for respect for ideas that you do not agree with," the moderator said. "We are fortunate to have such a representation of divergent points this evening. First is Andrew Refior, Professor of Political Science, who will speak in support of the war. Second is William Bedfast, Assistant Professor of History, who will speak against the war. Third is Captain Jonathan Griffin of ROTC who will speak in support of the war and the draft. And last is Harry Greenbergh of the Draft Resistance Union, who will speak in opposition to the draft. Professor Refior will speak first."

Not only was there a difference in the views of all four, there was a marked difference in their appearance. Professor Refior was neatly dressed in a sport jacket and tie with his white hair and mustache combed and trimmed.

Captain Griffin, dressed in his uniform with a hat lying on his lap, sat erect and straight. Professor Bedfast looked like he should be sitting in the audience with the students. He wore jeans, an old "Berkley" sweat shirt, and had not shaved for a couple of days. Next to him sat Harry with long red hair tied in a pony tail, wearing jeans, and a T-shirt that said "Suppose They gave a War and No One Came."

The audience quietly clapped after Professor Refior spoke in support of the war, but interrupted Professor Bedfast with cheers as he railed against the American military and the war. The placed exploded with people standing and cheering as he ended his talk with an emphatic comment flinging his arms wildly in the air. "Not only is the war immoral, illogical, and illegal—it is also Un-American! It is an abomination against humanity and civilization. And—it represents the worst in American ideals and principles. The war stands in direct opposition to the great principles that this country was founded upon."

It took several minutes for the audience to return to their seats and quiet down as Captain Griffin took the podium. He began speaking forcibly, as if addressing his ROTC cadets.

"Freedom is never free. Each generation of Americans must be prepared to step forward and do its share of protecting our way of life and institutions—just as generations have done so many times before in our history. In the American Revolution we needed to win our independence; during the Civil War we needed to eradicate slavery from the United States so all Americans could be free; and during World War II we needed to stop fascism. Now we must halt the spread of communism in Southeast Asia because if we do not stop it there, it will continue to grow until we will have to stop it at our own shores."

There was coughing and shuffling of feet in the audience as the mood of the crowd changed. Bob could feel the growing resentment of the crowd, and he was part of that energy. Captain Griffin stopped his address to the audience and turned to face Professor Bedfast.

"You say that our involvement in Vietnam is un-American. Well, I respect your right to your opinion, and I will defend your right to that opinion. But I will never be able to agree with that opinion. It is an opinion of ignorance and cowardice." He turned back to the audience and, although he still spoke evenly, his voice was becoming more agitated as he pointed to his chest.

"You may think you are an American. You may even say you love your country. But unless you are willing to put on this uniform and defend it from those who will destroy our way of life, then you are Un-American and will never be a true American!"

"Bullshit," a young man in the front said as he jumped to his feet. "That is nothing but pure bullshit."

Captain Griffin turned to respond to him, but a female student on the other side jumped up and screamed.

"America is bigger than uniforms. You are a fascist military pig!" Pandemonium broke out as the moderator tried to restore order and civility. He stood by the red-faced Captain who continued to argue with the young man in the front. The moderator pleaded for order, but it was too late. A paper airplane floated onto the stage. The back rows of the audience stood and clapped and shouted "bullshit—bullshit—bullshit." Bob and Jim had been standing all during the presentation and now both joining the cheer.

The Captain's face was now almost the color of Harry's hair, and he was so angry that he had trouble talking. Finally in response to the moderator's pleas, the crowd began to quiet. The noise had diminished just enough to hear what Captain Griffin was saying as he angrily shook his fist at the young man in the front row that had first started the verbal melee with his shout of "bullshit."

"You son-of-a-bitch—you arrogant little son-of-a-bitch. I'd like to have you in boot camp for one week." Turning to the crowd he said. "I'd like to have all you dumb sons-of-a-bitches in boot camp for one week."

Wadded paper flyers flew on to the stage as the clapping and shouting intensified. The cheer in the back changed to "baby-killers" and quickly spread to all. The moderator led the Captain and Professor Refior off the stage and out a side door as more paper flew from the crowd. Harry and Professor Belfast walked into the crowd and were greeted enthusiastically. The excitement still remained, but the audience began to quiet down as many left the lecture hall. Harry was engaged in animated conversation with a group of students at the front, while Professor Belfast had an admiring crowd, including several coeds, gathered around him. Bob and Jim walked out to the parking lot. Like the crowd, the old truck was still warm and started with the first try.

"Wow—that was interesting," Jim exclaimed as they drove off of campus. "Do you want to stop at Dagwood's for a sandwich? I didn't have any lunch or dinner."

"Sure," Bob said and in a few minutes maneuvered the old Ford into the parking lot of Dagwood's, a small bar located near the campus. They took a booth on the wall and ordered hamburgers, after two large steins of beer had been placed in front of them.

"I've always wanted to steal one of these steins," Jim said. "I've tried a couple of times, but I always get caught, and they get real pissed about it. I knew a guy in the dorm that had four."

"Well, maybe you can sneak one out this time," Bob said as he took a sip of beer. He was still agitated and could not believe that Jim was thinking about stealing empty beer steins after the meeting on campus. "What did you think about the Teach-In?"

"Are you talking about the circus that we just attended?" Jim smiled and ordered two more steins of beer. "I think that they're all assholes, and that junior general is the biggest asshole of all."

"I never thought much about Vietnam until a friend of mine was killed there, and now living with Harry that is all I hear. When I go to one of these Teach-Ins or listen to Harry, I really wonder if what we are doing in Vietnam is right."

"Well it's stupid, but Harry has too much of a hard-on about the place. If he got laid more, he wouldn't worry so much about the politicians. He reminds me of an old Sunday school teacher I had when I was ten. This guy was always preaching to us about what to do and what not to do. When I lost my eye, he tried telling me that the accident was part of God's plan. Bullshit!—Why can't God have a plan where I have two eyes? These pious, 'save the world' guys give me a pain in the rear, and Harry is one of them."

Jim placed the empty stein on the table and picked up the full one. Bob was surprised at the bitterness in his voice—sarcasm and humor was always there, but seldom bitterness. Jim took a long drink and then asked, "What are you going to do about the draft? You finish in the spring and our buddy Uncle Sam will have a graduation present of a trip to Vietnam. Fortunately, I don't have to worry about that with this eye, and I won't be graduating in the spring."

"I don't know what I'll do."

"Have you thought about Canada?"

"Yes—but I don't think I could ever leave permanently. I'd never be able to return to see my family, and besides I like the United States. I'm certain that it would devastate my family if I left the country."

"Yah, I know what you mean—but can you join something that you don't believe in? And is it worth going over there and dying for nothing?"

"I think that the war is wrong, but I don't want to leave the country, and I don't want to go to jail—so what the hell is there for me to do," said Bob. He looked into his beer while Jim stared at him across the table. "My best friend was killed there, and he was Jenny's brother. If I don't go and do my duty what does that say about my friend who died there, and what will Jenny think?"

There was a pause as each looked across the table at the other. "Maybe I'm just a coward," Bob said.

"I doubt it." Jim placed both hands around the stein and peered at the golden liquid as if it were a religious artifact. "I don't envy your position. All I have to worry about is where to score my next lid. Sometimes I think God is just jerking us around and laughing at us while we struggle with our lives. Maybe instead of the loving God that they taught me about in Sunday school, God is some sadistic bastard that gives us all these impossible choices—and then sits back and laughs while we sweat our balls off trying to decide what to do."

They both looked at their beer and their silence fit nicely with the bar that now was deserted except for the bartender and waitress. Jim held his beer up and said, "Beer, man—beer. 'Tis the stuff to drink for the fellow who it hurts to think." And he emptied his stein.

The waitress came to the table and said they were closing. As she returned to the bar, Jim slipped two of the four steins under his coat and stood up. They walked out the front as the bartender hollered: "Good night and drive safe."

A light snow had begun while they were inside, but it brushed easily off of the windshield. The truck had not sat long and again started the first time. The deserted streets of East Lansing took on a soft clean look with fresh snow under the street lights. They drove in silence as the first December snow floated down and scattered cowardly when Old Jezebel invaded its territory, reclaiming its assigned space once the pick up continued down the street. Bob thought about the evening's events and about his approaching draft notice. What was the right thing to do?

Tommy had done his patriotic duty and now lay near the Methodist Church in Lawsonville. What did "patriotism" mean and what was his "duty"? He thought about Jenny. The last few weeks he found new and deeper feelings for Jenny, and he was certain that she felt something for him. Was he falling in love, whatever that term meant?

What would she think if he didn't serve after her older brother had been killed in support of the country? If only his dilemma of Vietnam could be solved as easily as Jim stealing the two beer steins.

CHAPTER 10

"Eight-five, ninety, ninety-five, a hundred." Bob laid the last five dollar bill on the counter and slid it toward the East Lansing police officer.

"You need to sign the two places I have checked and initial the box at the bottom of the page," the officer said. "They will bring Mr. Greenbergh here in about fifteen minutes."

After processing a line of angry parents and bewildered students, the balding sergeant seemed thankful when Bob appeared and politely counted out cash without an angry monologue. Many before him had tried to post bail with a personal check, which he had politely refused—cash only. He had also had to deal with angry parents who had been called to East Lansing to bail a son or daughter out of jail because of the demonstration on campus and who were now directing their anger at the aging police officer behind the counter. He fielded all questions and comments politely and professionally as he shuffled papers back and forth and gave the same explanations about procedures over and over. Bob sat in a chair waiting for Harry who was somewhere in the East Lansing City jail—placed there from the demonstration on campus against Dow Chemical Corporation.

Dow had been on campus recruiting graduates for employment and the anti-war movement had targeted them as symbols of corporate American that were benefiting from the Vietnam War. Harry had led the demonstrators in a sit-in. Some had left when directed by the campus police, and those who had refused were now were lodged in jail with a hundred dollar bail and a future court date.

As Bob waited in the chair, he noticed one lady still in line. She complained about Michigan State University, East Lansing, and especially the police department. Her son was here unjustly and she was going to let someone know about it. She was also dressed differently than students who were posting bail for roommates or friends. She wore a full length fur coat with black high heel boots and flashed several large diamond rings on both hands.

"This is not right," she said to the sergeant. "William did not do anything wrong, and it is a hideous mistake that he should be placed in this filthy disgusting jail. You will be hearing from my lawyer, and I'm going to name every one of you police officers in the suit that I will file." The sergeant had finally depleted his supply of patience, and he snapped.

"In your damn suit lady, be sure and spell my name correctly," he said angrily as he pointed to his name tag over the left shirt pocket. "It pisses me off when people spell my name wrong. Do you want me to write it down so you won't make a mistake?"

The lady stopped her tirade and was quiet for the first time since entering. The sergeant realized his mistake and quietly added.

"I'm sorry, madam. My supervisor is Captain Jeremiah Willingham, and he will be here tomorrow morning at eight o'clock. He'll be happy to take any complaints or concerns you might have. Now if you'll just sign these, we can release your son."

She signed the forms, placed a hundred dollar bill on the counter without saying a word, and took a seat next to Bob. In a few minutes a grinning Harry walked through the door that said "Police Officials Only." Putting his arm around Bob as they walked into the December evening toward the University he said, "Well, now I have another chapter for my autobiography."

"I can't believe that they arrested you on trespassing charges. It's a public university," Bob said. "Isn't MSU supposed to be a land-grant college and help the public and all of that crap?"

"The placement director said that we were blocking the recruitment process, and the university had the obligation and right to remove us. The cops said the same thing when they came. I think they were just looking for some charge to get us out of there. We were an embarrassment to the university. I was hoping to make the national news, but I think we'll just be in the *Lansing State Journal*. Thanks anyway for bailing me out. I'll get the money for you tomorrow."

"Don't thank me. Thank Woody."

"Woody?"

"Yup—good old Woody. The cops wouldn't take a personal check from me, and Jim had spent all of his cash on two lids of grass. But you know Woody always has cash since he doesn't believe in a checking account. In fact, at first he was going to give me five hundred bucks because that is what we thought bail would be."

"I wouldn't have thought that he would help me, especially since it was a protest against the Vietnam War."

"He didn't hesitate for a minute when I asked if he had the money. He just forked it over. You know Woody. If you're a friend of his, there's nothing that he won't do for you."

"I'll be darned. I wouldn't have figured Woody for the money. I'll see that he gets it back tomorrow."

They reached Grand River Avenue and waited for a car to pass before crossing. There was little traffic and even fewer people walking on campus. Snow was on the ground, but because there was no wind, it was not very cold. They stopped under a street light and Harry asked. "Did they give you the keys to Betty at the police station?'

"Yes—I got 'em in my pocket." Bob pulled them from his jacket and handed them to Harry. "When's your court date?"

"It's in two weeks. Some of those who had to be carried out of the building were charged with resisting arrest, but I think that charge will be dropped and they will just have to face the same charge of trespassing. The University and East Lansing probably want this to go away quietly—but I'm not going to let it! I'll have my day in court, and I'll have my say about Dow Chemical and the Vietnam War," Harry said as he became more animated.

"Bob, the University is part of the problem. I can understand it better now. It isn't just the idiots in the Pentagon who decide to send Americans to die in Vietnam. It's the whole system with its corporate profits that feed off the labor and suffering of common people. It's Michigan State that trains the police for South Vietnam and provides chemists so Dow can make better and cheaper napalm. Where do CIA agents come from? Where do the majority of army and navy officers come from these days—not West Point and Annapolis! It's the universities that provide people with slide rules and Eversharps and teaches them to calculate profits and count bodies." Harry made a sweeping gesture with his hand.

"Here's the problem that we can fix. Check it out, Bob, and you will find that almost every trustee at MSU is on at least one board of directors of a major corporation—Dow Chemical, General Motors, Ford, and IBM. President Hannah is buddies with all of the corporate leaders, and he's on several boards himself—plus all of the money that the University has in trust and the experts that they employ here on campus—all available to corporate America. This university is nothing but a partner with the military industrial complex that is running the world and screwing the poor and weak. Vietnam is just one place where they're doing it. But we need to begin to change it here at Michigan State. Here we can change things."

Bob was losing interest as Harry continued on about Vietnam, the military industrial complex, and the universities of America. Generally Harry was soft-spoken and very concise in making points in an argument, and Bob found him very attuned to his listeners, whether it was Bob at the apartment, arguing politics, or counseling a young man on the war. This was not one of those times.

"Jenny is waiting for me at the Union, and we're going back to her place for a while. Where is your car?"

"Betty is parked by the stadium." Harry paused and looked at his roommate who shivered in the night air, and he smiled.

"Oh I see. I get Betty Buick and you get Jennifer McKnight. I hardly think that is a fair arrangement," Harry said as he gave Bob a light push on the shoulder.

"Well, you're the one who wants to save the world. I just want to be with a beautiful girl," Bob said as he climbed the Union steps. "I'll tell Jen that you found your true love in jail."

"Go to hell," Harry laughed. "She doesn't deserve you—she deserves me."

Bob entered the doors of the Union, searching for Jenny. He found her reading in the lounge. Throwing his jacket on the sofa, he flopped down and rested his head in Jenny's lap.

"The jailbird is out," he said as he flung his legs over the end of the sofa. Jenny put the book face down on the end table and placed one hand on his chest while the other hand played with his hair.

"Good. I'm glad. What did they finally charge him with?"

"Trespassing—he has to appear in court in a couple of weeks. He's really fired up now. All of the way from the police station he was rattling on and on about Vietnam and the military industrial complex. He would still be talking to me if I hadn't come to meet you."

"I like Harry. I know that he's passionate in his opposition to the War. Every time I talk with him he gives me something new to think about."

"I'll get you a date with him, "Bob teased.

"Harry is nice, but I prefer you," she blushed and looked across the room. It was an expansive room with chairs and sofas—most vacant but a few occupied by students who were quietly reading or writing. She was staring at nothing, and Bob looked at her wondering what she was thinking.

"A penny for your thoughts."

"Oh, the thing with Harry this afternoon got me to thinking about Tommy." She paused but continued to play with Bob's hair as he lay in her lap. "I have not thought about him in a couple of weeks, which is strange. Now with Harry and the demonstration this afternoon I can't help but think about Tommy. Do you ever think about him?"

"Yes."

Quietly he looked up, seeing her from a different perspective than he had before. Her brown hair flowed over both shoulders, and he gazed up into her face. She had a cute nose. These last few weeks he was taken by her beauty—a beauty that he had never noticed in the previous years. Those long brown eye lashes fluttered occasionally as she stared away. He knew that they covered deep brown eyes and he thought of "cow eyes"—a nickname Tommy and her family called her.

"When Tommy joined the marines, I was proud of him—we all were proud of him, and when he came home on leave before Vietnam, he looked really handsome," Jenny said softly. "I thought that he'd do his duty and then come home and farm with Pop—or get another farm somewhere around Lawsonville. I was shocked when Mother called me at school and told me that he had been killed in Vietnam. I couldn't cry or anything. I was just numb. Even that next week when Pop came and got me and took me home for the funeral, I still couldn't cry. I didn't feel anything; everything was in a fog, and I still don't remember much of the funeral. I did go to class and finish the term—that's about all that I can say for that time." Bob sat up and took Jenny's hand.

"No one cried at the funeral. I saw you standing next to the grave at the end and you looked so lost, I wanted to come over and hug you, but you had all of your brothers and sisters around you."

"I wish you had."

"I never even said anything to your Mom or Dad. I was going to the next day, but I didn't, and then I went back to school. That summer I was always going to stop and speak with your folks, but I never knew what to say, so I just wrote a letter and sent it."

"I know. I saw it, and it was nice."

"I still remember the day of his funeral. I stood by myself off to the side after carrying the casket to the grave. It was a warm April day," said Bob and he paused. "It was the kind of day when we would've been in the woods, or at the Schmidt farm, or playing down by the creek. And someone would have fallen into the creek, and your mom or my mom would have given us all hell."

"Maybe not slipped, but pushed," Jenny said with a smile.

"I also remember how angry I was that day. I wasn't sad—later I became sad when I thought about him—but then I was just angry. Furious that my best friend had died and I would never get to see or talk with him again," he said. "Perhaps I was also angry because I began to question about the war. That was at the end of our sophomore year, and up until then I always thought that the government was right about everything. At that point I began to wonder about things, after Tommy was killed in Vietnam."

"What are you going to do about Vietnam? You graduate in June, and then you will be drafted," Jenny asked.

"I don't know. I guess serve my time."

"I always thought it was the right thing to do, and I was proud of Tommy when he joined. After he was killed, I would get angry at those who were protesting the war. It just seemed to me that they were not supporting our troops—and making fun of Tommy. And that made me mad. Now I just don't know anymore." Jenny paused and stared across a room that now only contained them. "Maybe I've been listening to Harry too much, but it seems to me that the war is pointless and is going to go on for ever. I don't think that we can win and we can't quit, so how are we going to end that terrible situation. And I wonder how many more American boys will die over there like Tommy did?" Jenny touched his face as the lights flickered off and on in the Union.

"Looks like they are closing the place up and kicking us out," he said.

"Yes, they are. Will you walk me to my apartment?"

"Sure—maybe there will be a creek along the way and I can push you into it—just like the old days."

CHAPTER 11

"And here's Johnny."

Ed Mc Mahan introduced the *Johnny Carson Show* as Bob put his coffee cup down. Jenny sat next to him on the couch with both hands wrapped around a mug while Johnny began his monologue about the events of the day. After the Union closed they had walked to Jenny's apartment located in a quiet residential neighborhood within walking distance to the campus. She had moved there mid year of her junior year. A large room functioned as a kitchen and living room, and there was a small bedroom with an adjacent bathroom.

Since Fall, Bob spent many of his evenings with Jenny. They usually studied together on the week days and then hung out on the weekends. He had not skipped a class all term and had not been to Emma's since the classes started. He had just finished his last final and would be going home for Christmas break in two days. This was a marked difference from his life-style a year ago, but he was finding that he enjoyed being a serious student—besides he felt better in the mornings and there was more money in his checking account.

His new behavior was not lost on his friends. Harry was happy that he was spending time with Jenny studying and not partying. Harry was clearly infatuated with Jenny, and it was a mutual admiration society. Jim and Woody were polite around her, and Woody always teased her about "how she had reformed Bobby." Jim said very little, but he lived in his own world of "getting high and getting by." It was Woody who missed a ready companion to go bar-hopping. Woody harassed him endlessly.

"I got some fine ladies at Emma's just waiting to put out for a good looking college boy like you. Can you help me out here, Bobby?" Woody would say with mock seriousness. "No, I suppose that you can't—you got your own foxy lady, so the Woodpecker will have to lay pipe by himself."

When the first guest arrived on the Carson show, Jenny snuggled close and kissed him on the neck. He returned the kiss and while the television illuminated the room and someone droned on about the newest movie, the two were intertwined on the couch. Bob held her tightly with one hand while the other rubbed her back. Jenny's blouse slid up and his hand moved to the small of her back. She had the fragrance of spring flowers. He was so lost in the enjoyment of kissing and holding her that he did not realize what his fingers were doing. On their own they wandered across an expanse of skin and rested on Jenny's bra. There they lingered for awhile and then two fingers slid under the metal clasp. Suddenly she sat up straight and pushed herself away from him.

"Jenny, I'm sorry," he said seeing the startled look on her face. "I wasn't trying anything."

"I know, Robert," she said as she took and held his hand, but still stayed away from him. "It is not you—it is me."

"There it was again," he thought. In the last few weeks there had been several "It's not you—it's me." At times she seemed to want to be close, and many times she started the physical contact or encouraged it, and then she would suddenly draw away from him. He was confused, thinking that it was something that he did.

"Jenny I wouldn't do anything to hurt you, or something that you did not feel right about. You are special and I care about you. If I get carried away, it is because I'm stupid and not thinking."

"I know, Robert. And you probably don't believe this, but I want you to touch me and I want to touch you. It's just that something happens and I can't, then I need to distance myself."

"Is it something I do or say?"

"No"

"Well, what is it?"

"It is nothing that you do or say. It's me."

Bob looked into Jenny's face as she sat away from him, but still held tightly to both of his hands. He could see anguish on her face as a single tear rolled down her cheek; the smile that he enjoyed so much was gone. Yet for all of her discomfort, he could feel the anger and frustration rising in him. "I need to leave before I say something that I will regret," he thought.

"I had better get going."

"Please stay awhile."

"No, I need to go. I have a bunch of errands to do tomorrow before I go home. Harry has already left for Christmas, and there are a few things to do around the apartment since no one will be here for two or three weeks."

"Please stay a little longer. You didn't do anything wrong."

"I need to go."

He pulled his hands free and kissed her lightly on the cheek. He picked up his jacket from the chair in the kitchen and turned to say good-bye. Jenny still was on the couch with her feet folded under her. She looked so alone and sad that for a moment he wanted to hug and hold her. But if he did, where would his hands end? He did not want rejection again, and he did not want to verbalize his anger—it was best to leave.

"Robert, don't go."

"I have got to get going. I'll give you a call when we are both home," he said as he closed the door. Jenny was left on the couch with Johnny Carson. He went down the short hall and into the cold night. As he zipped his jacket, he gave a vicious kick to a piece of frozen snow that sailed into the street.

"What in the hell does she want? I'll be damned if I'll ever call her again or even go out with her if she calls me."

But he knew that this was not true. It only took a block and several chunks of kicked snow until he was missing her. Mid-Michigan had received a heavy wet December snow that morning and the streets and sidewalks had been cleared. Now several hours after sunset, the slushy snow had frozen into hockey pucks of different sizes. These he attacked as he swore. Speaking only to the illumination from the street light, he gave a large chunk of ice a shattering kick.

"Damn it! I'm tired of this shit. Does she think that she's the only one who suffered with the death of Tommy?" He stood on the sidewalk and sent another ice ball flying. Wheeling around, he was quickly back at Jenny's apartment building. Taking the stairs two at a time, he charged up to the hall where a single light shone near her apartment door. Stopping, he checked his watch—midnight. He started to knock, but decided that it was too late, and began to walk slowly out of the building. He stopped at the top of the stairs, and with no ice to kick he clenched and unclenched his fists. He wanted to be with Jenny; he wanted to tell her how he felt—even though it was always difficult to talk about his feelings. He went back to the door and knocked softly. Almost immediately it opened and there stood Jenny wearing sweatpants and an old "Lawsonville Football" shirt that must have belonged to Tommy.

"I'm glad that you came back. Come on in," she said as she took his hand and led him back into the room.

"Look Jenny, we need to talk."

"I know."

They sat on the couch with the single light from the kitchen revealing her red eyes. Jenny started to speak, but it was Bob who charged into the conversation.

"I know that sometimes I get carried away, but I want you to know that I would never do anything to hurt you. I care about you. You're not just some girl that I met at a party I'm trying to hustle. Jenny, we're old friends—we grew up together, and besides you are Tommy's sister. Sometimes I'm stupid and do stupid things."

"I'm more than Tommy's sister. I'm not that skinny tomboy that you used to have corn cob and apple fights with at the Schmidt Farm."

"I know. You're definitely not skin and bones—believe me, I know."

"And I want to touch you and be held by you—as strange as you might think it sounds."

"Well then what the heck! You want to be close and then the next minute you're pulling back and pushing me away. This doesn't make any sense. If it's something I do or say, please let me know so I can change. You are driving me nuts with this hot and cold." Realizing that he had raised his voice, he paused, took a deep breath, and then continued.

"I know that Tommy's death affected you greatly—just as it did me. If that's what it is—then tell me!"

"No, it's not that. It's me. I want to be close, and then when we are, I draw away. I know that. I also know that it's not fair to you. I know that you don't want to hear 'it's me and not you,' but I'm the problem."

Pausing, Jenny pulled back from him and sat straight on the couch. She took a deep breath and looked at him. He waited while the only sound that filled the room was the furnace blowing warm air.

"There's something that I need to tell you, but you must promise to listen to it all. You can't interrupt, or leave, and you have to hear it all. I need to tell you. I have wanted to tell you this many times since that evening at Schmidt's Farm in October, but I just didn't know how to say it, and I was afraid of what you would think of me, and that you wouldn't want to see me again. I just couldn't bear that. I care for you, Robert. I care for you deeply. In fact, I have fallen in love with you," she paused and touched his forehead with her finger tips and slowly drew them down his cheek bone and chin, and then pulled them away.

"I love you, Robert. I probably was in love long before we came to Michigan State. But now I must tell you what happened to me, if there is to be a chance for us. I may lose you, but we can't go on as we have for the last few weeks. This will be hard for me to say, and you must give me some time to get it out. Will you listen and not leave?"

"Yes"

The furnace shut off and now the quiet was deafening as he waited. She sighed deeply and then began.

"Something happened to me here at State the fall after Tommy was killed." She paused. "Someone forced himself on me—physically—more than I wanted. In fact, I didn't want any of it." Jenny again paused. "Do you understand what I'm saying, Robert?"

"Rape? Do you mean rape?"

"No, some people might call it that. But it wasn't rape, because I'm to blame. But, it was ugly—and dirty—and awful." She took a deep breath.

"It was the first time, Robert, and the only time, and it was not what I had imagined it would be like. I have wanted to tell you, but I was afraid of what you would think of me."

"Oh, Jenny—"

"Let me finish. This is hard."

"Jenny, you don't have to tell me."

"I know that I don't have to, but I need to. I owe you an explanation, and I need to do this for us. But most important, I need to do it for me," she said. "I've never been able to talk to anyone about this,—you're the first person that I have told. But I really need for you to listen."

As he sat on the couch facing Jenny she appeared to draw away from him, although she continued to sit in the same spot. A few minutes ago he had entered her apartment ready to force the conversation, and now he was speechless as he was lost in this small place. He had a vision of two burly men holding her down as she screamed and kicked while another man with long greasy hair and dirty hands wearing a leather jacket appeared. The scene was in an alley way next to full cans of garbage with a distant street light. Scenes of filth and violence flashed through his head in the instant that she caught her breath and continued.

"It was a year ago last September and I was at a fraternity party with Brad. Do you know Bradley Whitcomb?" she asked.

"Wasn't he some big shot in student government? Someone said that you were pinned to him."

"He was a member of Sigma Sigma Sigma and President of the All-Greek council, and no I wasn't pinned to him—although he wanted to be. I met him at the end of my freshman year, and we dated all during my sophomore year. He was handsome, polite, and thoughtful. I guess that I also liked the idea of dating someone who was a greek, and the Tri-Sigs are pretty important fraternity on campus. He was especially nice when Tommy was killed in April of our sophomore year. He came to the funeral and visited me a few times that summer. I don't think he felt very comfortable in Lawsonville, but he called at least once a week during the summer after Tommy's death. He's from the city, so Lawsonville was quite a change for him. Mother was nice to him, but you know Pop—if it isn't a John Deere tractor, he doesn't have much to say."

"I remember seeing him at the funeral," Bob said. He thought how the blue blazer, button-down oxford shirt, and khaki slacks stood out among the local farmers. It was Brooks Brothers' attire against J. C. Penny and Sears—the catalogue won the round that day because of sheer numbers.

"We had dated all year, and he was always thoughtful and kind. After we began to date steadily he had wanted to go all the way, but I just wasn't ready. He didn't seem like the right one. Anyway, when Tommy was killed, Brad was very supportive and thoughtful. I had a hard time realizing that Tommy would never be coming back, teasing me, picking on me, and calling me 'cow eyes' as he always did—and would never be there to fix every problem." She took a deep breath and sighed.

"Even that summer when he was visiting me at the farm, and we were parked on Wood Road, I had to push him away because his hands were going too far. He said that sex would help me get over Tommy's death, and that we should make love. But I said no. But I didn't think too much about it because I figured that he was just a guy, and all guys are interested in sex." She sat still with both hands folded in her lap. Her voice carried no emotion, and although she spoke softly, he heard and would remember every word she said.

"That fall we were at a Tri-Sig party playing this drinking game. I don't normally drink any alcohol—sometimes a glass of wine, but Brad wanted me to join the game because he said it had to be played with couples and he needed a partner. There were three other Tri-Sigs and their dates, and it was with shots of beer. Have you ever played one of those games, Robert?"

"Yes, I have," Bob replied. His mind flashed quickly to last summer when he and Woody had gone to Lake Michigan to visit some friends for the weekend. The game had been played with shots of bourbon, and he had woken up in the morning in a lawn chair—naked. It took him an hour to find all of his clothes.

"At first the beer tasted awful—and then not so bad. And then I began to feel really good. I know all of us were laughing at everything. Suddenly I started to cry, and I didn't know why. Everyone was trying to make me feel better, and then suddenly I threw up on the floor. I ran into the bathroom and got sick again, and by this time my head was spinning. I stayed in the bathroom until I felt better, but I was so embarrassed. The party had been at the fraternity house, and I went into Brad's room to get my purse and jacket and have Brad take me home, but then I got dizzy again, and I lay down on Brad's bed. I must have passed out or something." A tear ran down her cheek and another tear started down the other cheek.

"I came to with someone on top of me kissing me, and his hand was under my blouse and my slacks were pulled down. It took me a couple of seconds to realize that it was Bradley and what he was doing. I told him NO and tried to push him away, but I couldn't do it. He wouldn't stop. I was crying and begging him to stop, but he was too strong—or maybe I was too drunk. I don't know. I know that it was just awful, and I felt so ashamed when it finally stopped. When he got off of me, he stood at the end of the bed and pulled his pants up, and then that's when he told me how beautiful I was. He said that he just couldn't help himself; he had done it for us. Now we were a couple. He kept saying things, but I wasn't listening. I was sobbing and trying to straighten my clothes. The more he said about how beautiful I was, the uglier and dirtier I felt." She paused. "Do you think I'm ugly?"

"No." Bob reached out and pushed a strand of hair from her forehead back behind her ear, then lightly brushed Jenny's cheek. "I think you're the most beautiful girl on campus. In fact, you are the prettiest woman that I know."

"Thank you." She took his hand and kissed it and then laid it back on the couch. "I felt ugly for so long and didn't want to be around anyone. After that October evening at the Schmidt Farm, I began to feel pretty again—and I wanted to be with you. You make me feel pretty, and that is a feeling that I haven't had for some time."

Jenny took a couple of deep breaths as the furnace kicked on again. Bob sat in a room that still seemed expansive and listened as hot air was blown into the room. He did not know what to do or say. He wanted to do something, but was afraid that it would be the wrong thing. He saw a young girl in bib overalls and brown pig tails following him and Tommy everywhere. She was not a bother, but was just there as he and Tommy roamed their Tom Sawyer world. Now suddenly something insidious and ugly had entered that world, an ugliness that he could not understand but hated. Jenny continued.

"Brad was between me and the door, and when I got up to leave he grabbed me and wouldn't let me leave. I was crying and maybe I was hysterical, but he said that I had to calm down before he'd let me go. He said that this is what everyone did and that now I was his girl and everything would be fine if I would just calm down. He wouldn't let me go, so I kicked him hard where Tommy told me to. Tommy said all guys are sensitive there. Do you know where I mean?"

"Yes, I do."

"I ran out of the fraternity house and back to my dorm room. My roommate was gone for the weekend. I got sick again, but I thought that if I took a shower at least I might begin to feel clean. I showered several times a day for the next week, and I still couldn't get rid of the feeling of filth."

"Did you report it to the police or tell anyone?" Bob asked.

"No—how could I? I was drunk, and I was in his bedroom. If I hadn't gotten drunk then it wouldn't have happened. It was my fault."

"That's not right. He's a jerk, and he shouldn't have done it. Do your parents know?"

"No, I couldn't say anything to them. Tommy had only been dead a few months, and now they would have this mess—their daughter drunk at a fraternity party and drunk on her boyfriend's bed. And then having sex with him. Even though it was my fault, I know Pop would have killed him. I have seen him lose his temper. He shot an old ram sheep we had one time after the ram knocked me down and broke my arm when I was nine."

"I remember that," Bob said. He remembered Mr. McKnight as quiet and calm, but with a temper that would explode—but never toward his children or wife. And Jenny had always been a favorite, so he had little doubt how George McKnight would react if he knew what had happened to his Jenny.

"I wish that Tommy was around. He always looked out for me and fixed everything. But maybe I couldn't have told him. After a couple of weeks, it just got bottled up inside of me. I didn't socialize anymore, and I started going home more on the weekends. I just couldn't stand to be here at MSU. I thought about dropping out of school, but in class I could at least forget about what happened. So I stayed and moved into this apartment at term break."

"Jenny, I'm so sorry. I didn't know. I'm so sorry."

"I know you didn't know. There was no way that you would have known. After that night I could not stand to have anyone touch me—until that apple fight back last fall. And then I enjoyed just talking and laughing with you. I wanted to kiss you that evening and when you did kiss me, I really enjoyed it—as I always do. But when we are kissing something will cause me to push away from you, and that is what I mean by 'my fault.' It is nothing that you do or say. It's me that is the problem," she said. "I know that it is not fair to you. Am I bad and do you just hate me?"

"No—I could never hate you. I like you too much." He reached and touched her leg.

"I have found myself falling in love with you these last few weeks, and I have been afraid of losing you if you knew what had happened. I guess that maybe I have always had crush on you. You and Tommy always let me tag along and looked out for me. You protected me."

"I didn't do anything. It was Tommy that would kick anybody's butt who messed with his sister. Remember how he gave Johnny Snyder a black eye when he called you 'a dumb farmer bitch,' and how he held Fred Jenson's head under water in the stock tank because he made you cry."

"If he hadn't done it, you would have." For the first time a small smile appeared. "You two were always so wild and adventuresome; you and Tommy were my heroes and protectors in those days. I just tagged along."

"A nice tag-a-long," Bob said as he gently rubbed her leg. He thought a moment what Tommy would have done if he knew someone had hurt his "cow eyes" sister. It would have been very unpleasant for Bradley Whitcomb.

Now the tears were flowing down both cheeks, and Jenny took the back of her hand and wiped them away. Bob wanted to hold her but was afraid. He took his hand from her leg. He did not know what she wanted or needed, and he was afraid to say anything. Her anguish and his confusion caused inaction.

Finally he said, "Did you ever see Brad again?"

"Yes, he brought my things over the next day. He wanted to talk, but I couldn't stand to be in the same room with him. He wanted to go out again, but I didn't want to see him. He phoned a few times and would talk with my roommate, but I told her to say that I was at the library each time he called.

She couldn't understand why suddenly I stopped seeing him. I never told her what had happened, and then I moved into this apartment. I saw him once on campus before graduation. He'd been accepted to law school at Yale."

"I feel so bad," he said. "I never knew this happened to you. What can I do?"

"Would you mind holding me for a little while?"

"That's not a problem," he said softly and reached for her. He held her and lightly kissed her hair. They sat on the couch for several minutes with her head on his shoulder and his arm around her. He gently rubbed her shoulder with one hand and held her hand with the other.

"One more thing," she asked. "Would you mind spending the night with me? Just sleeping—nothing else."

"No. I would like to do that."

Later when he crawled into her bed with his jeans and shirt still on, she could not seem to get close enough to him. She curled with her back to him and took his leg and laid it over her own two legs. Her head was on his left arm and her head was under his chin so that he once again smelled the fragrance of flowers. She put his hand in both of her hands and held it next to her cheek.

"Thank you, Robert," she said and fell to sleep.

Bob lay listening to her breathing with a jumble of feelings surging through him like the waves on Lake Michigan hitting the shoreline. First tenderness for Jenny and her pain, and a desire to hold her would roll across him. That would recede from the shore as he was hesitant to touch her and bring more pain to her. Then a new wave of anger would crash over him and he wanted to put his hands around Bradley Whitcomb's throat. He did not care how big or tough Bradley was, there would be an "ass-kicking" that only Tommy could appreciate—perhaps he would just shoot him.

He would use a twelve gauge shot gun—pump action with five in the magazine and one in the chamber. At home he had always tried for the clean kill shot so the prey did not suffer, but for Bradley he would shoot only at the feet and the hands. He racked the slide action and another shell slid into the chamber. He would use bird shot because buck shot or slugs would be too quick. He would need an entire box of shells.

CHAPTER 12

"Damn her."

Bob swore as he shut the door and stepped out onto the porch. Immediately, several purring cats were rubbing against his leg. He placed his foot under a bobtailed yellow tomcat and flung him off of the porch, watching him twist and turn as he sailed toward the barn.

"God-damn useless cats," he cursed and immediately felt remorse. He was actually fond of the cats that lived in the barn and always gathered at the back steps of the house in the evening before milking time. They knew that dinner was at hand and made a nuisance of themselves with purring and rubbing.

His anger was directed at his mother, not the cats. They had just made the mistake of being present to receive the fury he couldn't express inside. The problem began at supper when his mother commented about his late arrival the night before. He had taken Jenny to a movie and afterward they had parked on a back road and talked. Neither realized the time, and it had been two o'clock in the morning when he finally got home. In East Lansing this would not have been a problem because the campus was still alive, but now he was back in Lawsonville—dead—boring—Lasonsville. At supper his mother had hoped that he would not be out all night "tomcatting around," because "there was nothing a responsible person could do after eleven pm—unless it was to get into trouble—especially get a girl in trouble."

After a week home, he was ready to return to East Lansing and was thinking that it had been a mistake to leave. Perhaps he should have stayed in the apartment and come home only on Christmas Eve and then returned the next day. Already she had asked him twice "how had he done in school," and there were the constant mothering that his younger brothers accepted, but infuriated him.

"Robert, do you have a clean handkerchief?"

"ROBERT! Would you please tuck that shirt tail in!"

"You're not going to wear that tonight, are you?"

A few steps down the path and the cold December air dissipated his anger while several meowing cats tagged at his feet. He knew that his mother intended her comments for his good—it was just that she still saw him as twelve years old. He was not unhappy that he had come home because his father could use his help, and he did enjoy it—when he put some distance between him and his mother. Besides, Jenny had also returned for winter break, and he saw her almost every day.

He could hear the twenty Holsteins bellowing as they waited to exchange their milk for feed. The wind blew the snow around his feet. It would not have bothered the waiting cows, but it sent a shiver through him, because he was not wearing long underwear. At least he wore his heavy boots so his feet were warm in the two inches of snow on the ground. It was not unusual to have snow the middle of December, but there was heavy snow in the forecast and there would surely be a Bing Crosby Christmas next week—to the joy of children and the dismay of his father who still had corn to pick. Off to his left behind the corn bins he could hear the steady twang of a hammer striking metal. His father was in the workshop trying to repair the conveyor on the combine to finish picking the sixty acres of corn still in the fields. He had been quieter than usual at supper, which was an indication he was worried about something. After eating he stood and said to Bob, "Milk the cows tonight, Bobby. I need to fix the combine. We need to get that corn in, and I don't like the look of this weather."

Since he had gone away to college, the milking chores had fallen to his younger brother, Joe. Joe was at a wrestling meet, and his dad would have done the milking—as he had done in previous years for Bob when school activities kept him from his duties. Now weather, harvest, and a broken combine kept his father from relieving the Holsteins of their daily production.

He stepped into the barn and stopped for a minute. He could still hear the bellowing outside the milking parlor door, and he could smell the fragrance of alfalfa hay in the mows. He looked at the structure of the barn—built with rough cut beams on the inside, red painted boards on the outside, and tin on the roof covering everything.

He thought for a moment of the many hours he had spent in this barn. There were the times in the summer of storing fresh cut hay in the mows for the winter. If it was hot outside, the temperature in the mow would be even higher, and there would never be any breeze to cool the sweat dripping off his forehead. He would work without a shirt, and hay chaff would stick to his arms, face, and chest. As he stacked the hay sometimes a bale would fall back on him, and then hundreds of tiny alfalfa twigs would scratch and brand him. No one ever left after a day in the mow without red welts on his chest or arms where the hay won the battle.

When he first stacked hay at ten years of age, he was happy to think that he could work with the older boys and not spend the day with the children playing. He was proud to be considered an adult, but he quickly realized that hard work was required of adults. The first year the bales of hay came up the elevator so fast, and they were so large that he had a difficult time putting them in the symmetrical mound that was built in the loft of the barn. The older boys did most of the work, laughed at him, and put hay down his pants. He would have to go someplace where no one would see him, and remove them. The hay would be gone but there would be an itching and burning sensation on his butt and groin all day. But he did not complain because that was the price that he paid for hanging out with older boys who knew about girls and drove cars. They also knew a lot of neat words.

It was in the haymow with older boys that his knowledge and vocabulary greatly increased. Words like "vagina" and "period" were used along with new swear words, and although he had no idea what they meant, he knew the right time to laugh. These were cool words to throw around in his conversation, and it was fun to be with the older boys as they discussed the topics of the day—girls and sports. He did learn very quickly that this expanding vocabulary should be used only in certain locations.

His first summer, an older neighbor boy used the word "cocksucker" with authority as he spoke to each teen in the mow. Bob was "little cocksucker." The new word was also applied to any bale that broke on the elevator and to his football coach—it also labeled the sheriff deputy who had stopped him the night before because his car made too much noise. That evening, Bob used the new word to refer to his brother. Unfortunately, his mother was standing in the room.

He immediately realized the error as he saw the horrified expression on her face. He frantically tried to explain the situation as he was propelled toward the bathroom with his mother in control of his shirt collar and his feet lightly touching the floor. His second mistake was in trying to explain and beg for forgiveness, thus his jaw was moving as the Ivory soap was jammed into his mouth.

The next morning after milking his father said, "Bobby, you need to watch your language in the house. Your mother is pretty upset with some of the words that you use. Just remember that there is barn language and house language and never use the barn language in the house. Do you understand?"

"Yes sir," he replied. His father never yelled or struck his children, but Bob had been afraid after his mother's reaction that that rule might be broken. Much to Bob's relief his father quickly walked away.

"Cocksucker—I'll be damned," his father chuckled softly as he measured the grain out for each cow locked in her stanchion.

A bang on the milking parlor door brought him back to the reality of Holsteins who were suffering the elements. He walked through the milking parlor to the outside door toward the increasingly louder bellowing. He was surrounded by a familiar smell of fermenting grain and pungent manure. The parlor was neat and orderly with feed at each open stanchions waiting for the cattle to enter and then to be closed around their heads.

He opened the outside door and quickly stepped aside as the cows rushed by him even louder than before. The cows knew which stanchion was theirs and they raced to it, placing their head through the iron uprights to begin eating their allotment of grain. When they finished, there would be hay to eat until they were turned back outside. Bob walked down the center aisle and closed the stanchions. Sometimes he did not even lock them in place. The older cows stood quietly chewing while they were milked and would remain in place until forced outside. It was the young cows that would try to escape or kick and stomp when the milking machine was attached to their udder. The older ones knew the procedures and patterns; it was the young ones that fought against the established order.

Before he began the milking, he turned on the radio and adjusted it to a station from Chicago. He listened to the Beatles, Bob Dylan, and the Motown sound as he worked. The cows never complained about his selection of music, only his father did. His father always listened to a local station with farm news and country music while Bob always looked for a station from Detroit or Chicago that played modern rock and roll.

Most mornings or evenings Bob knew his father never turned the radio on if he milked by himself. But if one of his boys were with him, he would be sure and turn it up loud with the exclamation, "Now we're going to hear some good music, not that cat-a-ma-growl stuff you listen to. You're going to really enjoy Tammy and Loretta this morning."

"I just can't stand that sick, tired music in the morning," Bob would say as he selected the station that he wanted, and his father would only grin. The joy came not in the music but in teasing his son about it.

With each cow secured, Bob began placing the milking machines on the cattle. After each one was milked, he dumped the warm liquid and moved the apparatus to the next waiting cow. The milking didn't take long; it was a job that he had done hundreds of times without thinking. After it was completed, he let the cattle out of the barn into the feed lot where more hay waited for them. They stayed there until the morning when the entire procedure was repeated again. There were only a couple times a year when the weather was so terrible that the cows were left in the barn.

Once the cows were outside eating and ruminating, he cleaned the barn and prepared it for the morning. Turning the radio off, he carried the last of the equipment into the parlor and began washing the milking machine. As he finished, his father walked into the milk house and sat in the corner on an old stool.

CHAPTER 13

"Damn conveyor."

Sam Hartman took a pack of Camels from his jacket, removed a cigarette, and returned the pack to his pocket. From another he took a single match, struck it on the concrete floor and lit his cigarette. He extinguished the match and held it for a moment while he inhaled, then after rolling the burnt part in his fingers, he returned the match to his pocket.

"I can't get the conveyor to work," he said. "I'll have to buy a new chain tomorrow."

Although Bob had seen his father smoke several times, it still seemed strange to watch him light up here. He also knew that later, when his father was far from the barn, the burnt match would be discarded. There were only a few places and times that his father indulged a habit that he had acquired years ago in France and Germany. His mother did not allow smoking in the house, and Sam would not light a match in any wooden building, but the milk house was constructed of concrete. The milk house and the open fields were the only place he smoked, and usually too many chores still to do after milking left little time to enjoy a moment with a cigarette. It was only in the long hours on the tractor in the fields that Bob regularly saw his father with a cigarette.

"How did milking go?" his dad asked. "Did that old black bitch give you any trouble?" He looked out the window not particularly interested in the answer. The snow and a full moon shed an eerie light on the field of corn waiting to be picked.

"No problem," Bob replied. "Midnight was fine this evening. It must be the calming music that I play."

His father did not seem to notice the reference to the "battle of the bands" that usually occurred between him and his son. He continued to gaze out the window and smoke while Bob finished the cleaning. Turning his gaze from the window and exhaling, he quietly asked, "How did school go this term?"

"It went fine," Bob replied.

"Did you get that mess from last spring cleaned up?"

"Yah." Bob, placing the remaining milking equipment on the rack, was thankful that he did not have to view his father's stare. He knew what a disappointment it had been last spring when the letter came from the University telling him not to return in the fall, and how they were thrilled when he had been able to talk his way back into school. There was a long silence as his dad continued to smoke, and Bob continued cleaning up.

"Is there a chance that you might get drafted because of that mess from the spring?"

"I have a II-S deferment until graduation in June."

"Good," his father said. "It will mean a lot to your mother to see you graduate from State. You will be the first from her side or my side of the family to graduate from college. She doesn't want you to get stuck on this farm or working in a factory like many of the boys do here."

Bob put the last pail on the rack to dry and went to the sink to wash his hands. His father still sat on the stool smoking the cigarette. There was no wind outside and one could hear the cattle moving in the feed lot. Occasionally there was a bellowing or the sound of one of them rubbing against the barn. The compressor that cooled the fresh milk in the tank began to run.

"You know, Tom Beemer's boy was drafted last month and Harry Jorgen's boy joined the Marines about the same time. I think there are about four or five Lawsonville boys in Vietnam right now," his dad said.

Bob dried his hands. He hated the way this conversation was heading. He did not want to get into a conversation about Vietnam or the draft. He didn't want to hear lectures about "rightness of the war" or "doing your duty" or "I served in World War II and now it is your turn." He could never argue with his father. It was easy to oppose or irritate his mother, but it was different with his father. He didn't want to see or hear disappointment because he could not enthusiastically support American foreign policy. His doubts, which were growing in East Lansing, did not wear well in Lawsonville. Arguing with his mother had been a common occurrence for several years, but he could never challenge his father, and he knew that his dad, a World War II veteran, would obediently support his President Johnson.

Sam Hartman stubbed the cigarette out and placed the butt in an old oil can on the window sill. He would never throw a butt down anywhere near a farm building so the can already contained several remains of solitary smokes. He looked out again on the corn and an uneasy quiet settled into the milk house. Although the chores were done, Bob felt awkward about leaving his father sitting in the milk house. The stillness wrapped around him, afraid of where the conversation was heading, he tried to think of some diversion.

"Do you think you'll have the combine running tomorrow so that you can finish picking?"

"Yah—it'll get done some time," his dad replied absent-mindedly.

Bob was surprised at the lack of urgency in his reply. Usually anything about the harvest of crops was a matter of primary concern. Now he seemed to be someplace else other than this old wooden stool. Again there was a long pause, but this time Bob was not as frightened, rather curious as to where is father was.

"I don't think George ever got over Tommy being killed in Vietnam. He doesn't say too much, but it's strange when you lose a son. I hope you don't get drafted," Sam Hartman said. Then he added with a sense of disgust in his voice that Bob rarely heard, "Johnson and those boys in Washington sit in their cushy chairs and send boys to Vietnam to die. I don't know why the hell we are over there. We ought to stay home and mind our own business."

"Dad, were you drafted or did you join the army in World War II?"

"I joined up as soon as I graduated from high school in '42—just a dumb farm boy who wanted to see the world and have some action."

"Did you go right to Europe?" This was the first time Bob had ever heard him talk about his experience in World War II.

"No, my unit shipped out from the east coast after training and went to Africa. We were in Africa early in '43, but the fighting was pretty much done, and we were only there mopping up. It was hotter than hell and really boring. I thought that there was nothing to this soldiering. I was full of piss and vinegar and dumb as a stone. Part of the unit went to Sicily and then to Italy, but my group went back to England to train. And train we did.—Again I was bored and wanted some excitement, but all we did was train and drink English beer—which tastes like cow piss."

"By the spring of '44 we knew that something was going to happen pretty soon. We knew that a big push was going to occur across the Channel, and everyone in the division was taking bets on where we would land. I was pretty excited about it and just couldn't wait to get to the battle lines."

"Finally in June we went to France on D-Day. We were one of the first waves to hit the beach, and we really took a butt kicking. I was already seasick even before they opened the door on the landing craft. The first few guys out were hit, and the rest of us went across those poor bastards. The Germans were up on the high ground and were shooting at us like fish in a barrel. I slipped getting out and got dumped into the water and probably would have drowned if someone hadn't dragged my sorry butt to where I could stand up."

His father talked to a window that looked out on snow-covered corn where the wind had picked up and now whistled around the barn. Bob leaned against the sink entranced by the story his father was telling. He knew that his dad had served in World War II, but he never talked about it. He had heard his mother mention a few times, "Sam had a difficult time after the War," but the subject was never discussed at the dinner table or anywhere else.

"I got to land, and we were pinned down with guys dead or dying all around us. The Germans were having a field day shooting Americans lying on the beach or anyone dumb enough to try and stand up. There were guys crying for their mothers and begging for help, and there wasn't one God-damn thing anyone could do for them. A friend of mine from Warsaw, Indiana took one in the stomach. I helped him put his guts back in and was holding them in place when he died. I was just sitting there holding him when some sergeant kicked me and told me to get moving. I sure was getting the action that I wanted." Sam Hartman turned to his son on the other side of the milk house.

"You know when your mom and I were first married, I was going to butcher a pig each year—we didn't have much money and that would have helped a lot. When I hung that hog up and opened him up his guts spilled out—all that I could think of was my friend from Warsaw. I couldn't finish the job. I sent that hog over to Brown's Packing House, and everything else that we have had butchered here on the farm. I know it costs a little more than if I do it, but I just can't. I don't think your mother ever understood why I wouldn't butcher any livestock on the place."

Bob watched his father as again another cow rubbed against the barn and the compressor continued to run. He was mesmerized about the stories about D-Day—these stories that he had never heard before. He knew that this conversation was meant for him, and yet, it was as if he was not even present in the milk house, and his dad was someplace far from this small farm in Michigan. He had heard other people mention that his father was a World War II veteran and hero from several battles in Europe. Once Bob over heard someone ask his dad about joining the American Legion and his dad had refused, mentioning something about, "tin star soldiers." Sam Hartman lit another cigarette, and this time he dropped the extinguished match on the milk house floor—not his usual pattern. After a long exhale, he continued on with the story.

"We finally got off of that damn beach, and the next few weeks were tough as we proceeded inland. The Germans were dug into every hedgerow in France and wouldn't give any ground without a tough fight. They sure to hell knew how to use those hedgerows. We had to force them out, and it was tough fighting all of the way. I was a big farm boy and could cover the ground pretty well, so they put me in a group that was always scouting ahead. It seems like every time we went out to search, we came back with one or two less GIs. Amazingly, I never got hit. The only injury I got was when my knife slipped opening a C ration and I cut my palm. The Captain gave me the Purple Heart for that."

"We moved through France toward the Rhine River and Germany. It was hard going, but I survived somehow—a lot of my buddies didn't. Some times there would be fighting, and then some times the Germans would just give up. As we neared the Rhine, we began to take a lot of prisoners. I captured several

Germans one afternoon, and they gave me a medal for that. The truth of the matter was I just walked into a French village, and a German officer walked out from behind a building with his hands up. I couldn't understand a word that he was saying, but I figured I'd take him back to our bivouac area. He kept jabbering about something and pointing. We walked behind this building and there were all of these German soldiers hunkered down looking like whipped pups. I marched them all back to camp. I really looked like something with about twenty Germans with their hands in the air and me following them with a rifle. The truth was that they were so hungry that they were begging to surrender. When the mess sergeant fed them, they ate like wolves. Marching them into camp, I think I only had four or five bullets left."

"A week later some Colonel shows up in a fresh starched uniform smelling like a French whore and pins a medal on me and tells the whole company how brave I was, how I was shortening the war effort, and how I was saving American lives. He didn't say anything about my buddies who were shot in France, but just talked about me who had done nothing. What the hell did he know about the War, sitting back at his desk with a clean shirt everyday and three squares?"

His dad sat on the stool with the cigarette burning in his hand. The compressor had stopped and the only sound was the wind outside because the cattle had finally quieted.

"The worse time was after we had crossed the Rhine and about a week or two before the end of the War. We were moving pretty fast through Germany, and what little resistance we encountered was old men or boys. They were pretty poorly equipped and were always in pitiful shape. They seemed to be happy to be captured—at least then they got something to eat."

"One day traveling along a road we took fire from a big old house on the outskirts of a village. Two of our squad were hit, and we went after the shooters. The Sarge was right next to me as we moved up, and he took one right in the head—a good man who had been with us since Normandy. As everyone else covered me, I threw a grenade and then ran into the building. There were three of them still standing. One reached for an old Enfield. I put a bullet in his head and shot the other two who were moving. All of them were dead then."

"When I checked on the one that I had shot in the head—he was just a kid about twelve years old! All of them were kids, and I don't think anyone of them was over fourteen or fifteen. Later we found out that the building was some type of school or something."

"Anyway, a week later the War ended, and another week after that, a big-ass General showed up and pins another medal on me—with a lot of high sounding words about how I was a hero." There was a pause and then softy he added, "A damn medal for shooting kids."

There was quiet again except for the wind. It had picked up a loose piece of sheet metal on the roof to provide a rhythmic thump—thump—thump—thump in the background. Like watching a train wreck unfold, Bob could not take his eyes off of his father as he relived his war experience. He had never seen his father this way and was beginning to feel uneasy in this new situation of revelation, and yet he could not move nor do anything except listen.

Total darkness had now enveloped the barn. The full moon and the snow still lit the milk house, so neither had realized how late it was. Bob reached over and flipped the light switch, and the trance was broken.

"Oh, you'd better get up to the house and see if your mother needs anything. I'll finish up here," his dad said.

"OK—I'll see you later," Bob added, knowing that everything had been cleaned and all of the evening chores were completed. As he left, his father was lighting his third cigarette to sit with the ghosts of his past.

CHAPTER 14

Again Bob sat in Dean Jenning's office.

But he was not as anxious and nervous as he had been in the fall. Instead of clutching a folder of letters supporting his return, a packet of registration material lay on the chair next to him; instead of a jacket and tie he wore jeans and a flannel shirt; and instead of sweating and fidgeting, he stretched his feet out and surveyed the confusion as he waited for the Dean. A hold had been placed on registration, and until the Dean of Students signed a permission form, he could not register for winter term. Miss Crampton was standing at the counter sorting through a pile of papers while students waited in line to have problems solved.

"I really need the blue form to register. What will I do if you don't have it?" Panic was written on the face of a student caught in a bureaucratic nightmare. Bob had been there before, and he knew that once in the catch-22 of university regulations and forms, it was difficult to get out.

"Don't worry. I know that it is here," said Miss Crampton as she patiently thumbed a stack of papers with her usual calm and professionalism. "Here it is."

She handed the blue piece of paper to him as a thankful expression spread across his face; he was out the door. Another student stepped forward with the next problem. Miss Crampton efficiently answered questions, signed forms, and directed frustrated students. She wore a blue miniskirt, and Bob remembered her sitting at a desk—with a skirt seductively sliding up a nylon leg. Standing at the counter there was little chance of revelation of the top of nylons.

He pulled his legs back and repositioned himself in the chair. He was the next in line to see the Dean, but a tearful coed had gone into Dr. Jenning's office twenty minutes earlier. As he waited his turn, he thought back on the last term and how his situation had changed from the fall. He had met the academic conditions of the university and would graduate in June. The biggest change in his life was Jennifer Mc Knight. He liked the way she looked and smelled, but more important he simply liked being with her. And under the jeans and sweat shirts she wore most of the time was a body that was soft in all of the right places—and there were eyes that always followed him. They teared at old movies, sparkled when he touched her, and were surrounded with a touch of mascara and eye shadow. They were a wonderful deep brown that he wanted to fall into.

The coed emerged from the hall to Dr. Jennings's office. The tears had stopped, but there was no smile on her face, only a look of panic as she left. Miss Crampton turned to him. "You may see the Dean now."

Bob stood up and followed the same path he had in the fall. Dr. Jenning sat at his desk writing in a file folder. The office had the same arrangement and order as before, the athletic pictures were on one wall, and the books were neatly arranged on shelves on the other. The piles were neatly piled on the credenza behind his desk, but some were stacked on the desk. Bob knocked lightly on the open door and stepped into the room.

"Excuse me, Dean Jenning. I need you to sign a release so that I may register."

Dr. Jennings looked up and laid the pen down. He smiled and leaned back in his chair.

"I saw your grades from the fall. You did quite well, Mr. Hartman. A 3.8 GPA is quite different from the 0.0 that you had in the previous semester. Most students in your situation drop out of school. Not many make such a dramatic leap forward, as you did. What caused the change?"

"I tried a little harder this time." Bob stepped into the office and stopped in front of Dean Jenning's desk. "Just get me out of here," he thought. "I don't want any lectures or long discussions about the advantages of a college education."

"It does make a difference when you take your finals, doesn't it?"

"Yes, sir."

"Any plans after graduation?" Reaching across the desk, he took the form from Bob and signed it. He did not return it, but laid it on his desk and again leaned back in his chair with his arms folded behind his head.

"None. I'll probably get drafted this summer."

"Yes, you probably will. The draft is a difficult question. In my day it was a lot easier. There was a war everyone supported that made sense in those days. I was drafted after I graduated from Ohio State and sent to Europe. It's more difficult for you young men today. I'm lucky—I have two daughters, and they don't have to face the question of selective service. But my sister has two boys—one is a Marine captain in Vietnam, and the younger one just left for Canada last month. Both are good boys, but it sure has been tough on her." Dr. Jenning paused. He looked weary from the day's problems, and he seemed to be thinking about some place other than his office. Bob repositioned himself again. He did not know what to do with his hands.

"Did you ever think about the Peace Corps? With your agricultural background you would be admitted, have an opportunity to see the world, and do some pretty interesting work. You would also be deferred for two more years."

"I have considered it," Bob lied.

"Well, the best of luck to you. You did an excellent job last term, and you should be proud of your accomplishment. You should graduate in June with honors, and then you will have to decide what you are going to do," the Dean said. "You're the only success that I have seen today. I have spent the day with sad stories and excuses—registration week is always difficult."

He handed the signed form to Bob and returned to the papers on his desk. Bob left the office and walked past Miss Crampton who still had a line of students before her. With the signed form he was allowed to enter the maze of registration at the Intramural Building. There were several gymnasiums on two different floors that he would have to traverse successfully before he would be officially enrolled.

He was a rat running a Skinner box of rewards and punishments. Bob was given a packet of cards bearing his name and student number, each a different color. At various stations along the path he left the assigned card and then proceeded to the next station. There were strict paths that he must follow and assistants along the way. Rather than helping, they more resembled wardens to make sure that everyone moved in the correct order. Bob proceeded along quickly and entered the huge arena where class selections were held. He remembered as a freshman how he had spent two hours going from station to station trying to complete a schedule of the classes that he needed. At each point someone indifferent to his needs and frustration met him at the end of his wait in line.

This time he secured his classes quickly and finished registration—there had been none of the usual "No, you can't do that," "I don't know why it is that way—it just is," and "There is no need to get angry now." He stopped at the campus bookstore and purchased the required texts. Bob had made plans to meet Harry at the Union in the afternoon. He had arrived at campus the day before, but Harry had returned from New York a week ago. Harry had come back early because, for the first time, the University was allowing the draft resistance group to have a booth on campus. As the leader of the group, Harry was determined that everything be prepared, and they would have someone at the booth everyday during registration. For the first week it was going to be just Harry.

Bob walked up the steps of the Union and entered a long hall towards a cafeteria at the end. Along one side was an open lounge where he and Jenny had spent time in the fall either talking or studying. Now in this area and down the hall were the representatives of different campus organizations that students could join. There were activities—sailing, judo, lacrosse; there social organizations—Black Union, International Students; and there were political action groups—Young Democrats, Young Republicans, SDS. Other organizations were represented, some of which he did not know existed. At the end of the hall sat his red-headed roommate at a table with a large sign over the top—DRAFT COUNSELING.

Bob slid into the empty chair behind the table while Harry talked with a student. He looked at some of the free mimeographed papers on the table. Most were explanations about various deferments, and there were some on emigration and conscientious objector status. Also, anyone could buy *Guide to the Draft*, buttons, posters, or bumper stickers.

"I'm thinking about applying for conscientious objector," the inquiring student said. "I don't graduate for another year, but I don't want to go to Vietnam. This war is stupid, and I don't want to be a part of it. What do you have to do to be a CO?"

"Well, you apply to your local draft board," Harry said, "and they make the decision as to whether they'll honor your request. If they do classify you as a conscientious objector, then when you're drafted you will have to complete two years of alternative service that they approve."

"Is it difficult to get?"

"It depends on the draft board. But they have to allow you to apply—that's the law."

"Somebody told me about a conscientious objector that's in the army but doesn't have to fight. That would keep me out of Vietnam."

"That is an I-A-O classification. You would be in a medical unit of some sorts but wouldn't carry a weapon. But you are still supporting the war effort and are part of anything that the military is doing. There are just a few people that feel comfortable with that classification."

"I don't know if any of these will work for me," the student said. "There is a guy on my floor in the dorm whose brother did not get drafted because he took some pills that shot his blood pressure up during the physical. Maybe I'll look into that." He picked up several sheets and a bumper sticker—BOMB WASHINGTON—NOT HANOI.

"I don't know about any medicines that'll do that. But if you have any other questions or need some help, we have an office in East Lansing you can call anytime during the day." Harry wrote the number on a piece of paper and handed it to him. Folding the paper, the student placed it in his shirt pocket, took several brochures, and stopped at the next booth—the MSU Sailing Club. Harry turned to Bob and shook his head with a disgusted look on his face.

"That's the way it has been most of the day—people just looking to avoid the draft. No one really gives a crap about whether Vietnam is right or wrong."

"Each one you get not to go helps your cause, doesn't it? What's your saying—'Suppose they gave a War and no one showed up?' Well, if you can get enough people out of the draft, the politicians will have to change their policies—won't they? So the reason that they don't go doesn't matter that much, does it?"

"I guess that's a good point—one less McNamara cannon fodder," said Harry. He put the stacks of mimeographs in order and straightened the bumper stickers that were in disarray. He watched the crowded hall for a moment and then he turned to Bob.

"Are you going to be back at the apartment tonight? I have to work here until six o'clock."

"I'm going back for a little while. Woody and I are going to Emma's tonight for hamburgers and fries."

"Oh, are you a free man tonight?" Harry said feinting surprise. "And pray tell, has the fair Ophelia let you loose for one evening?"

"Screw you—Jenny has some type of meeting with an honorary that she's in. They meet once a term, and besides, I can go anytime that I want."

"Me thinks, thou doth protest too much," Harry laughed. "Besides you know anytime that you are not available, I would be more than happy to escort her any place."

Bob stood up and mixed the neatly stacked piles of bumper stickers into one mess spread on the end of the table. He picked up his bag of books as Harry restacked the bumper stickers.

"Jenny does have a thing for red heads." He headed away from the table and turned and called back. "She hates them."

CHAPTER 15

Bob woke with a headache. His tongue stuck to the roof of his mouth with a horrible taste. He needed a drink—of water. It was still dark—he needed to get up and start milking—surely his father would be in the barn by now.

Then he realized that he was not in Lawsonville but in East Lansing, and he panicked that he had missed a class. Clearing his head, he realized classes had not begun yet, and he saw that he was on the sofa in Jenny's apartment with a blanket over him. He was not certain how he got there, but he was certain that he needed a drink of water. He went to the kitchen and took a long drink from the faucet and then returned to the sofa. He had been sleeping in his underwear and socks—as was his habit—but his clothes were neatly folded on the floor—as was not his habit. He covered his head and felt the texture of the couch as he tried to return to sleep. The last he remembered was being at Emma's and drinking shots of Jack Daniels with Woody. There were other fuzzy details, but the one huge detail that concerned him was how he had arrived at Jenny's and what foolish things he had done or said in her presence? Was she mad at him?

The next time he poked his head out from under the blankets it was daylight, and Jenny was at the kitchen table reading. He sat up and wrapped a blanket around his shoulders. She looked up from her book and smiled.

"Sleeping kind of late today, aren't you. Do you want anything?"

"I would love a Coke, please, if you have one."

She got a Coke from the refrigerator and a glass from the cupboard. Bob looked at a clock and saw that it was ten and through a head that was pounding, pulled up the details of last night. Woody and he had left Emma's and had found it great fun to slide the car on the icy roads—until Woody drove it into a mound of snow and it wouldn't move. Bob could not budge it because the rear wheels kept spinning. Placing his jacket under the one wheel and an old blanket under the other, enough traction was created so Bob pushed the car free. He did not see the jacket with his folded clothes so it might be in Woody's car or more likely lying along a snowy road. Across from him was a damaged chair that somehow he felt responsible for.

"Thank you," he said as he took the drink and pointed to the collapsed chair. "Did I do that?"

"Yes. You were quite entertaining last night, or maybe I should say this morning."

"I'm sorry. Are there any other damages—or anything that I said that I need to apologize for? Woody and I drank too much last night, and I can't remember some of the details of the evening." The Coke did not set well in his stomach, but the wetness and carbonization were wonderful in his mouth.

"You mentioned that you were stuck in the snow in a ditch and that you'd used your jacket to free the car. You said that you drove back to the apartment complex and that Woody passed out in the car and you walked over to see me. I was up reading because I thought that you might come over. You called me about every half hour from Emma's, so I wasn't surprised when you showed up this morning," Jenny said. "Don't worry about the chair. It was an old one from home. You picked me up in your arms and twirled me around when you lost your balance and fell backwards into the chair with me on top of you. I was afraid that you had hurt yourself, but you were laughing so hard I knew that you were okay. And then you wanted to tickle and wrestle, but you were easy to escape from. If you'd have been sober, I would have had a very difficult time getting away from you. You did a lot of talking and eventually you fell asleep on the couch."

Bob sat up with his feet still on the couch with a blanket wrapped around him. The elevation did not help his head, but his headache was not his worry—what had he said? Jenny left the kitchen and sat on the end of the couch. She rubbed his legs through the blanket and gazed at him, saying nothing.

"What idiot things did I say?"

"Oh nothing—after the chair incident we sat on the couch and you talked about Tommy. You mentioned several times how he was your friend and that it wasn't fair that he was killed in Vietnam. And then you said that you didn't think the war was right, but how could you not go if Tommy had died there," Jenny said. She paused and smiled as she rubbed his leg again.

"You were quite funny. All you wanted to do was talk and kiss. You fell off the couch twice trying to kiss me—and I was having too much fun teasing you. You'd lean over and I would move, and then you would end up on the floor laughing. I've never seen you talk so much. Usually it's me who does all of the talking, and you're the silent one. I guess that I just have to give you some alcohol to loosen your tongue."

"It makes a fool of me."

Bob put his feet on the floor and left the blanket wrapped around his legs. Putting arms on his knees, he placed his head in his hands. Jenny slid next to him and rubbed his back. He wondered how she could be near him because he must smell terrible. He knew that after one of these marathon drinking feats he always reeked of stale beer, cigarette smoke and sweat. He needed a shower and a new brain—one that was not still swimming in alcohol.

"Besides kissing me, you complimented me."

"Oh no, what did I say?"

"Just that I am no longer skinny and that you thought my 'cow eyes' were wonderful. You also wondered why I wear sweat shirts all of the time, and why I don't wear a skirt now and then?"

"Oh no," he groaned and put his head further into his hands.

"That's okay, Robert. I wasn't offended." She hugged him. "Sometimes a compliment is nice to hear."

"I'd better get going. Harry will wonder where I am."

He started to rise, but hesitated when he realized that he had on only his underwear. Then he saw his folded clothes on the chair and knew that Jenny must have taken his pants and shirt off after he passed out on the couch. If he had undressed himself his clothes would be thrown in a pile in the middle of the room. He pushed the blanket back, put on his pants and shirt, and then remembered that he had no jacket. It would be a cold walk back to his apartment.

"Why don't you come back this evening? We could watch television or go to a movie," Jenny said. "I could fix some dinner here."

"Television would be fine. I think that I'll take it a little easy this evening."

The walk back to the apartment was not as bad as he had feared. It was almost noon, the sun was shining, and a warm breeze was melting the snow. The coolness helped his hangover and the three aspirin that he took when he got home helped also. He took a quick shower, pulled the blinds in his room, and crawled into bed.

He woke and looked at the clock—four o'clock. He felt much better—almost human. He took another shower and dressed. Jenny had said for him to come around six, so he had an hour to kill. He walked out to the living room where Harry sat reading.

"Rough night last night?"

"Yes it was—brown bottle flu. But I'm on the mend now."

"I saw Woody this morning as he was leaving for work, and he looked pretty rough. It was good that he only had to work half a day. You two need to stop and think about what you are doing. He doesn't remember driving home; he wasn't even sure who had driven."

"He started out but ran into a ditch after Emma's. It took us awhile to get out, and then I drove home."

"Well, you'd better be careful."

"We're just a couple of sots who don't have to attend the meetings every week," Bob joked. Harry did not laugh.

"I know all of the drinking jokes," Harry snapped. "What if the police pull you over, and worse yet, what if you were in an accident and someone was injured. If you two idiots hurt yourself or smash your car is one thing, but what if you kill some innocent person because you're too drunk to function properly. What are you going to feel like then?"

Bob squirmed under the glare of his roommate. He had heard this from Harry before. He would listen, but ignored everything he said because it was too much fun to be out with Woody. Last spring he avoided these conversations and eventually, Harry gave up giving advice. Harry was just worrying about a friend, Bob knew, but he did not want to be lectured to.

"I've got to get going. I'm going to have dinner at Jenny's, and then we are going to watch television there."

"I won't give you any more sermons—you're not going to listen to them any way. I just don't have time to bail you out of jail or go to your funeral when I have to worry about the idiots in Washington."

"Well I'll tell you what I'll do—if I'm in an accident, I'll make sure that Westmoreland and McNamara are in the back seat. Will that satisfy you?"

"Get out of here." Harry threw a pillow at him, which he caught and threw back. "Say hi to Jenny—she's the only one that seems to be able to keep you out of trouble. Are you coming home tonight?

"Yes, I'll be home."

He grabbed a jacket and left. As he walked toward Jenny's apartment, he realized that it had been warm and sunny—not typical for Michigan in January. He regretted that he had spent the entire day in bed because of a hang-over. Sleeping had been such a waste, but he had no one to blame except himself. At least he felt much better on the way back to Jenny's than he had felt this morning when he had made this same trek.

The lectures from Harry were well intended, but he did not like them. He got enough of those from his mother when he was home—he did not need them from Harry—"self-righteous, goody-two-shoes" Harry who was out to save the world but first had to save Bob Hartman.

CHAPTER 16

"It's wonderful to be here. It's certainly a thrill."

The Beatles played in the background as Jenny placed the dinner dishes on the counter. Bob offered to help, but she insisted that she would do it. Her single bedroom apartment was so small that it was only a short step from the table to the kitchen sink. He had not eaten all day, and, as his hangover from the previous night dissipated, it was replaced by hunger.

"That was great, Jenny. I don't cook. Harry tries hard, but he isn't much of a chef, so I eat a lot of junk food. This meal was like my mother cooks at home."

"Four younger brothers and sisters always needed a big meal. And then Pop and Tommy would come in from the barn or the fields, and they had to be fed. Tommy was a big eater—Mother always said that he would eat anything that didn't eat him." Jenny placed the last of the dishes on the counter.

"There are always big meals at home," he said. "Everything is grown or raised there—not much bought at the store. We can and freeze everything from a big garden, and then we butcher our own meat."

"Same here—Mom thinks the Depression will return. She tells stories about when she was a little girl on the farm on Briggs Road during the thirties.—'Waste not—Want not' is her saying I've heard a million times."

Bob went into the living room and sat on the same couch he had slept on the previous night. He felt much better now after the meal than he did this morning. Jenny stacked the dishes in the sink and sang.

"You're such a lovely audience. We'd like to take you home with us. We'd love to take you home."

Bob leaned back and locked his hands behind his head as he continued to watch Jenny. "She's such a babe, why is she spending the evening with me?" he thought. "I'm lucky that she's even talking to me after last night."

When Bob arrived at the apartment, he was surprised to see her wearing a skirt with a matching sweater. He also noticed that she had make-up on, which she usually did not wear. It was just enough to make her enticing. She wore a small barrette bow that pulled her brown hair to one side, it gave her a Veronica Lake effect—but it was definitely the Jennifer Mc Knight look.

Jenny left the kitchen and sat next to Bob as he slid down the couch to make room for her. He again stretched and kicked his loafers off, but kept his feet on the floor. He was not touching Jenny, but he would have liked to put his head in her lap. Her skirt was stylish and short and the hem was way above the knee—with his head in her lap he was worried what might happen, or what she would think. He felt good—his headache was gone, his stomach was full, and he was enjoying being here.

"We're lazy tonight, aren't we?"

She picked up one leg and put it in her lap, and he lifted the other one there. Then he really stretched and yawned. Jenny slid her hand under the cuff of his jean and absent-mindedly twirled the hair on his leg.

"You're quiet, as usual," Jenny said. "I guess that I should have your friends bring some beer over for you. Now I have to do all of the talking."

"I had enough last night to last for a long time. Beer makes me babble when I should be quiet. What is it your friend Shakespeare says: 'A tale told by an idiot'?"

"'Struts and frets its hour upon the stage—full of sound and fury—signifying nothing.'" She pulled one of his leg hairs out.

"Darn—that hurts!" He half sat up and grabbed her hand and put it on the outside of his jeans.

"Math majors who know only slide rules and the Pythagoras Theorem must never quote Shakespeare to English majors," Jenny said grinning as she put her other hand back under the cuff of his jeans and again rubbed his leg. They sat without talking. Finally Jenny asked, "Do you ever think about Tommy? Last night was the first time that I've ever heard you talk about his death in Vietnam."

"Yes, I do."

Bob felt her hand gently rub his leg under the cuff while her other hand laid on the outside of his jeans. He felt uncomfortable talking about his feelings. It was much easier to make a joke about everything, but he sensed that Jenny wanted to talk about Tommy's death.

"At first I guess I was just numb. I still remember that spring afternoon at the cemetery and what a nice day it was, but I couldn't feel anything. I remember how your family looked, and I felt so sorry for all of you. I wanted to do something, but I didn't know what to do or say. And so I did nothing," he said.

"At first when I returned to State I thought about him a lot, and then that summer when I went back home, I thought about coming over and talking with you, or saying something to your mother, but I didn't do anything. I do think of him more now that I spend time with you, but it is weird how his memory comes up. It's when I return home and am around the farm that he crosses my mind. I thought a lot about him when I was home at Christmas—especially when I was out in the barn milking. One time I was in the hay mow throwing hay down and the pigeons were cooing in the top of the barn, and I began thinking about how many times we had tried to kill them with BB guns—never with any success. And then it was like someone punched me in the stomach, and I realized that I would never see him again. I sat down on a bale for a moment before I went down and finished the milking. I guess I thought that we'd always be friends and be screwing around for ever—just like we did when we were kids. You remember how we were always in trouble?"

"Yes," Jenny said. "Either Mother or your mom would be so angry at you two. And Pop, if he knew, would just smile and walk away. I just stayed in the background and watched while you two tried the craziest things, and you always got caught. I wasn't brave, like you."

"Don't you mean foolish?" Bob said with a grin. "Gosh, your mom would get so mad at him and whack him a good one—and me sometimes too, and we would both try not to laugh. I remember one time we had a cow pie fight. We were both covered with manure, and I had my Sunday shirt on. My mom was so mad she made me bend over. She was whacking me with a broom—and then Tommy laughed. She turned and broke the broom across his back. It didn't hurt him, but it sure did surprise him."

"We both faked crying so we could get out of her way. After we went to the milk house and washed off the manure, we were in the hay mow and he started using that funny voice of his to tell about it, and I got to laughing so hard that I wet my pants. He had a big red welt across his back for a couple of days, but he never said anything to your folks about it."

"No, I'm sure he didn't," Jenny said. "I could just hear what Mother would say: 'Don't you be sassing Mrs. Hartman,' and then she would take after him with the fly swatter. Pop would just smile and shake his head. 'Old Bobby and Tommy are at it again.' I think that he was amused by things that you and Tommy did."

"Do you think of him?" Bob asked after a period of silence. The smile left Jenny's face, and she stared blankly at him.

"Yes I do—especially these last few weeks. I was numb at first, like you. I wanted to cry. I thought that I should cry—but I just couldn't. Mother sat and cried for weeks. Pop just went to the barn and worked more that usual. I don't think any of us saw him that much; it was almost like he slept in the barn or in the fields."

"Mother couldn't do anything for a few days, and it was up to me to feed the family and take care of the house. That spring I came home every weekend and tried to get things in shape around the house and cook some meals until

Mother got back on her feet. Somehow I got through the summer, and then in the fall when I came back to State, that thing with Bradley happened, and Tommy's death got put aside, or it got mixed up with all of my other problems at that time. It is only in the last few weeks as we have become close do I think about him."

Jenny stared beyond him with her hands resting on his legs. He wanted to grab her so that every part of her touched him—but he didn't. He laid his hand on hers. That broke the spell, and she looked at him and smiled.

"I think of Tommy a lot as I hear more and more about the war in Vietnam. At first I thought it was the right thing to do—you know—all the communism stuff that we were taught in school. He was there defending the country and doing his duty. But now I just don't believe it, and I think that it's probably a mistake that we are there. But if it's a mistake to be there, what does that say about Tommy's death? I just don't know anymore." She squeezed his hand.

"I do think that he would be happy that we have become close," she said. "He always thought that you were special—just like I do."

Bob sat up and pulled her close. Jenny kissed him lightly on the cheek as he buried his face into brown hair. He kissed her on the neck and laid his hand on her knee. His fingers lightly caressed her knee as he pulled her closer. He felt soft skin and then his fingers touched the hem of her skirt. He thought of Bradley Whitcomb and that night at the Tri-Sig house and knew that Jenny must be thinking he was trying the same thing. He was not Bradley Whitcomb.

"I didn't—I didn't"

"What?" She held his hand and looked at him with surprise.

"I wasn't trying anything. I just—I just don't want you to think that I was getting out of line."

"You aren't," she said. A sly smile spread across her face. "Maybe I am."

Jenny unbuttoned the top two buttons on his shirt and gently touched his chest. There she made little circles, and then leaned forward and kissed him where the circles had been traced. She opened the rest of the buttons. He could smell the fragrance of her hair and a surge of feelings rushed over him so fast and unexpectedly that he gave the smallest shudder as she placed his hand back on her thigh. Her skirt rose as his hand rested on flesh above her knee. His fingers begged to slide upward.

Jenny gave a small sound in her throat, like the soft cooing of a pigeon in the very top of a barn. She pulled away from his chest and looked into his eyes. His hand remained immobile.

"Oh, Robert," she said, and she touched his cheek. "I love you."

He looked into a quiet face with deep eyes that invited him to plunge like a diver from a ten meter board—knowing that there was no danger of injury and that he would not strike bottom. He kissed her hard as his hand moved up and her hand moved down.

When Bob laid back down on the couch, Jenny followed, and his hands went under her sweater and slid up to her bra. One hand held her waist and the other tried to unhook her bra as she passionately kissed him. His fingers were on the clasp, then under the clasp, and again on top of the clasp. It wouldn't let go. She sat up, pulled her sweater over her head and shook her hair. The barrette was gone and brown hair hung over each shoulder. She pushed several strands back from her face and unclasped her brassiere and dropped it on the floor.

"Two hands," she said with a smile.

As she sat on his stomach and he looked up at the brown hair flowing over her shoulder and the brown eyes with long eyelashes looking at him. A smile spread across Jenny's face. He touched her breast while the other hand held her waist. His fingers slid across soft skin. She made no effort to remove them as his fingers explored and enjoyed.

"Uh—I—uh—I don't—uh I don't,' Bob stammered as the feelings rushed him to action, and yet he hesitated.

"What?" Jenny said. A puzzled look came to her face.

"Uh—I don't have any—uh—you know. I don't have—," he could not bring himself to say the word around her that a sense of responsibility caused him to think about.

"Oh." The puzzlement disappeared as a smile returned, bending down said whispered softly. "It's OK, Robert. This is a safe time." She leaned back up and put both of her hands around his face.

"You know, Mr. Hartman, you are not very good at wrestling. You are pinned. And for someone who was a football star, it is pretty bad to get pinned by a weak girl, like me. I hope that no one finds out what a poor athlete you are." Jenny's grin now had a mischievous twitch at the corner of her mouth and a twinkle appeared in those deep brown eyes.

Bob's hand remained on her breast, and as his fingers explored there he became excited. Her skirt had slid up so that Jenny's inner thighs rested on his chest. It was skin touching skin as he looked into her eyes. Her quirky smile caused him to pull her down on him and kiss her passionately. He held her as he rushed to remove her remaining clothes. Jenny joined in opening his pants. It was a race that he won.

They made love on the couch. There was a moment when she gave a small cry that he would remember forever. As she collapsed down on him, he held her so tightly that he thought that she would not be able to breathe. Relaxing his grip, she lay still on top of him. As he noticed the ceiling for the first time, he listened to her breathing and felt her hair next to his face. Finally she sat up.

"Let's go to bed," she said. She took his hand and led him into the bedroom. Again they made love. Afterwards she slept next to him with her head under his arm and their legs intertwined. Bob played the previous hours over and over in his head. The chronology of the events he could recreate, the details of Jenny's body he revisited with awe and wonder, but it was the feelings that had surged through him and had chiseled their mark on him that he could not understand.

Bob had had sex with women before—but nothing like this. It had been pleasurable, but when it was done he had wanted to leave immediately—only courtesy caused him to remain and talk. And when it was in the back of Woody's car there was no need to talk—only to help with her clothes. Each time he promised to call in the morning after he wrote their phone number down. But he never did.

Now he wanted to talk. He wanted to talk for hours and tell Jenny everything—mostly he wanted to say again and again how beautiful and wonderful she was. He wanted to touch her and make her safe, but mostly he wanted to never leave this bed. These feelings that now surged through him were all new.

Eventually he drifted off to sleep thinking that in the morning Jenny might be embarrassed and regret what had just happened. He would have no regrets.

CHAPTER 17

The wind blew down Shaw Lane and cut through Bob's thin shirt and light jacket. He did not notice the cold in his chest so much because his fingers and feet were numb. Foolishly he had worn no socks to class, and now the snow and slush had soaked his penny loafers so that his toes were numb. When he left Jenny's apartment this morning, it had been a warm sunny March day and with April only a few days away. It looked like an early spring had arrived. The reality of Michigan weather appeared with a spring snow.

Bob had just finished his last final of Winter Term and could enjoy a week of spring vacation. Since January, he found himself spending many evenings and nights at Jenny's apartment. At the first he would return to his apartment and spend the day there if he did not have class. Then in the evening he and Jenny would study together, and when he walked her home, she would ask him to stay. By February he had a tooth brush and shaving things there, and then Jenny said. "If you bring your laundry over I can do it with mine." He hated doing laundry, so he brought his shirts and a couple of pairs of jeans.

"Don't you have any underwear or socks?"

"I'll take care of those," he said, too embarrassed to mention underwear.

"Robert, I have brothers, and I have seen you in your underwear—and less."

Now his clothes were always neatly folded and piled on a shelf in the bedroom. Jenny had offered him a drawer in her dresser, but he refused. It still felt strange spending so much time in her apartment, but he enjoyed it. Although he saw Harry almost every day, he spent very few nights in his apartment. Harry teased him about what a good roommate he had finally become.

"Three years I've tried to reform you with little success. Miss Ophelia does it in a few weeks.

The wind was still blowing hard as Bob tried unsuccessfully to jump a puddle of slush. Now the bottoms of his jeans were wet and cold slush was in his loafers. Since the wind continued to cut him above and the slush freeze him below, he stopped at a dormitory to warm up.

He had come to campus early to study for his final in an American history class. The weather was warm but cloudy in the morning when he arrived at the Library. The past few days had been very warm for the last week of March, and all of the signs of spring had erupted on campus—Frisbees, shorts, and sandals. For those hundreds of students who were planning on making the trip to Florida, it seemed that the trip was unnecessary—why not enjoy the warmth here in East Lansing. Now Michigan weather was teaching a lesson to those who had forgotten that there are only two seasons in Michigan—winter and the Fourth of July.

After going over his notes on Progressives, World War I, and the Jazz Age he had emerged from the Library with an inch of snow on the ground. It had stopped snowing and the warmth had made it slushy. He had noticed some crocuses by the Library almost buried, but they were not complaining as the purple and yellow pushed the white aside. When he emerged from the exam, the weather had again changed. The wind had increased in intensity and sleet was in the air. The slush was hardening, and everywhere people hustled from building to building trying to avoid any exposure to the wind and sleet that now punished the campus.

Bob went to the grill in the basement and paid for a tuna bagel and a cup of coffee. Sitting at a table, he slipped his wet penny loafers off to let his feet dry and put his wet jacket on a chair. The feeling was returning to his feet and the coffee warmed his insides. He was the only one in the grill, which was odd. He remembered that when he lived in the dorm, at any time the grill was open there would be dozens of students there. Some would be quietly studying in the corners, but most of the tables would be taken by "grill rats" that were smoking cigarettes, drinking coffee, and avoiding class and study. Now with only one day left until the official spring vacation at MSU, even the haven for malingers was deserted. He slipped his wet shoes on, and since he had missed lunch got another bagel. He had forgotten how good the bagels tasted. They had been one of several new foods he had learned about when he entered MSU; homemade bread and biscuits had been the diet at home—not bagels.

As he warmed, Bob thought about the exam he had just taken and was certain that he had done well; he had received a ninety-six per cent on the mid-term exam in February. Jenny had urged him to take Dr. Brown's American History class. She had a history minor in connection with her English major, and since he had completed all of his required classes and only needed a few electives, he enrolled in the class.

"You will really enjoy Dr. Brown's class. He has so much knowledge about everything, and he will give you a different way of looking at American history," she said. "Besides being knowledgeable, he is one of the kindest professors that I have ever had. When I was a sophomore I took his honors class filled with juniors and seniors. I was over my head, and Dr. Brown realized it. But he was so patient and helpful that I was able to pass the class and actually receive a good grade."

Jenny had been right—Bob enjoyed it except for a few individuals who insisted on monopolizing the class time with extraneous questions, almost always tied to American foreign policy in Southeast Asia. They were not really questions but rather statements of opposition. Although Bob shared some of their views, he became weary of the distraction from the assigned topics that he found interesting; everything in late nineteenth and early twentieth century America was a spring board to the Vietnam War for these radicals. Each time Dr. Brown listened to the student's comment or question, and then patiently led the conversation back to the topic at hand.

"That is an interesting point, but have you considered."—or—"Thank you for your comment, but you may have made an error at . . ." And then smoking the ever present Camel cigarette, Dr. Brown would gently point out the mistaken logic or lack of knowledge. He would proceed on with the day's dialogue between professor and students until he was again interrupted. Only once had Bob seen him become agitated. A student with long hair and a full beard who wore the same shirt covered with anti-war buttons each class period had been on a tirade for several minutes about Dean Rusk and Robert McNamara and their "stupidity and arrogance of power." Finally after two interruptions, Dr. Brown lost his patience.

"Young man, your assertion of 'stupidity' is not shared by everyone. These are very complicated questions that require more than comic book solutions. And as for 'arrogance of power,' let me assure you it is a fearsome responsibility to lead men into combat and possible death. I know, I had to make those decisions in Italy." Dr. Brown paused, and continued more calmly.

"I personally know Secretary Rusk and have had an opportunity to meet Bob McNamara a few times. Let me assure you that they take their Constitutional responsibility very seriously, and there's nothing arrogant about the decisions that they make. They agonize immensely over these difficult questions about how to protect our country. I have more sympathy for those who have to make decisions that will cause hundreds or thousands to die than those who complain about the draft."

Dr. Brown took another long drag on the Camel and returned to the topic of the rise of fascism in Europe. Everyone could sense the tension in the class room as Dr. Brown finished his lecture. There were no more disruptions about the Vietnam War—until the next class meeting.

Bob finished his second bagel and left the grill. It had stopped sleeting, but the wind was still piercingly cold. He jogged the distance to his apartment with shoes that seemed molded to his feet. A soaking hot shower brought feeling back to his body, and after he had dressed he went down stairs to the Sin Den, where Harry and Jim were.

Tomorrow, Jim and Harry were planning on going to Washington D.C. for a peace rally, and Bob had agreed to go. They were to meet a group of people in Ann Arbor and then everyone was to ride to Washington together. Harry had made arrangements for the three of them to travel to D.C. and to spend a night there. Bob had agreed to go because he would be free for spring vacation and the only plans that he had were to return home and help his father. He was also becoming more opposed to the War, and he had never been to Washington. He grabbed a piece of pizza and sat on the couch next to Woody, who was watching the evening news. Harry and Jim sat at the kitchen table talking.

"Bob, Jim isn't going to go tomorrow," Harry called from the kitchen with a strong sense of frustration in his voice.

"Why? Why are you backing out now?" Bob asked as he stood up and walked to the kitchen.

"I have a paper due," Jim said.

"It's spring vacation, and the term has ended. How can you have an assignment due now?"

"It was due today as part of the final examination, and I didn't have it done."

"Now that really surprises me," Harry said sarcastically.

"The professor says that he'll accept it if I have it turned into his office by eight A.M. on Monday. And since Martin Luther King won't be giving his 'I have Dream' speech on the steps of the Lincoln Memorial, I have a dream of passing the history of philosophy class that I failed last term."

"Did you do any of the assigned readings?" Harry asked. The meticulous plans that he had made and the time schedule were falling apart. Harry had been working on the details of the trip for two weeks, and Bob knew that a small deviation from the prescribed plan would be very irritating and frustrating for Harry, who always needed everything planned and all functions to move with precision and punctuality.

"I haven't done many of them, but I've gone to class so that puts me way ahead of last term. If I can just get though Immanuel Kant and the German crap, I should be able to write something for Monday."

"Well, we were counting on you." There was a pause as Harry looked at Jim. "I guess it won't matter about the drive out to Washington; there will be more room in the van. I'll just have to tell my cousin that there's only one person instead of two that she has to find room for when we arrive."

"I can go in his place, if you have room?" Woody asked from the living room.

"That would be great," Bob exclaimed.

"I don't know," Harry said with hesitance. "This march is not about getting drunk or getting laid."

"The news says that there is suppose to be a group of former Vietnam Vets there. Maybe I will find someone that I was with me in Nam."

"Let him go, Harry. There should be room now that Jim isn't going. Having Vietnam Vets in the march should make it more effective. And Woody can help share the costs." Bob had been a little apprehensive about traveling with Jim, Harry, and a few strangers, but with Woody along the trip would be more relaxed and enjoyable.

"Just don't get thrown in jail or do something stupid," Harry admonished.

"Isn't this about making love and not war," Jim adding his sarcastic humor now that he was off the hook about attending. "You are taking the king of love making to our nation's capitol."

"Yes Papa, I'll behave myself," Woody said with a grin and his middle finger pointed upward. "Just let me call my boss and tell him that I'll be using one of my vacation days tomorrow."

Woody walked into the bedroom and closed the door while the three of them were in the kitchen. Harry looked down at the piece of paper in front of him that had all of the details of the trip listed and shook his head. Jim spoke softly.

"You might be surprised at Woody on this trip, Harry. Ever since the Tet Offensive, Woody has watched the evening news each night. It has gotten to the point where I almost wish he was watching Bugs Bunny again. Some of the footage that he saw during Tet was of areas of Vietnam where he had been stationed."

"Well, I guess that it will be OK. I just don't want him screwing around. This is a big demonstration against the Vietnam War, and since it's in Washington, there'll be major press coverage. I know that there'll be people from all over the United States marching with us."

"Woody doesn't say much about his time in Vietnam, but something the last few weeks has increased his interest in it on the news. I don't know if it was Tet or something else," Jim said and then added: "The news says there are supposed to be over a half of a million demonstrators—I don't think that one Elwood from East Lansing is going to affect the march that much."

"And now that I'm free from doing my patriotic duty in Washington, I shall do some reading for my paper and let you plan the logistics of your attack." Jim picked up a copy of *Playboy*.

"I thought your report was on Immanuel Kant not Miss April," Harry sniped.

"My dear Professor Greenbergh," Jim said as he struck a comic pose in his bedroom doorway. "Don't you know that you can only understand the esoteric nature of nineteenth century German philosophy by first understanding the duality of Miss April's bosom? You know I'd never look at the pictures of naked ladies in this magazine. I only read the intellectual articles and interviews." He went into his bedroom as Woody re-entered the room.

"I'm going. What time do we leave in the morning?"

CHAPTER 18

"Come Senators and Congressmen, please heed the call. Don't' stand in the doorway and don't block up the hall."

The tires of the Volkswagen bus kept time as Elaine sang Bob Dylan. Elaine was a University of Michigan coed riding with Harry, Bob, and Woody to Washington. The three from East Lansing had joined four other students from Ann Arbor for the trip. One of the U of M students owned a Volkswagen bus, and all seven were now journeying east to Washington on the Ohio Turnpike. They had left Ann Arbor in the morning and the weather had been sunny and warm as they traveled through Ohio. In Pennsylvania, it was a pleasant spring day.

"Come mothers and fathers throughout the land. And don't criticize what you can't understand. Your sons and your daughters are beyond your command." Everyone except Woody joined in on, *"For the times they are a-changing."*

Next to Bob in the back, Elaine, a large woman, occupied much of the seat. She seemed to know every song recorded by Bob Dylan, Tom Paxton, and Joan Baez. When the van passed Pittsburg, she removed her jean jacket to reveal only a tie-dyed T-shirt. Almost everything was exposed and Bob thought Elaine could use a brassiere—a very large brassiere. Woody sat on a cushion on the floor of the van. Mary, a Spanish major, and Derek, a philosophy major, were also on the floor on large maize and blue bean bags. Derek, Mary, and Elaine lived together on an organic farm outside of Ann Arbor. Mary was friendly until she learned that Woody was an auto mechanic not a college student. She turned her conversation to Bob while Derek slept the morning away. and Elaine continued to sing.

Harry rode in the front with Jose, the driver. Jose was a graduate student and an avowed Maoist who liked to quote from Mao's *Red Book*. He and Harry were in constant discussion and argument. Bob could only hear parts of the debate about history and class struggle, so he dozed much of the afternoon. Around four in the afternoon, Mary produced a joint and a bottle of wine and offered it to everyone. Only she, Elaine, and Derek, who was now awake, smoked, but Woody took several long swallows on the Boone's Farm Apple Wine. Woody and Bob brought out pickled baloney, cheese, and crackers and offered it to everyone. With disgust Mary informed everyone that she was a vegetarian. Elaine also jointed Mary in the values of vegetarianism, but she took pieces of baloney and cheese when it was passed. Derek lit a second joint. Jose, the driving Maoist, stopped talking revolution and informed everyone he had just stopped eating meat, and now avoided all alcohol and drugs because of Zen Buddhism. This conversion six months ago had made a profound change in his life. The avoidance of meat had made him feel better and was allowing him to focus more on the things that he needed to accomplish—the elimination of desire and suffering, which in turn was the way to world peace. Becoming a vegetarian had changed and improved his life and caused him to see that eating of animal flesh was directly related to the amount of violence in the world. Bob never understood the connection, but smiled as he thought what his father would say to this idea and how these "farmers' would survive eating at the Hartman farm where the table was filled with two types of meat each evening that had been grown on the farm.

"We need to go to Washington Circle which is near George Washington University. If we get off at this exit we will be able to take Wisconsin Avenue through D.C.," said Harry as they neared the suburbs of D.C. "There should be some people there tonight since Washington Circle is one of the staging areas for the Peace March."

Jose guided the van off I-70 and followed Harry's directions to Washington Circle. It was dark, but Harry had been to Washington several times, and with the aid of a map, he directed Jose to within a few blocks of Washington Circle.

"Do any of you need a somewhere to crash tonight?" Harry asked. "I've made sleeping arrangements for Woody and Bob, but my cousin can probably locate a place for you three. She's a graduate student at Georgetown and she'd be able to help. I'm sure she can find somewhere for you to sleep."

"No, we're OK. Derek has friends here, and they are expecting us sometime tonight," Mary said. Everyone took their bags out of the van, and Jose locked it.

"Remember, I want to leave at six tomorrow night. We might stay until seven, but no later. I need to get back to Ann Arbor to write a paper," Jose said as the Ann Arbor group moved away from Washington Circle.

Bob, Harry, and Woody turned for Washington Circle and arrived in a couple of minutes. The Circle was packed with milling people who flowed out onto the street. Passing cars honked support for the numerous signs already appearing or at people who wandered in the street. The weather was much warmer than in Michigan, which added to a carnival atmosphere among those gathered.

"Give me a few minutes to look for Becky. She said that she'd be here by eight o'clock, so I'm sure that she's somewhere in this crowd." Harry left Woody and Bob standing at the center of Washington Circle as he began a loop of the outside.

"Some mighty fine looking ladies demonstrating for peace, Bobby. Maybe you and I could hook up with a couple of them." Woody grinned and gave him a poke in the ribs.

"Jesus, Woody, don't you ever think of anything else. Here we are in Washington taking a stand against the War, and all that you can talk about is getting laid. Man, you're thinking with the wrong head."

"Just trying to bring love into the world—just a little love for the old Woodpecker." Just then Harry appeared through the crowd accompanied by a red-headed girl who was as tall as he was.

"Bob, Woody, this is my cousin, Rebecca Greenbergh. She is a graduate student at Georgetown and has a place for you two to stay tonight," said Harry. "I'm not going with you guys because I'm meeting someone with the National Draft Resistance Board this evening. They have a workshop that will give me some ideas about our draft resistance organization back in East Lansing. The meeting will go until at least to midnight, and then we can stay there for the night. I'll meet you in the morning back here for the march to the Capitol."

"We need to meet at the Washington Monument," Becky said.

"Ok, the Washington Monument in the morning."

"My place is about a half hour walk, so if you grab your stuff we can get started," Becky said.

"I think I'll wander around here for a while. I've never been to Washington, so I'll just take a look-see," Woody said. "Don't worry about me. I'll find some place to crash for the evening."

"Damn it, Woody. We came out here to demonstrate and not party. Don't screw around and get thrown in jail." Harry's face flushed the color of his hair. Seldom had he lost his composure, although Woody had the ability to create a red face in him where others failed.

"Let's see," Woody stroked his chin with mock thoughtfulness. "Been in jail in Lansing, Mount Pleasant, and Kalamazoo—and there was the Philippines in the Army. Nope, I've never been in a Washington jail—should be interesting. Can I use your name for a reference?"

"Just don't be late tomorrow. I won't be here because I am going home to New York for a week after the march," Harry said quietly, having regained his usual composure. "There're some veteran groups here that are participating in the march tomorrow. You might want to hook up with them."

"I'll try to hook up with the veterans—not the veterans of wars—the veterans of the streets," Woody said with that grin still on his face. "I don't swing from that side of the plate."

Harry went in one direction, and Becky led Bob in the opposite. Woody wandered off in a third direction with a grin of wonderment on his face. Bob and Becky walked and talked west along Pennsylvania Avenue and then on to M Street through Georgetown to 34th Street and Becky's apartment. They climbed to the second floor, and she unlocked the door and turned on the light. It was a large apartment with kitchen, bed, desk, and a sofa—all in one room.

"Make yourself at home," she said. "The door next to the desk is the bathroom. Would you like a glass of wine or a beer?"

"No thanks. Just a coke—if you have one?"

Becky went into the kitchen while Bob dropped his bag on the floor and sat on the couch. She returned with a glass of wine and handed it to him.

"I just have beer or wine," she said sitting on the sofa next to him. Bob took a sip while Becky did the same. He felt uncomfortable and uncertain as to what to say.

"What are you doing graduate work in?"

"Anthropology."

"Where did you get your undergraduate degree?"

"I have a BA from Smith in Sociology."

"How long have you been in graduate school here at Georgetown?" Bob said as Becky continued to look at him. She moved closer.

"This is my first semester here."

"Harry says that you were in the Peace Corps for two years before beginning your PhD. Where were you?"

"Africa"

"Where in Africa, and what did you do there?"

"I was in Uganda for two years. I taught English and mathematics in a local school. It was like a junior high school with boys in one class and girls in another. They separated the students by sex there," she said as she placed her hand on his shoulder. "In the afternoon we were supposed to do some community health work. There was a team of four of us, and my job was to work with the young girls on reproductive health issues. It was what we would call 'sex education' here. It was difficult to talk with the local girls because we were outsiders, and the information I needed to share went against local customs and taboos. It was usually an old grandmother or aunt who talked with young girls about this topic."

"Did you like it? I've thought about joining the Peace Corps after graduation."

"It was a great time, and I would recommend it to anyone. You experience things in the Peace Corps that you never experience anywhere else. And it would get you out of the draft." Becky had laid her hand on his shoulder. There it remained for a few minutes before it began to walk its way to his ear and up to his hair.

"What was it like there—anything dangerous or exciting happen to you while in Uganda?"

"Lots of things."

She laughed and took her hand from his head and finished her wine. She related how a jeep she was riding in turned over on a muddy road at night and the native driver had been killed, but she escaped with only a broken wrist. Then she talked about a two week trip to South Africa that she and two other volunteers had taken.

Bob excused himself to use the restroom and when he returned there were two fresh glasses of wine on the table in front of them. Becky talked more about Uganda and continued to lightly touch him or fondle his hair. Bob drank the last of his wine, stood up and stretched.

"I'd better get some sleep. It's been a long day, and we have to go back to East Lansing after the march tomorrow. Where do you want me to sleep—on the floor or on the couch?"

"The sofa is not very comfortable. You can sleep in the bed with me. It is large, and there is plenty of room for two."

"The floor will be fine. I sleep on the floor a lot." There was a nervous tone in his voice.

"Don't be silly. The floor is cold and hard, and there is plenty of room in the bed. We'll just sleep; I have to be up early also for the march. You can use the bathroom first if you like."

After brushing his teeth and washing, he came back to the room and Becky went into the bathroom. Bob kicked off his shoes and lay on top of the covers. He felt strange lying there. She came out of the bathroom in only her bra and panties and laid down besides him.

"Get under the covers silly," she ordered. She crawled under with him and moved close. She put her head next to his and threw her leg over his. Holding his hand only for a moment, she placed it on her butt. He could feel a thin layer of cotton between his fingers and her bottom. She kissed him several times lightly on the neck and then the ear.

"Let's make love," she said.

"I can't. Uh . . . I can't, I have a girl friend."

Part of him wanted to respond to Becky's advances, and his body was moving in that direction, but then he thought of Jenny. A small wave of lust washed across him followed by a much larger wave of guilt. His hands wanted to go one place, but his mind was back in East Lansing with Jenny, and it told the hands to stay where they were. Jennifer McKnight wouldn't understand why he was in bed with Becky and why he was unable to resist her advances.

"Well, I see you're not gay," she said as she laid her hand on his crotch. "Let's make love. I'm on the pill, if that is what you are worried about?"

"I really can't. We—We're engaged."

"But she's not here and I am." Becky nibbled on his hear.

"We're going to be married in June, and she wouldn't understand."

"That's OK. This is just for tonight. And she's not here. No one will ever know."

"I know. I—I still—uh, still can't do it. It is tempting, and you're very beautiful, but I can't."

He rolled away from her. He lied about the engagement, but he had to do something. Even when he pulled away there was no space between them and she slid her hand under his shirt while the other hand remained on his crotch.

Bob looked at the ceiling enveloped with guilt and lust. He wanted Becky to continue, and he wanted to be part of it, but he couldn't get Jenny out of his mind. Becky lay quietly next to him; she began to rub his stomach.

"Well if you can't make love, we can at least take care of this problem," she said as she unzipped his jeans. The waves of lust grew while the waves of guilt shrank.

CHAPTER 19

Bob woke early and slipped out of bed without waking Becky. Silently, he put on his pants and shoes, and used an envelope on the desk to write a note to say good-bye. Grabbing his jacket and bag, he quietly let himself out into a Washington morning. Becky still slept in the bed.

It was clear and bright with daffodils blooming in front of the apartment. Even at this early hour the air was warm in a cloudless sky; there was the promise of a beautiful day. This was Michigan Spring—in another three weeks.

He wished that he would have showered and changed his shirt—at least brushed his teeth. He had left without saying anything to Becky because he was afraid of what might have happened if she was awake. Guilt pushed him out of bed, just as morning chores had done for years.

"Hell," he thought. "I'm not married, and Jenny is just a friend. I should go back to the apartment and wake Becky. We'll never see each other again, and Jenny is in Michigan. Becky is here."

But he knew that if he returned, it would hurt Jenny deeply—if she found out. He worried that the guilt might show on his face, or a slip of the tongue would let Jenny in on the secret. Walking away meant he would not have to see the pain on Jenny's face. And he also knew that "Jenny was just a friend" was a lie that he was telling himself. As he walked in Georgetown looking for a restaurant or coffee shop, he realized he missed her. He wished that she was with him now, jabbering away as she did when the two were together. She would have talked constantly about the scenes in D.C., and he would have enjoyed the childlike excitement that was part of her. But she had to remain in East Lansing to write her senior honors thesis.

Bob finally found Washington Circle around ten o'clock. He had eaten breakfast in a small café on M Street, but then had gotten lost and ended up by the Potomac River. After he bought a tourist map he realized that he had wandered too far south when he crossed Rock Creek, and that he was only a few blocks from where he wanted to be. When he entered Washington Circle, he saw people there getting ready for the march. Finally, he found Woody sitting on a bench by himself. He walked by several people who were making signs and sat next to Woody.

"Man, you look terrible. And you smell worse," Bob said as the odor of stale beer and cigarettes wafted around him. "What have you been doing—drinking all night?"

"I ran into some vets, and they offered me a beer. You know how it goes, one turns to two, and two turns to nine. We ended up drinking all night and telling tales. They're here to protest the war. These guys are really against the War, and they've some pretty interesting stories to tell. I think I finished my last beer about six this morning, and I came back here to wait for you. I knew that you'd be here sometime this morning. How was it last night with Harry's cousin?"

"It was fine. I crashed on her floor and took off this morning before she woke. Do you need some aspirin? I have some if you want any."

"No, I'll be OK—as soon as I get some sleep. Where is the van? It was dark when we came here last night, and I can't remember which one of these streets we were parked on."

"It is right back there behind you." Bob turned away from him and pointed to a street running straight north from the Circle.

"It's two blocks that way and it's on the right side," he said. "But you don't have a key. Don't you remember that they locked the van, and I doubt that anyone is there now?"

"You forgot what I do for a living." Woody pulled a coat hanger from under his jacket on the bench. "I found this in the trash a few minutes ago. I bet that I opened a hundred cars with a simple piece of wire when I was driving a tow truck."

"What if they don't want you in their van?"

"Screw Ann Arbor Boy. If he doesn't like it, he can kiss my East Lansing ass with his stuck up friends watching." Woody said as he stood. "What time is the march?"

"We're to be at the Washington Monument at noon, and the march begins at one o'clock."

"I'll be there. Just give me a couple hours of sleep, and I'll be ready to kick ass and take names. I may walk with my vet friends from last night. If I don't see you at the beginning of the march, I'll catch up with you at the Capitol."

"Don't be late or get lost. Remember we leave at six." Woody, walking toward the van, waved his hand to acknowledge Bob's admonishment. Bob sat on the bench for a few minutes more enjoying the sunshine, and then he set out down 23rd Street into the George Washington University area. The day was pleasant as he wandered aimlessly knowing that he had two hours before he had to be at the Washington Monument. Large cities fascinated him because of where he had been raised. The only large cities that he had ever visited were Chicago and a trip to Detroit to watch a Tiger baseball game. He again thought how much Jenny would have enjoyed being here with him, and he missed her.

He walked all the way to the Lincoln Memorial and sat on the steps and looking across the Reflecting Pool to the Washington Monument. Two bags of potato chips, a Heresy bar, and a Coke were an early lunch; he sat in the sun enjoying the sights and sounds of everyone moving around him. Most were young students who were probably in Washington for the same reason that he was, but there were also families and foreigners. The Tidal Basin and the Cherry blossoms were off to his right. They were not in bloom yet, and Becky said it would be another week or two before they would be. He walked down the steps of the Lincoln Monument and looked back at Lincoln sitting in his chair; he tried to imagine where Dr. King had stood and given the speech that he had heard on television, and then he headed to the Washington Monument. He knew that Harry would be there some place, and he hoped that Woody would make it, too.

The area around the base of the monument was filled with a crowd that ran from the ordinary to the ridiculous. Many were young college-age students, but Bob was surprised by the number of older marchers—many were mothers who carried signs of protest. He stopped at a large crowd that had gathered around a small makeshift stage on which two guys with guitars were singing.

"Lyndon Johnson told the nation, have no fear of escalation. I am trying everyone to please. Tho' it isn't really war, we're sending fifty thousand more, to help save Vietnam from the Vietnamese."

Bob joined in the clapping even though he did not know the words to the song. Everyone sang enthusiastically and two girls in front did a dance as the singers began the next verse softly.

"Here I am in this rice paddy, thinking about Big Daddy, and I know that Lyndon loves me so. How sad it is to remember, way back in November, when he said I'd never have to go."

Just then a man with a bullhorn came from behind and announced. "Marchers line up—Please line up now." The duo continued with more verses, but the audience moved away to the east and began to line up for the march. More directions were issued.

"We'll march down Constitution to Pennsylvania and then to the steps of the Capitol. Please walk in the street and not on the sidewalk. Don't respond to any hecklers or supporters of the war. There may be a right-wing group trying to disrupt our demonstration. It's important that we show Washington and the nation that we are serious and united against the War in Vietnam. Remember we are marching for peace, so don't respond to taunts and violence."

Bob had not seen Harry or Woody but he did see a large banner—MICHIGAN FOR PEACE—STOP THE WAR NOW! He joined in with the group, although he recognized only a couple of the students. There were older marchers—one was Professor Bedfast from MSU.

Bob was caught in the spirit as he marched down Constitution Avenue. Not only was the weather warm and sunny, but there was a spirit of purpose and hope that moved with the demonstrators. It was almost a carnival atmosphere, but with a very serious intent—stopping the war in Southeast Asia. With the singing and chanting, he was caught up in the moment of euphoria, and he felt the energy and resolve of the thousands of those marching toward the Capitol. A few along the way on the sidewalks held signs in opposition to them—AMERICA—LOVE IT OR LEAVE IT, or SUPPORT OUR BOYS. But most of those not in the march simply watched as a collection of people in different dress and of different ages paraded by them to the Capitol.

The strangest group was dressed in suits and carrying brief cases under a sign—WALL STREET FOR PEACE. He thought that they were just college students dressed that way because he could not image the business community associating with this crowd. There were grandmothers, mothers, and people in clown suits all singing and marching. Just before his group hit Pennsylvania Avenue and made the turn toward the Capitol, they passed a group of veterans marching. Some wore their old fatigues from the service, but none had a military haircut—except Elwood Rademaker.

Bob saw Woody on the other side of the street and started to join him, but then notice that he was pushing a wheel chair with a vet who had both legs amputated. Woody was staring straight ahead and keeping pace with the other veterans. They were not moving as fast as the rest of the crowd because several members were on crutches or in wheel chairs. They marched as a group, each supporting any who needed assistance. Woody was doing his share. Bob returned to the Michigan group and made the swing on Pennsylvania and in two blocks they were at the Capitol.

There was a large platform erected in front of the building and he sat with the Michigan contingent. He had marched with four MSU freshman girls who had driven from East Lansing for the demonstration and were going to Florida for spring break. Not all of the marchers had arrived, and no one was speaking on the platform. The organizers were having difficulty with the microphone and there as a series of "tests," "tests," and "tests"—interspersed with the "test" were shrieks and squawks as the audio system would not cooperate. Ignoring the problems, the gathering crowd enjoyed the pleasant weather. Bob sat on the grass with the four and listened to them talk about the next stage of their spring vacation—the drive to Fort Lauderdale. One of the girls tried to light a cigarette, but the breeze kept extinguishing the match.

"Here let me help you." Bob took the book of matches from her hand.

Leaving the match still attached to the book, he lit it. Cupping his hands around the book and the lit match, he offered it to her. This was something he had seen his father do several times when the wind was blowing. She leaned toward him and held his hand while she lit the cigarette.

"Thank you," she said. "I hope Bobbie Kennedy will speak." She held the cigarette awkwardly and exhaled smoke into the clear air of D.C.

"I think that he's campaigning somewhere out West," Bob said. "My roommate, who helped organize this, said that he did not think there would be any presidential candidate speakers today. It would be nice to see McCarthy or Kennedy appear. I'm very certain that Humphrey won't be here."

"Or Robert McNamara," the other girl said. "Perhaps Tricky Dick will show up." Everyone laughed.

Several people spoke against the war. William Sloan Coffin Jr. and Dr. Benjamin Spock were the only individuals that Bob recognized. There were others criticizing American actions in Vietnam. He knew that Harry would recognize all of them, but he did not. After an hour of speakers, interspersed with protest songs, he got up to look for Woody.

He sat with the same group of veterans that Bob had seen him with earlier. Most were listening to the speakers, but Woody was listening to two vets in wheel chairs who had a conversation going. Bob walked up behind Woody and stood.

"God-damn it. It's a load of shit over there," one said. "I joined after college, so I could choose where I went. The Army promised me that I would serve my time in Germany, but they sent me to Nam anyway. I was only there a week when I stepped on a mine."

"They lost my papers and shipped me to Vietnam right after basic training," another vet with long hair and beads said. He wore a military jacket with "Airborne" on it. "I was supposed to have two weeks leave before I shipped out. I was going to Thailand or the Philippines, but they sent me right after basic. I tried arguing with them, but the Sergeant said 'get your ass on the plane.' Then they notified my parents that I was AWOL and had a warrant out for my arrest. It took the idiots four months before someone realized that I was in Vietnam." He flicked a cigarette butt out into the street. "Hell, if they were going to mark me AWOL, I should have gone AWOL. At least then I would have my legs."

Both were quiet and Woody said nothing. They all turned their attention to the podium where Peter Paul and Mary were singing.

"How many times must the cannon balls fly before they're forever banned?" They finished *"Blowing in the Wind"* and everyone cheered and clapped. Bob checked his watch and tapped Woody on the shoulder.

"We should head back to the van. It's four o'clock, and it might take an hour to walk back. I'm not sure how to get there, but I do have a map that I bought this morning," Bob said.

"Lead on, Bobby—you have the map."

They moved away from the Capitol toward the White House. The sidewalks were crowded with demonstrators leaving the Capitol, and traffic had returned to Pennsylvania Avenue. At the National Archives, half way to the White House, the sidewalk was blocked. Several demonstrators were passing out leaflets and a crowd was gathering in opposition. Bob and Woody stood at the edge to see what was happening.

"If you got a haircut you could probably think better. All of that long hair hanging on your head has affected your brain."

The man speaking was about Bob's father's age, and there were several standing with him who clapped and laughed at his comment. The speaker's face was beginning to reach the color of the American Flag that he had stitched on his jacket.

"Read this," said a young man with long hair and a Duke University T-shirt, offering a pamphlet. "It will tell you how the government has lied to us, and why we're really in Vietnam."

"I don't need to read—I'm an educated American," he shouted. "I know all that I need to know, and that is that communism is spreading like wild fire in the world, and if we do not stop it in Vietnam, then we will have to stop it here in America."

"That's not true."

"Crap, if it isn't. The commies are in Cuba and South America. They took over China and tried to take Korea, and would have done it if we had not stopped them there. Now they're trying the same thing again in Southeast Asia. If we don't stop them, they will take all of Asia just like they did in Europe."

"That's not true. That's not true at all. We are oppressing the Vietnamese people. They are trying to gain their freedom, and we're involved in someone else's internal struggle, and we're supporting corrupt politicians who have no concern for the well-being of their own people. We are involved in a civil war in Vietnam. Let the Vietnamese fight their own civil war just as we fought our Civil War over a hundred years ago."

A short round-faced man with dark hair that carried traces of white pushed by the man with the American flag and spoke with an accent.

"Freedom—you have no freedom under communism. I was in Hungary when the Russian tanks come. There they tell you everything to do and believe. You want communist here in US of A, telling you what to do? That is what will happen if you do not stop communist. They want to take over all of world and make so no one have freedom."

A young girl with long blond hair in a pony tail and wearing a Brown University sweat shirt offered a pamphlet to the Hungarian and spoke calmly.

"Sir, what we are doing in Vietnam is the same that the Russians did to you in Hungary. We are the Russians today."

"Are you crazy little girl. We are no Russians. Why you not home. Does your Poppa know where you are and what crazy you talk?"

"Yes, he knows where I am, and he supports me in opposition to this illegal and insane war," she said as her voice now had lost its calmness. "He was a paratrooper at Normandy and fought all through France and Germany. He understands that we're not under attack like in World War II and that this is just the American government putting their nose into the business of a small Asian country and that young men are dying in a war that is immoral and illegal."

There were several cheers but even more boos as others joined. The pamphlets being offered were accepted, wadded up, and then thrown on the ground. The noise level was rising in the divided crowd. On one side were demonstrators—all had long hair and wore jeans and T-shirts or sweat shirts. On the other side were males who were older with short hair cuts. Most of them wore casual clothes, but a few were in suits and ties. All were yelling at each other.

"Let's get the hell out of here," Woody said. They went around the crowd and continued up Pennsylvania Avenue. After they had left the arguing group he said, "I'm not the sharpest crayon in the box, but at least I could see that no one was listening to each other."

"You're right," Bob said. "When talking with a fool, make sure he is not doing the same thing."

CHAPTER 20

When Bob and Woody arrived at the van, Elaine and Mary were already there with two other guys. They sat in the door smoking cigarettes, with an open bottle of wine at hand. Bob wondered if the girls had even marched to the Capitol.

"Where are Derek and Jose?" Bob asked.

"Derek met a girl last night, and they're hitchhiking to Boston today. Jose decided to stay here in D.C. for a few more days. He has friends here, so he is going to come back to Ann Arbor next week."

"Doesn't he have a paper to write?" Bob asked. "How are we going to get back to Lansing?" Bob looked at Woody who just shrugged.

"It's OK. It's Derek's van, and he gave me these." Mary took the keys from her jeans and held them for everyone to see. "This is Tony and Chuck. They are hitchhiking to San Francisco, and we are going to give them a ride to Ann Arbor, so they can spend of few days with Elaine and me. They've never been to Michigan. Will one of you drive?"

Tony and Chuck stood up and shook hands. They both had long hair and beards and looked like they had worn the same clothes for several days, just as everyone did. Already in the van were two different bags and a guitar and banjo case. The bags were actually backpacks tied to aluminum frames. There was a big peace sign on one and the other had various patches sewed on it.

"I'll drive," said Bob as he took the keys from Mary.

They left Washington a little before six and drove north on I-70 past Hagerstown. Tony uncased his guitar and took several minutes to tune it. He did several fingering exercises and then began a steady beat as the van began to climb the hills of western Maryland into Pennsylvania. The banjo case remained closed, but Chuck opened another bottle of wine and offered it to everyone.

"Do you know any Jefferson Star Ship or The Who songs?" Mary asked.

"I don't play that commercial shit; I play the blues. Have you ever heard of Leadbelly or Mississippi John Hurt?"

"No, but play some."

They drove into Pennsylvania with a new type of music that Bob had never heard. Elaine tried to sing but did not know any of the words. Mary would ask for a popular tune, but Tony refused to play anything that he considered "bullshit music." At Breezewood they filled the van with gas and purchased snack food to share. Woody bought a pack of cigarettes.

As they drove west through Pennsylvania, the guitar was cased and a joint was rolled. Everyone took a hit on it in the back, and it was offered to those in the front.

"No thanks, I got to drive," Bob said.

"None for me," Woody responded. He stared out the window. He had been unusually quiet since they had left Washington.

"You can get in the back and burn one with them if you want. I'm fine driving,"

"Not my style, Bobby—not my style."

Woody lit a cigarette and continued to look straight ahead. It was strange to see him smoke and Bob had never seen him buy a pack of cigarettes before. He usually bummed one from someone when he had been drinking or was with a woman who was smoking. Other than those occasions, he very seldom smoked tobacco, and Bob had never seen him smoke marijuana.

"How come you never smoke any dope?" Bob asked. It was quiet in the back as they continued west. "Jim has it in the apartment all of the time."

"Jim-bo smokes my share and the rest of Lansing's." Woody said as he exhaled smoke. "I got really stoned the first week that I was in Nam. I was a new fill-in, just in from the States to a company that was deployed in the field. The second night some of the guys were smoking local weed, and they offered me some. I was the new guy and too afraid to refuse. I'd drunk beer several times in high school before I went into the army, but I'd never been stoned," Woody paused, then continued. "Let me tell you, the dope that they have in Nam is tough shit, not that puppy chow those rookies in the back are smoking. I saw some guys get really stoned on just half a joint there."

"Well anyway, sometime after dark we came under rocket attack. I was so stoned I just stood and watched. It was like ten Fourth of Julys all at once. Someone grabbed me and pulled me into a foxhole. It wasn't the one I was supposed to be in, but hell, I wasn't going to argue. When the attack was done, everyone crawled out from the hole or bunker they were hiding in. Where I was supposed to be took a direct hit. Those poor bastards never knew what hit them. Of course I was so stoned, I didn't understand anything. It wasn't until the next day that I realized how close I came to being sent home in a body bag, and that was just the first day there." Woody put his cigarette out in the ash tray.

"I saw some crazy shit over there. I was always straight when we were on patrol in the bush, but a lot of guys weren't. When we weren't on patrol, I did become good friends with Mr. Daniels and Mr. Beam."

As they drove west on the turnpike another joint was offered to the front of the van and again Bob and Woody declined. With the wine and marijuana consumed, the gas station feast of snacks began with much laughter. Shortly the giggling stopped, and sounds of passion were mixed with the marijuana smoke from the back. Bob wondered who was with whom, but then they may not even have known or cared because they were so stoned.

As the van approached Pittsburg and the last moan emitted from the back, it became quiet and only the whine of the tires could be heard. Woody still stared and smoked. Bob played the events of the day over again in his head. It was the march and the different kinds of people and their dress that he kept remembering. He was carried away by the spirit of the march—a spirit of opposition to the War and an unshakable belief that they could change the policies of the United States government in Southeast Asia.

That feeling that he had during the march down Constitutional Avenue was like what he had seen in tent revivals that he had been forced to attend when he was young. People were "filled with the Spirit," as they called it and sang, danced, and said strange things. He never experienced it, but it was always fascinating to see. And the "joyful praises" from the audience always help counteract a boring sermon that he could not understand. The only "spirit" that moved him was a slap on the head from his mother with orders: "Stop fidgeting, Robert."

They were past Pittsburg and into Ohio. The exits for Cleveland were appearing as he drove at 70 miles per hour. At 55 the front end shook, but at 60 the van sailed smoothly, bouncing only when it hit an expansion joint in the concrete. This rhythmic thumps and early morning were beginning to have an affect on him. Bob glanced at Woody who had not said anything for over an hour; he just smoked and stared. Bob thought about asking him about the vets that he had marched with in the parade, but he had a feeling that the experience was something Woody did not want to share at this time. Still he needed conversation to keep from falling asleep at the wheel.

"What was it like in Vietnam, Woody? Did you shoot anyone? Were you ever scared?"

Woody didn't say anything, but just took another cigarette and lit it and then looked out the side window. Bob realized that he had opened a topic that his friend did not want to talk about. Woody seldom mentioned Vietnam beyond the girls and the drinking. When he volunteered to come to Washington, Bob figured that it was because the possibility of free and easy sex. But now he wasn't so sure. It seemed that the trip to D.C. had impacted Woody. Bob regretted asking the question.

"Skip it, Woody; those were dumb questions to ask."

"It's okay." Woody turned back from the window and looked at him.

"It's a shit hole over there. It was incredibly beautiful. The jungle has greens that I can't describe. The little villages and the country side are neat, and I suppose that if I wasn't so scared of getting shot, I would have enjoyed some of the scenery more. It's the smells that I remember the most. The cities and the jungle have a smell that you never forget. Every once in awhile I get a whiff of something that will jar my memory of my time there—and I think about Nam. It is never a pleasant smell that takes me back." He took a deep drag on the cigarette and paused for a time. Then he continued, speaking even more softly. Bob focused as much as he could on his friend while driving.

"I don't know if I actually killed anyone or not in combat. We wasted a lot of people, but there was so much fire power thrown out from everyone in the squad, it was hard to tell whose bullets did what. I suppose some of mine may have killed someone. We would go through a village after a fire fight, and there would be all of these dead gooks—women, kids, and old people. We would bag them up, if we had time, and count them as dead VC. We would have a high count of enemy killed and the brass would pat us on the back and send us out to do more. I don't know if they were VC or not. All that I know is that if someone is shooting at you, you shoot back with everything that you have. Have a few buddies get killed and you don't worry about shooting women and kids, Bobby." Woody stopped and the only sound was the steady thump of expansion joints. He continued to speak so quietly that Bob had to lean towards him to hear.

"The one that bothers me, and the one that I still remember is the old lady that I shot in a rice paddy one afternoon—for no reason." Woody coughed a couple of times and cleared his throat.

"We were riding in a truck. Our whole company was being moved to another area. We'd taken a lot of flak where we had just been. Three or four guys had been killed and several wounded so badly that they had to evacuate them in helicopters. But the area had been secured, so the brass brought in a green company and sent us to another area. We thought we were going into another hot area, and we were right. We were such a large convoy that there wasn't much danger, unless we hit a mine, and they had swept the road before we moved."

"We were passing through these little villages when someone decided to shoot some of the livestock as we went through—ducks, pigs, chickens, and dogs—stuff like that. Someone blasted a water buffalo in a rice paddy. Man a 50 caliber does a hell of a number on a pig or a water buffalo. We never stopped, just kept going and shooting. A few times we fired into huts, but I don't think that there was anyone in them. We were all laughing and goofing around. Some of the guys may have been high, but most of us weren't—just being stupid—like when you were kids, and you and your buddies rode around at night throwing M-80s and cherry bombs out the window." Woody paused and again the expansion joints sang in the quiet with soft snoring from the back.

"We came out of a village and this old Mama-san was standing in a rice paddy. When she saw us, she ran away. I wasted her right there in the paddy, and I don't know why. I still can see her floating face down in that field, and even now I can't think of any reason why I did it. I just did it. And no one in the truck said anything, and we didn't stop. We just went on riding and laughing and doing the shit that we did over there. To this day, I still can't figure out why I did it." He stubbed the cigarette out in the ash tray staring again, and then he said. "You want me to drive awhile. I'm not sleepy at all."

"Sure. There is a rest area just two miles ahead. We can switch there." Bob pulled the van into the parking area and the two just changed positions and continued on to Toledo. Bob dozed lightly as Woody drove out of Ohio and into Michigan. It was daylight when Woody pulled the van into the parking lot in Ann Arbor next to his car. Bob looked in the back and for the first time the morning light revealed four naked bodies sprawled on the floor.

"What should we do with them? Wake 'em up or just leave them?" he asked.

"No just leave 'em," Woody said. "They may want to get at it again when they wake up. Let's go home."

They got out into a spring morning that was cold but sunny. The air had a bite to it that felt good and clean after the heavy air of tobacco and marijuana they had endured for the last ten hours. Traffic was still light on I-96 as they drove toward Lansing and although his eyes burned from the long drive, Bob could not sleep.

The events of the last two days were fresh in his mind, along with a desire to see Jenny. She was back in Lawsonville, and he would see her in another day when he went home for the rest of spring break. He could not forget that "revival" feeling from the march in Washington, but the strangest item rolling in his mind was the conversation with Woody on the way back from D.C.

CHAPTER 21

"Bob, get up. The cows are out."

Bob jumped out of bed and into some clothes when his mother called up the stairs. He had been awake, lying there thinking about the trip to Washington and the march to the Capitol. After returning from the Peace March, he spent only one day at the apartment, then hitchhiked to Lawsonville. He had the remainder of the week at home until he would have to return to East Lansing for Spring Term. Walking into the kitchen, he grabbed his jacket off a hook by the door. His mother sat at the table writing checks.

"Somebody just stopped and said we have cattle in the road. I think that they're the heifers, not the old cows, and somehow your brother Joe is responsible. Sam just went outside and the air was quite blue as he left. He loves his cattle and sons, but they both make him mad at times. I wish the good Lord would give him a little more patience, and he did not take the Savior's name in vain so often."

Bob went to the barn where his father would be. It was sunny and warm; wonderful weather for early spring, although it was not uncommon to get a late snow storm early in Aril. He changed directions to the tool shed when he heard a hammer strike metal. His father was straightening disk blades.

"Where are they, Dad?"

"They are probably over in McKnight's field by now and back by the power line, or they still may be by the county ditch. You'd better push them up by Schmidt's and into the woods. I'll have the gate to the lane open, and then we can bring them back to the barn. Don't let them get into the pothole or you'll have a hell of mess," Sam Hartman said. "You'd better take Roscoe with you. There will be six heifers. That damn brother of yours didn't hook the hot wire last night like I asked him to do, and now he's at school. I wish he would use his head for something other than to hang his hat on. With that kid around it'll be a miracle if I live long enough to collect social security."

Bob whistled and a ball of black and white fur bounded from behind the disk, tail wagging furiously.

"Let's go, Roscoe. Let's go chase cows."

Bob whistled softly as he walked along the road with Roscoe splashing in and out of the water standing in the ditches. At one point he laughed out loud at his father's comment about his brother. He had heard that one, and several similar ones, about himself when he had been in high school. By the time that Joe returned home this evening the incident would be forgotten.

Bob set out down the gravel road to the area that his father said the heifers would be. Redwing blackbirds flew from the fields along the road. A chill was still in the air, but it would warm by noon if the sun continued to shine as it was. This afternoon when he was to meet Jenny, he would not need a jacket.

"Boy, I sure do miss her," he said as Roscoe pushed a rabbit out of a fence row and with a yelp took off after it across the corn stubble. Bob whistled and yelled. "Get back here you worthless hound dog—we're chasing cows, not rabbits."

Roscoe jogged back and rubbed against his pants as Bob patted his wet and matted fur. A burr-filled tail whacked his pant leg. Bob put both hands around the head that had a tongue hanging out panting, and scuffed him.

"Let's go get those cows. You want to go with me this afternoon to the Schmidt's farm when I see Jenny? She likes you, even though you are a worthless hound dog. You won't bite her will you? Remember we just bite cows." The tail increased motion and intensity.

They continued down the road and crossed into McKnight's field. The six heifers were in the back feeding on young grass under a Detroit Edison power line. Bob pushed them across the field and up the lane past the old Schmidt house and into the woods. A barking Roscoe drove them and Bob just strolled behind. A couple of times a heifer would try to bolt from the chosen path, but Roscoe was right on her. If the barking did not drive her back, then a couple of well chosen nips on the heels convinced her of the error of her ways. When they came out of the woods, the gate to the lane was open and Sam Hartman stood ten yards from it. The heifers went in the gate and headed up the lane to the barn with Roscoe still in pursuit. Sam Hartman closed the gate as Bob walked out from the woods.

"Thanks, Bobby."

"I didn't do anything. Roscoe did all of the work. I think it makes his day when he has cows to chase."

"You're probably right. The only thing I think he enjoys more is when we used to have hogs, and then he could grab their ears and hang on."

Sam Hartman reopened the gate, and both he and Bob walked through. This time he latched it, and they walked toward the barn. The grass in the lane was nibbled short but on the other side of the fence green sprouts were emerging. The trees were close to budding, and already laced in the dead brown woods were the white spots where the dogwood was blooming. The redwing blackbirds were now singing in full voice as the wind and the sun warmed the surrounding fields.

"Your mother said that you were in Washington in that Peace March, and that's why you didn't come home last weekend. I saw the March on television. It looked like there were a lot of people there."

"Almost a half a million."

"Did you go by yourself?"

"No, I went with a couple of friends, and we rode out with four others from Ann Arbor. There were quite a few people in Washington from Michigan." A steel post was leaning inward. Bob stopped, and being careful not to touch the attached electric wire, straightened it.

"Thanks," Sam said. When they reached the barn yard, Bob closed and latched the gate into a small pasture where the six heifers now grazed.

"Do you think the war in Vietnam is wrong?" his father asked.

"Damn," Bob thought. "I don't want to discuss Vietnam with my dad. How can I say that I don't believe in it because he's a World War II veteran." He unhooked the gate into the barn yard and swung it open. It would be left open for cows to go to the woods to graze now that the heifers were secure in the adjacent pasture. Sam stood watching two young Holsteins run and kick their heels. Bob knew his father was waiting for an answer, and he chose his words carefully, hoping to avoid any political argument, but also not able to lie to his father about his growing doubt about Vietnam.

"I think that we're involved in a civil war that the Vietnamese should settle themselves."

"We sure do a have knack to put our noses into everyone's business."

"I think it was a mistake to get involved, and now we just don't know how to get out." There, he had told his father that he didn't support American involvement in Southeast Asia.

"I sure hope that they know what they are doing because there seems to be a lot of boys dying over there. Most of those son-of-a-bitches in Washington don't know anything except hot air and how to spend money. If they had to do an honest days work, they would probably have a heart attack." Sam Hartman turned to his son.

"Do you know a William Whitefield?"

"I played 4-H softball with a Billy Whitefield."

"Yes, that's him. His dad is on the Farm Bureau Board with me. Anyway, he was killed last week in Vietnam. And there are two boys who live in town that have been wounded over there, according to the paper. One is pretty serious and is at a hospital in Washington D.C." His father looked at him for a moment and then moved to the barn, but continued to speak.

"I don't think George McKnight is over losing Tommy. I sure hope the politicians in Washington know what the hell they are doing." There was a long pause as Sam Hartman stared at the barn and not his son. Bob did not know what to say. He turned to Bob and clapped him on the shoulder, and changed the subject.

"Talk to your mother, Bobby. I know that she can be a pain in the neck. But she worries about you, as she does all of her children. She thinks that prayer and worry will solve everything," he grinned and added. "I don't think that she'll be able to change and save me, but she has hope for her children."

His father entered the barn and Bob went back to the house. He unpacked his dirty laundry from school and brought it downstairs, placing it next to the washer. He played with Sarah, his younger sister, while his mother went to town to run a few errands. His three other siblings, Joe, Mary, and Billy, were at school. As Sarah watched Captain Kangaroo on television he thumbed through the latest edition of *The Readers Digest*.

Just before noon his mother returned and fixed lunch for Sarah and him. His father continued to work outside. Bob did not take his father's advice and ate silently. Helen Hartman asked about his trip to Washington, but Bob mumbled just a few responses.

"Pastor Floyd was talking about those hippies that were in Washington demonstrating. He says that this is all the work of Satan and it just demonstrates that we are living in the end times, just like the Bible says. When you have young girls running around without brassieres and hippies having sex in the streets of our nation's capitol, it just goes to show that Old Lucifer is doing his work."

"Don't you think that napalm is also the work of the devil?'

"I don't know much about napalm, Robert, but if Americans are using it against godless Communists, then it must be the thing to do."

"So killing and burning children is OK, but someone going naked is a dreadful sin?"

"You know what I mean. I don't know how anyone would want to be naked in public—that just isn't right."

"What's happening in Vietnam isn't right. And if you're looking for the work of Satan, take a look at Washington D.C. A little nudity seems to me less harmful than blowing up innocent women and children. But then what do I know because I'm just a hippie in Washington." He got up and went outside, letting the door slam behind him.

He was so angry a cat was kicked off of the porch. As he went by the barn, he whistled for Roscoe who came running with his tail wagging. About half way down the lane his anger lessened, and he regretted his parting comments. He and his mother always seemed to have words, and he knew that he was part of the problem. Why couldn't he just ignore her, but she was always correcting him or putting her nose in his affairs.

Bob had called Jenny from East Lansing yesterday, and she had suggested that they meet at the old Schmidt Farm this afternoon. He was early, but he could spend some time wandering in the woods and fields. Even though it was early, there might be a few morel mushrooms, and the floor of the woods was carpeted with trilliums. He wandered among the flowers and decaying trees that had fallen. He remembered that when he was very young he had come here with his grandfather and father as they cut wood to heat their homes in the winter. Now his grandfather was dead and they heated with oil—a call to the oil distributor was simpler than spending the day cutting and stacking oak and maple. By the time he entered grade school, no one cut wood from here; now it was used just for pasture.

Bob walked by a huge oak in a small clearing that had weathered boards nailed on the lower limbs. Here Tommy and he had built a tree house and tied old hay ropes to limbs. These ropes were used to exit their tree house with a Tarzan yell or to drop on an imaginary lion or tiger. They were kings of the jungle until a knot untied on a limb and Tommy broke his arm. They were forbidden to use the tree house from then on, so they began to build log cabins. None were ever completed, and their remains were visible throughout the woods; late in the summer these half finished cabins disappeared as vines and blackberry bushes covered them. A track also circled through the trees where they raced an old go-cart that Tommy had salvaged from the dump. Now the track was kept clear by the cattle that walked on it, but a few years ago it had been the Indy 500 with several spectacular crashes into surrounding trees.

The woods were a patchwork quilt of spring flowers and memories. Along with all of his adventures with Tommy had been a girl with bib overalls, brown pig tails, and soft brown eyes. She tagged along and sometimes jabbered, and at other times she was silent. She was not as adventuresome, but she was always present; Bob just assumed that she would be there and did not think too much about her. She never broke the cardinal rule of telling what they did. When they returned to the forbidden tree house or smoked stolen cigarettes, she kept quiet.

It was this pig-tailed quiet girl that he was going to see now. At one time he had hardly ever thought about her, but now after not seeing her for a week, it was all that he could do to keep from sprinting to the Schmidt farm. As he moved up the lane with a bouquet of butter cups and violets, he felt like running and squirming like Roscoe had been doing all during their walk as he chased rabbits, squirrels, and birds.

When Bob walked around the barn, Jenny was sitting on the concrete horse tank they had sat on in the fall. Roscoe barked and Jenny whipped around.

"Robert." She ran and hugged him around the neck. "I've missed you."

"Here are some flowers for my lady." He kissed her on the cheek.

"Is that the best that you can do?" She took his face and kissed him passionately on the lips. Jenny took the flowers, and they returned to the horse tank and sat on the edge. Roscoe found a sunny spot of grass in front of them and began to chew on the burrs that were knotted in his fur.

"Tell me about Washington. Did Woody actually go with you and Harry?"

"Yes, he went. It was an incredible experience. There were so many people, different kinds of people, who are against the war in Vietnam. It was great weather and Washington is amazing. I wish that you had been there with me."

"I wish I could have gone, but that project is done, and now all I have to do is type it and proof-read it." She hugged him one more time. "I missed you so much. Tell me everything that you did there. What was it like marching to the Capitol?"

"We rode out with four students from Ann Arbor. They were so weird that they must have been English majors."

"By weird, you mean, they knew how to spell. Where did you stay that first night?"

"Harry has a cousin in grad school at Georgetown. Several of us slept on the floor there," Bob quickly changed the subject, remembering his stay with Becky. "What have you been doing since you came home for vacation?"

"I've been helping Mother. She always does a major spring cleaning in May, but the weather has been so nice that we started it last week. It has been nice helping her and seeing the kids, but I sure have missed you." She put both her arms around him and hugged him tight.

They continued to talk, perched on the horse tank, while Roscoe gave up on the burrs, stretched out in the sun and went to sleep. Every once in a while he would give a small yelp and his paws would shake and quiver. Bob mentioned how Woody had seemed different on the way back. He did not give details of Vietnam that Woody had shared with him as they drove through Ohio, but simply related that Woody appeared to have changed because of his trip to Washington Jenny wanted to know every detail about his trip.

At some point she put her head in his lap and took his hand and held it. Bob stroked her hair as she lay with bent knees on the edge of the horse tank. She wore shorts and sandals and had her toe nails painted a bright red. He lost his train of thought for a moment as he looked down at her legs. They were gorgeous—long and graceful—a model's legs that had perfect proportions. He looked back at her and was embarrassed. Jenny smiled and kicked one leg up.

"Why, Mr. Hartman, here you have been to Washington saving the world and now you are looking at this old farm girl's skinny legs."

"They're not skinny anymore."

"I just painted my toenails. This is definitely not the style for Lawsonville," Jenny laughed she put her leg down. "How come you came from behind the barn? I thought you would come across the field; that was where I expected to see you."

"I was walking back in the woods where we used to play. I stopped at the old tree fort that Tommy and I built. Do you remember it?"

"Yes. I do."

She was quiet and the smile changed to a thoughtful expression. Bob continued to stroke her hair.

"A penny for your thoughts. You seem to be some place far from here."

"Oh, I was just thinking about the last time I was at that old tree fort," she said. She gave his hand a squeeze.

"It was sometime in the summer after Tommy was killed. Mother had finally gotten so that she could take care of the house and kids, and I went for a walk in the woods where we used to play. I was still feeling numb from his death. I always felt guilty that I couldn't cry. No one in our family even cried at the funeral, although I used to hear Mother cry at night. But she never shed a tear in public. I just felt that if I could cry that somehow I'd feel better. I guess I still believed that it was all a dream, and that I'd wake up and Tommy would be there with a big grin on his face calling me 'cow eyes' or some other name."

"Anyway, I did climb up to the old fort and was just sitting there, when all of a sudden I began to sob. Later I came over here to the Schmidt's where we had played so much, and then I began again. I think that I spent the whole afternoon and evening here and in the woods crying. Afterwards it seemed to get better. Even now I still get sad, but when I let go with the tears, it always seems to help. I still miss him, but now I think mostly of the happy times. I do wish he was here with us today."

"What would he think of me here with you?"

"Oh he'd love it. He always thought the world of you and would be happy that you are dating his little sister. He'd probably have something funny to say." Roscoe got up, stretched, and barked. Bob looked at his watch and Jenny sat up.

"I'd better get back. I said that I would help with milking tonight because Joe has track practice after school. Would you like to go to a show in town this evening?" he asked.

"Sure, pick me up around seven." Jenny hugged him and kissed his cheek. "I sure did miss you, Robert."

Robert and Roscoe left for the woods and the evening chores. When he crossed a fence, he saw Jenny walking up the road to home. Knowing that his father would have started the milking, he hurried home. Closing the gate to the barnyard, he thought how wonderful to see and touch Jenny again. Yet even as enjoyable it was to be with her again, he felt a hesitance to share his true feelings about his trip to Washington. He was becoming more and more convinced that the war in Vietnam was a mistake, and that he could not be a part of it.

But Tommy had done his duty and gave his life there. Would he lose Jenny if he did not serve his country when he was drafted?

CHAPTER 22

"*No, don't come home a drinkin' with lovin' on your mind.*"

Woody was singing along with Loretta Lynn as he drove along a country road south of Lansing. One arm rested on the open window, the other on the steering wheel, while a beer can was wedged between his legs. Bob sat on the other side looking out the window holding his own can of beer.

"*Just stay out there on the town and see what you can find.*" Woody took a large swig of beer.

"Now Bobby, I know that you have your lady friend, but old Woody needs some lovin', so you got to help me on that 'find' part tonight. You seem to be nursing that beer along. Did you join the church?"

"No, I haven't joined the church," Bob laughed. He finished the beer, threw the empty can in the back and took another one from the floor. "Jesus, Woody, why did you get Stroh's? That stuff tastes like crap."

"I know Bobby, my boy. But we've got to support the breweries in Detroit. You'll really enjoy it in the morning when it leaves you. The rest of a case is in the trunk. Someone brought two cases of the Stroh's to work this afternoon, and when I left work early, I took one. Nothing tastes better than free beer."

That afternoon Bob had been sitting in his apartment reading in the afternoon when Woody appeared with a beer in his hand. For the last week he had spent every night at Jenny's but had decided that he needed some time alone.

"Let's go on a road trip, Bobby. It's is a beautiful spring afternoon. The sun is shining, the birds are singing—just right for drinking beer."

"No, I'm going to stay here. I've some reading to do."

"You can read tomorrow. I haven't seen you in so long; I think that you might have gotten married. Did you have a wedding and not invite me?"

"I'm not married. But, if I did get married, you would be the last person that I'd invite. You'd be hitting on all of the bridesmaids—you'd probably even make a pass at my bride."

"Just trying to bring a little joy into the world," Woody said as he drank his beer. "Why don't we go to Hell?"

"What?"

"You and I, we'll hop in the car and go to Hell, this afternoon."

"What are you talking about, you can't do that."

"Yes, you can. We can go to Hell, Michigan."

"There is no Hell, Michigan, Woody. Are you drunk already?"

"Let's go, Bobby. I'll kiss your ass in the middle of Grand River Avenue if we can't go to Hell."

After a couple of stops in country bars, they drove into Hell, Michigan. Woody grinned even broader than usual as they toured the little village, turned around, and headed back toward the Lansing area. It was dark, but they still cruised with the windows down as Woody continued to sing with every country song that came on the radio. From the light of the rising moon, Bob could see all of the freshly plowed fields; some were planted, but there still was a lot of ground that needed to be prepared for crops. He was certain that his father would have all of his corn in at home. If the corn and beans were done, Sam Hartman would be greasing and repairing haying equipment that he would need to use in a month.

"We aren't stopping at Emma's are we?"

"Just for a quick one, Bobby. There might be some ladies there looking for the old Woodpecker." Woody pulled the car into the parking lot that Bob knew well, but had not seen since January.

"No fights tonight, Woody."

Woody stopped the car and turned the ignition off. "Don't worry, Bobby. I'm in my lovin' mood, and I ain't in my fightin' mood."

The bar was already crowded, the juke box was playing, and couples were on the dance floor. The noise level was high. Several tables had just women sitting at them as Friday night a lot of single or divorced women came with their girl friends for a girl's night out. Bob knew that this was Woody's favorite night to attend. They stood at the bar and Gene, the bartender, put two drafts in front of them.

"Haven't seen you for awhile, Bobby," he said, wiping the counter. "Now Woody, are you going to behave yourself, or do I have to throw you out tonight like I did last week?"

"Now that wasn't my fault—and you know it. I didn't cause the trouble, and I left when you asked me to leave."

"Well he was a jerk, and you did leave quietly. I had to persuade him that it was in his best interest to find another place to drink. But why don't you try keeping your hands to yourself and your mouth shut?" Bob was sipping his beer as Lucille sidled up next to them and placed her tray on the counter.

"Two pitchers of Bud, and three Pink Squirrels, Gene."

"Say Lucille—why don't you and I go outside and play a little 'hide and seek' this evening?" Woody said as he patted her bottom.

"In your dreams, Woody."

"But I've been saving myself just for you."

"Well you keep saving, honey," she said as she took the full tray and headed across the room. "Because it ain't going to happen in your life time."

"Woody, you'd better give up—you're never going to get to first base with her." Gene laughed and rang the sale into the cash register.

"A man's got to dream. She sure is a fine woman," Woody said and then turned to Bob. "Are you drinking tonight or just nursing one along? There's a table of ladies that probably want to meet me, and I know that at least one will want to dance with this Woodpecker."

With a beer in hand Woody walked across the room. Bob took his beer and went to a corner away from the bar—opposite from where Woody was. Soon Woody was dancing on the dance floor. His dancing was more flailing and jumping, but his partner seemed to be enjoying it. Bob realized that it would be a long evening, and that he would be driving home—either Woody would be passed out in the back, or he would have found a lady to stay with for the evening.

Bob thought of Jenny and the fact that he had never brought her here. She didn't drink, so a bar would be an odd place for her. She did not seem to fit in with this crowd, but if he had asked her, Bob was certain that she would come and have had a nice time because she would be with him. She'd recognize that these patrons were working people like her father and his father; they possessed the same values and prejudices that he and she had been raised with in Lawsonville. She would certainly be polite about it. His thoughts were interrupted with a tune from the juke box that was out of place at Emma's.

"*I heard it through the grape vine, not much longer would you be mine.*"

Marvin Gaye crooned a silky melodic tune as the dancers continued to sway. This did not sound like George Jones or Ernest Tubbs.

Bob wondered who would play a Motown song in Emma's and figured that it was one of the four guys who sat a couple of tables over from him. They had arrived boisterous, and as they drank long-neck bottles of Budweiser, they got louder. They were not interested in dancing or any of the single ladies that were in the bar. Bob saw one of the guys roll an empty long-neck underhanded onto the dance floor. A dancing couple looked around in surprise, but then went to the other side of the floor and continued dancing. Another couple stopped, picked up the empty, and after looking around the bar, placed it on a vacant table. They returned to dancing. Bob smiled as the first one went onto the floor, but after the second and third, the trick no longer seemed funny—it seemed mean. One couple almost fell and several were becoming irritated when their dancing was interrupted. Bob could hear the four as they became drunker and louder. Several caustic and cutting comments were made about the patrons of the bar and the country music that was played.

With penny loafers and button-down oxford shirts, Bob figured that they were MSU students. It was just a matter of time before Gene asked them to leave or a local patron got into a fight with one of them. Lucille was polite when she brought them more beer, but Bob saw a disgusted look on her face that he had seen when she served rude patrons before.

"You need another one, Bobby," Lucille said as she picked up his empty glass. "You're awfully quiet tonight. Are you OK?"

"I'm fine—just not pounding them down like usual."

"I haven't seen you here much lately. Woody says that you have a girl."

"Yes, I have a friend. She goes to Michigan State."

"Are you nice to her?"

"Yes, I am. You know I'm always nice," Bob laughed. "Are those four guys over there causing you trouble? Do you want me to say something to Gene about them?"

"Oh, they're OK," Lucille said as she wiped the table. "You know most guys say something, or they touch you but don't mean a lot by it—just guys being guys. Most of them are married and are just having a little fun when the wife is not around, and even those guys that are not married know where the line is drawn. But guys like those four over there think they own you. To them you are just something that they can have fun with. They don't care anything about you or anyone else—those are the ones that I don't like."

"I can say something to Gene. He'll throw them out."

"No, that's OK, honey," Lucille said as she patted him on the cheek. "It comes with the job. I just don't like them thinking I'm a piece of dirt just because I wait tables in a bar."

"Hey, Nurse," one of the four yelled. "I got a thirst." The other three laughed.

"I get to see the wonder boys," Lucille said as she turned to the table of four.

Another long-neck bottle rolled out on the dance floor. Bob shook his head and wondered if he had been as obnoxious when he was as drunk as those four were. Two more bottles rolled out among the dancers. They were rolling them under the table so that no one could see where they were coming from. This time a dancer stepped on one and almost fell; her partner caught her just before she lost her balance completely. Bob walked over to the table.

"Why don't you stop it before someone gets hurt?"

"What are you talking about, hillbilly," one said.

"The beer bottles."

"I don't know what beer bottles you are talking about? It must be raining beer bottles from heaven." All four laughed and one slapped another on the back.

"Raining beer bottles from heaven." He took an empty bottle and raised it up with one hand and dropped it—catching it with the other.

"Raining beer bottles from heaven." He repeated himself and did the stunt again. Everyone else at the table was laughing uncontrollably. The juke box continued to play for the couples crowding the dance floor.

"Gene will throw you guys out of here when he sees what you're doing," Bob said.

"Who's Gene?"

"He's the bartender."

"That fat slob. That guy is so fat he hasn't seen his pecker in three years."

Everyone laughed, and comments continued to be made about Gene. It was obvious now that they were college students who had an absolute distain for everyone there. Three were about his size, but the fourth one across the table was taller and heavier. All were well-dressed and stood out from the working clothes that most of the guys at Emma's were wearing. Because Bob was seen as a local with his jeans and boots, he could feel their sense of superiority, to which Lucille had referred earlier.

"Well, you'd better cool it, and be a little nicer to the waitress."

"Or what the hell is going to happen? Are you going to do anything about it, Cowboy Roy?" Just then Gene yelled from the bar.

"You guys quit screwing around over there, or else you are out of here." They all waved good-naturedly and smiled. When Gene turned his back and walked to the other end of the bar, two of them put their middle finger up to his back; everyone laughed. Bob turned and walked back to his table.

"Queer,"

"Fag"

Someone made a clucking sound like a chicken.

Bob stopped, took a deep breath, and sat down. He stared at the table where all four were laughing. One flipped him off and another puckered his lips and threw him a kiss.

He could feel anger rising as he finished his glass of beer in one long drink. All four turned away from him, talking and laughing among themselves. The name-calling and the lack of respect for Lucille, or anyone here at Emma's, had him angry. But that fury was now fueled by the nylon windbreakers on the back of chairs that he hadn't seen until he walked over to their table. All four were members of Sigma Sigma Sigma fraternity.

CHAPTER 23

"*One o'clock, two o'clock, three o'clock rock. We're going to rock around the clock tonight.*"

Bill Halley sang and Bob's anger increased as he watched the four Tri-Sigs. The next beer that Lucille brought he drank in two gulps. Lucille brought another one.

"They are assholes," Lucille said.

"I know"

"Now don't you start anything, Bobby. There are four of them. And for God's sake, keep Woody away from them. He's dumb enough; he'll want to fight all of them at once."

As Lucille left him at the table, he took another long swig of beer which did not lessen the fury that was burning inside. The four had stopped throwing beer bottles on the dance floor, but they were just as loud and obnoxious as they had been all evening. People who had been sitting by them had moved to the other side of the bar, but Bob remained where he had always been—two tables away. They ignored him as they spent most of their time joking about the patrons of the bar and making lewd comments about the waitresses.

"Bradley Whitcomb would fit right in with those jerks," Bob thought as he drank. "He may be sitting in some cushy chair at Yale, but if he were still here at State, he would be here with his idiot frat brothers." One Tri-Sig stood up and waved an empty beer bottle.

"Nurse, Nurse, I got a thirst," he yelled and then, turning to his friends, "Bring your tits over here first."

They all laughed at the comment. When he sat down, he missed the chair and fell on the floor. He had trouble standing as his friend tried to help him up. Lucille went to their table and said, "That's it. I'm not serving you anymore. You can finish what you have left and then you'd better leave."

"How about if I have some of you then."

He pulled her on to his lap and held her tight as she tried to free herself.

"Are these Nortons real? Just let me feel them."

One hand held her waist while the other cupped her breast. Everyone was laughing and enjoying the show—except Lucille. Lucille freed herself and slapped him across the cheek, and without hesitation, he returned the slap with greater ferocity. She fell backwards into the table. Bob, who had started toward the table when she had been grabbed by the drunken Tri-Sig, was beside her immediately.

"You OK? he asked. There was a red welt on her cheek.

"Assholes!" she cried. "God-damn assholes."

Her shoulders shook more with rage than hurt. Bob turned and pushed an angry Lucille behind him. The Tri-Sig still stood while his three brothers watched.

"You can't hit women. You just can't do that here."

"Hell, she's just an old slut—just an old barroom slut."

"And you can't talk about her that way. You apologize and then get out, along with your asshole friends."

"Says who?"

Bob took a step toward the standing Tri-Sig, and two brothers who had been sitting next to him stood up, while the big one across the table remained in his chair, grinning. The one who had struck Lucille now had a fraternity brother on each side and a smile on his face.

"Is she your sister, Hillbilly?"

"Be careful what you say about Hillbilly's sister, Freddie," the one on the right said. "There mightn't be any sheep tonight for Hillbilly, and he'll want to take his sister home."

The fraternity brother on the left laughed so hard that he stumbled backward. The one in the middle remained still with his gaze focused on Bob. Bob saw him tighten his fists and lean slightly forward on the balls of his feet—a linebacker ready to deliver a jarring tackle seconds before the ball carrier arrived.

"Why don't you go sit down, cowboy, like you did before. You got a good ass-kicking coming if you stay around here." An arrogant smirk spread across the face of the one in the middle.

Bob clenched his fists, took another step forward but suddenly was stopped short by Woody who placed a hand on his chest and held him back. The other hand he extended toward the Tri-Sig.

"Whoa boys—what's the problem?" Woody said as he stood with both arms extended between the two.

"Your hillbilly friend is about to get his ass kicked,"

Woody left both hands extended, and Bob could feel the palm pushing against his chest. He turned to Lucille who was still behind Bob.

"You OK, Lucille?"

"Woody, don't get into it. There're four of them," Lucille warned.

"You want into this, Shorty. I got an ass-kicking for you too—just as soon as I'm done with your hillbilly friend."

"No sir, not me," Woody said as he dropped his left arm that he had used to separate the two. His right arm still remained planted on Bob chest holding him in place.

"I don't believe in fighting. I think that we can settle our differences in a peaceful manner. Peace, brother." Woody took his left arm that had been pointing at the Tri-Sig and held it up in a peace sign. His right hand remained firmly on Bob's chest.

He turned to face Bob with his entire back to the Tri-Sigs. His right arm still held Bob at full length, but he laid his left hand on Bob's shoulder. A puzzled look appeared on the Tri-Sigs's faces.

"Now Bobby, you know we have to love one another, and there's nothing ever good comes from violence. Haven't I tried to teach you that? You need to turn the other . . ."

Bob stared in disbelief at Woody. He couldn't believe his friend was walking away from this fight. Then he felt the right hand unclench his shirt and saw the blank calm stare on Woody's face. All hell was about to break loose.

" . . . cheek."

Woody whirled with cat-like quickness and the right hand that had held Bob smashed into the face of the much larger Tri-Sig. There was a soft thud of cartilage being crushed and then two other quick strikes. Bob had seen Woody fight before, but he had never seen him land such quick blows. The Tri-Sig bent over and covered a face that was turning red. The largest fraternity brother across the table was half way up.

"You son-of-a . . ."

Woody went across the table and tackled him before he could stand or finish his comment. They both rolled on the floor with fists flailing.

Bob took a step toward the brother on the right who had made the comment about the sheep and Lucille. He kicked hard up through the groin and the Tri-Sig rose six inches off of the floor with a groan. Later he would remember how in high school the football coach had tried to have him kick extra points after touchdowns. He never could hit the pigskin just right so that it would fly through the uprights. Tonight was a perfect kick. He smashed down with his right hand to the one bending over grabbing his crotch. His hand connected with full force, but when he swung his left, he was hit in the side of the head by the fourth Tri-Sig, who finally jumped into the action.

The blow dropped him to his knees, and as he tried to get up, a kick to his ribs followed. When the second kick arrived, he had rolled out of its way and, standing up, deftly knocked the other foot of the assailant. That Tri-Sig went down. Bob turned to the two at the table—one was still in pain on the floor but the other one now up with a bloody face waiting for Bob. Lucille jumped on his back, but he easily threw her off, and she landed on a table. He was only interested in Bob.

"Come on, Hillbilly."

Bob took a couple of steps toward him, then ducked and drove a shoulder into his midsection for a clean tackle. The bloody Tri-Sig had expected Bob to trade punches, so the tackle had taken him by surprise. He delivered a few harmless blows to Bob's back as they rolled onto the dance floor, Bob delivering way more punches than he was taking. He almost had the Tri-Sig pinned on the dance floor when he was kicked in the back by another Tri-Sig. Bob was now on the defensive as he tried to avoid the kicks that were raining down on him, yet keep the guy on the floor pinned. The advantage had suddenly shifted and things were going very badly for him. He stayed on the ground and like a bulldog, he had one Tri-Sig pinned at the throat, but the kicking was taking a toll. Suddenly the kicker screamed and fell. Bob turned loose of the one he had pinned and looked up at Gene.

"Get the hell out of here, you punk," Gene said as he swung a short baseball bat. He stood red-faced with his legs spread wide and the bat raised chest high.

The frat boy stood up by placing one hand on the table and snarled, "Go to hell, Fatso."

The bat crashed down on the hand, and skin and bones prevented the wood from making full contact with the Formica top. The Tri-Sig screamed and grabbed his mangled hand. The bat struck again across the forearm.

"You want some more, Buddy—because I've got a lot more to give." Gene raised the bat and shook it. "You boys like to beat up women. This here is Miss Pearl. Why don't you come forward and slap her around?"

The Tri-Sig retreated with his eye on Miss Pearl, holding his arm. The knuckles now were bloody as was with his face. Bob sat up and saw one fraternity member helping the one who he had kicked out the door. He still could not stand up straight. The final member of the group got help out the front door by a local patron.

"Jesus, Gene, I think you broke that guy's arm when you hit him. Remind me not to get you pissed off at me," someone said. Then he laughed. "Whoever kicked that guy in the balls sure did a job. I don't think that he'll be standing straight for a couple of days."

"Damn women-beaters," Gene said. "I'd like to have another go at them. Twenty years of Shore Patrol dealing with drunken sailors and marines. Those college hippies think they're something; Miss Pearl and I would complete their education in a hurry." He turned to Bob, who was sitting on the floor.

"What you boys need is an evener. This here evens the sides up in a hurry. Meet Miss Pearl." With that he held up his short club and shook it as someone came in door.

"They're gone now. That big one who was thumping Woody is going to need a few stitches in the cheek where you hit him. And another one isn't going to be writing any love letters to his girl friend with that hand for a few days."

"Good," Gene said. "I can't stand a man who will hit a woman. Guys fighting—I can understand that—but beating on a woman just isn't right, especially not one of my gals."

"Hell, Gene, we had everything under control. No need for you to get involved. Bobby and I were just about to take charge," Woody said.

He was sitting at a table behind Bob. As Bob stood he felt a sharp pain in his side, then he remembered the kick in the ribs. Woody's shirt was ripped, his left eye was almost swollen shut, and there were other scratches on his face. The knuckles on one hand were bleeding and one shoe was missing.

"Yea—you sure did have things under control. I don't know how much more control you two could have stood if Pearl and I hadn't showed up," Gene laughed. He turned to Lucille. "You OK, Honey?"

"I'm OK," she said. "Woody and Bobby came to save the day."

"I know," Gene said as he stood the last table up. "I was in the back trying to change a keg over and didn't hear the ruckus at first. I'm obliged you two helped Lucille. Let me get you a couple of beers on the house." With the tables and chairs back in order, he returned to the bar. Now Hank Williams was singing.

"Hey, hey good lookin', what you got cookin'"

Bob sat with Woody while Lucille brought over two glasses and a pitcher of beer. Everything was back to normal with a game at the pool table, Gene behind the bar, and the jukebox playing. Only now Lucille, instead of waiting tables, was cleaning the cuts on Woody's face. He rested his hand on her knee while she gently washed the scratches.

"How in the heck did you lose your shoe in that scuffle?" Bob asked. He took a sip of beer and realized that somehow he had bitten his tongue in the fight, and the beer stung. He decided that he had enough aches and pains without adding suffering to the inside of his mouth. Woody could have all of the beer.

"Well, I don't know. Maybe I was going to clip my toenails after I whipped that frat boy's ass."

"Elwood honey, you had two of those frat boys—not one. And they were doing the whipping."

"Ouch!" Woody said as he winced when Lucille pressed too hard near his left eye. "I know that I hit the first one and then took after the big boy. But

I'm just put out. Bobby was trying to start a fight, and he didn't even invite me. And that just ain't right."

"Woody," Lucille said softly as she wiped more blood off of his cheek.

"Well, I've tried to teach him to share, Lucille, but you can see how he is. He would have whipped all four of their asses and left me dancing on the dance floor. I've always had trouble with him wanting to hog all of the fight. I just had to get over here so I could join in and have some fun."

"Oh—that hurts," Bob said as he grabbed his side. Laughing at Woody's commentary might be more painful than the actual injuries.

They sat at the table with the free pitcher. Woody had no trouble drinking his share and most of Bobby's. He had put his shoe on that someone had retrieved for him. His injuries appeared to increase when Lucille came near the table, and she was spending a lot of her time there waiting on them personally. The bar was back to normal and another pitcher of beer had appeared when Woody leaned over to Bob and said, "Bobby, why don't you take my car back to the apartment when you get ready to leave? Lucille says she wants to drive me home. I'm hoping that I just might get lucky and she'll show me some real gratitude."

Bob looked at his friend with one eye swollen shut, a torn shirt, and knuckles that looked like fresh ground hamburger. He shook his head and tried not to laugh because it would hurt too much.

"You're amazing. Just simply amazing."

"Got to get it when you can, Bobby. Got to get it when you can—besides she's a mighty fine-looking women."

When Bob stood up to leave, Lucille came and gave him a gentle hug.

"Thank you, Bobby."

"No thanks needed." Bob winched with the hug as he felt the pain again in his ribs. "I had a score to settle with Sigma Sigma Sigma, and tonight an old debt was repaid."

Bob left Emma's with Lucille fussing over Woody. A couple of the patrons had joined Woody at his table and the details were changing with every free drink. One eye was completely closed, but there was a huge grin on Woody's face. Although Lucille was now being attentive to him as she waited tables, Bob was certain that after Emma's closed she would really express her gratitude. He slowly drove back to the apartment. It was after midnight when he walked into the apartment, but Harry was sitting on the sofa reading, looked up as he entered.

"Holy shit! What happened to you," he exclaimed as Bob gingerly sat down in a chair.

"Woody and I got into a disagreement at Emma's," Bob said, and then he related the details of the evening. Harry did not say anything, just shook his head in amazement. After finishing the story and explaining Woody's whereabouts, Bob stood.

"I think I'll take a hot shower. I'm beginning to ache all over. Man, I'll be sore in the morning."

"You sure will be."

Bob stood in the shower and let the water run over him. It was early morning so there was an unlimited supply of hot water. He could feel the soreness in his body and when he breathed deep, there was that pain again. He would probably have difficulty getting out of bed, but with no class in the morning he would use the weekend to recover. He thought back to those Saturday mornings after the Friday's when he had big games. He was always stiff and sore, but it was a good soreness that came with a sense of accomplishment. He felt like that now.

Stepping from the shower, he dried himself and looked in the mirror. Already his eye was turning black, with a yellowish tint on his cheek where the bruise was deeper. The soap and water had burned several places where the skin had been scraped, and he noticed several bruises on his thighs and stomach, having no idea how they got there. There were teeth marks on his left hand, but the skin had not been broken. Although the fight had ended, the adrenaline still flowed, and he smiled at himself in the mirror; his physical pain was over shadowed by a sense of accomplishment. He walked into the living room with the towel wrapped around his waist and saw Jenny sitting alone with a single light on.

"What—What are you doing here?" he asked in surprise.

"Harry called me and said that you'd been in a fight. He went to bed when I came in," she said as she came to him. She gently touched his face. "My God, what happened to your face?"

"You ought to see the other guy," Bob joked, and immediately felt a sharp pain in his side from the small laugh. The old joke about "the other guy" was true this time, thanks to Gene and Miss Pearl. He sat on the sofa and Jenny sat next to him as he again told the story. She held his right hand and gently touched his arm or face every once in a while. When he finished there was a long pause. Finally she said, "I hope this was not about me? Harry said that all four were members of Sigma Sigma Sigma."

"Nope—not at all—they were just some jerks that were way out of line at Emma's."

"Are you sure, Robert? I wouldn't want you to fight for me."

"I'm sure."

"It would be like you to think that you had to protect me. It's nice to be looked after, but that thing a couple of years ago is done."

"Nope, not at all. Woody started it," Bob said as he calmly lied into Jenny's eyes. The only thing that would have made the evening more satisfying was if Tommy had been there. With Tommy present, there would have been no need for Miss Pearl. Jenny said nothing, but Bob was not certain that he had convinced her about the Tri-Sigs.

She stood and took his hand. "Let's go to bed."

"I thought that you didn't want to spend the night here?"

"I want to be with you tonight, and I don't think that you want to walk back to my place. And I'm not sure that you are capable of it."

"No, I'm a little sore. But I don't want you to feel uncomfortable. I thought that you were concerned about what Harry might think."

"I don't think we are fooling anyone about us," she laughed. "And I really want to be with you."

"I'd like to spend the night with you, although my ribs are quite sore. What will we say to Harry, if we see him in the morning?'

"We can tell Harry that we are working on a paper. I'm an English major and everyone knows that you math majors can't put two coherent sentences together." She tugged at his arm and he stood with his other hand holding the towel.

"Shall we work on your grammar or is a lesson in spelling needed?"

He followed her into the bedroom.

CHAPTER 24

The crab apple trees were in full bloom as Jim and Bob walked toward the Red Cedar River. The pink and white blossom flowers stood above mowed lawns while red and yellow tulips edged the green. Students were stretched out on blankets or lying on the grass everywhere—some may have even been studying.

"Jesus Christ, this is stupid," Jim muttered as he and Bob crossed a patchwork of color that had been planted in previous years by MSU horticulture students.

"Aw stop bitching. You've been complaining for the last half hour. Canoeing on the Red Cedar will be fun, and we need your ID if we're going to get two canoes. Besides, what would you be doing if you'd stayed back at the apartment on a day like this—sleeping or watching the Tigers on TV?"

"Maybe I'd have sat outside naked."

"Yah—that'd be a great idea. Then the cops could come at noon instead of making their usual midnight trip," Bob replied cheerfully. "Besides, Jenny is bringing something to eat, she always has good food, and Woody will have the beer. Maybe we'll throw a tablespoon of sugar in to sweeten your sour puss."

"A jug of wine, a book of verse, and a tuna fish sandwich—ah paradise, paradise enow. I still think this is stupid," Jim said.

They came around a building and saw Jenny standing on the dock holding a basket. Bob and Jim used their students IDs to check out canoes, and then walked out on the dock. Jenny gave Bob a hug as Jim unfastened two canoes and put the paddles in each.

"I have the food. Where's Woody?"

"He'll join us at the Bogue Street Bridge."

"Why don't you let me canoe with Jenny?" Jim said, smiling for the first time today. "She could carry on a conversation with someone who at least understands the English language. You math majors speak only in symbols and equations."

"No way on that—you two will simply sit in the middle of the river quoting Shakespeare, and I'm stuck with Woody."

"You'd better let me have him, Jim," Jenny said as Bob held the canoe for her. "Sometimes he can actually speak in sentences that don't have equations or logarithms. I've trained him so that he knows the difference between nouns and verbs; we're going to work on adjectives today."

They pushed out and paddled upstream. On both sides of the river students threw Frisbees and footballs, or lay on blankets in the warm May sun. At the Bogue Street Bridge they picked up Woody who had two six packs of beer.

"I don't see why I had to wait here. I could have gone with you guys right at first," Woody grumbled.

"You can't have alcohol on campus. If we're gong to have beer on this canoe trip someone had to be here," Bob replied.

"Well, we're all twenty-one. If they did catch us with beer, blame me—the University can expel me."

"That's a problem since you're not a student, but the rest of us are. We could be expelled. Somehow whenever I hang around with you, Woody, I end up in trouble. After being on probation Fall Term, I don't want to be back in the Dean's office again."

They continued up the river with Jim and Woody in the lead melding with canoes bearing MSU on the side. Woody sat in the front drinking and paddling while Jim steered from the rear. The four were making good progress away from campus, although Jim was having difficulty keeping the canoe in the middle of the Red Cedar.

"I really did want to see what was on the bank, and I love going backwards, Jimbo," Woody said with a broad grin as he drank a beer while Jim tried to maneuver from the stern. Turning back to Bob and Jenny he added. "We're taking the scenic route here. I want to get a close up look at both sides of the river."

Bob held his canoe and looked at the lawns on the bank as Jim made a complete circle ahead of him. On one side were woods and swamps, and it was hard to imagine that they were just a mile from campus. On the other side were homes with mowed lawns supporting all the collections of urban America. Ahead were areas that were as pristine as those he had experienced on the Au Sable last year. The Red Cedar moved languidly and would provide an easy return in the afternoon. Bob had been here in late winter when the banks were covered with snow and also in early spring when rain and melting snow made canoeing dangerous and thrilling. Today there would be a leisurely pace with no danger, only sun, beer, and friends.

Around noon they began to look for a grassy spot for lunch. Jim and Woody were several yards ahead when they passed a large tree with a protruding limb over the water. Five feet above hung a fishing lure with several feet of line hanging down. As the canoe glided by the line, Jim stood and grabbed it.

"Jim, don't stand . . ." Bob called out. It was too late.

The canoe stopped forward progress and leaned to the right. Woody, who had no idea what was happening, reacted by jerking to the left, putting the edge under water. Woody used his arms to try and balance himself as a standing Jim plunged into the water. Woody followed from a sitting position.

Woody emerged from the baptismal with a shocked look and a flurry of profanity. Jim came next, farther away from the canoe and in the middle of the river. The river was shallow and both stood in water just above their waists.

Bob could see Jenny in the front with her shoulders shaking, politely trying to stifle her laugh. He was not as polite. He roared out loud and began to retrieve floating items from both sides of the Red Cedar.

He held his canoe in the river as Jim and Woody emptied the water from theirs and climbed back in. This time Woody was in the back and Jim in the front. An inventory was taken of what had been lost: one shoe, two pair of sunglasses, one shirt, and, of course, the beer. Both canoes were in the middle of the river floating as plans were re-evaluated.

"I am sorry for my language," Woody said sheepishly to Jenny. "I wasn't planning on swimming today."

"No apology needed, nothing new to me," Jenny said. "You've heard my Pop swear before haven't you, Robert?"

"Yes I have," Bob laughed. "He can teach you some words, Woody."

"I'm for going back since these wet jeans and shirt aren't very comfortable," Jim said.

"At least you have a shirt—mine is in the river with the beer."

"We'll call it a sacrifice to the river gods. This should bring us good luck," Jim said and then added sheepishly. "Perhaps, my philosophy paper due Monday will appear miraculously." Woody just glared. They began paddling downstream back to the canoe livery.

"Reverend Ellison will you be baptizing anymore this afternoon," Bob called out as they pulled away. Jim turned and grinned, but did not stand.

"I think Sinner Woody has been saved for today. He shall sin no more and go forward from this day with Christian charity and kindness," Jim said. He raised his right hand and made the sign of the cross then turned back to paddling.

In between a strong stroke, Woody slapped the water and sprayed Jim in the front and then returned to pushing the canoe toward campus. Bob and Jenny followed, but took a more leisurely approach. When they finally arrived at the livery, Woody and Jim's canoe was tied, and they had left.

After the student worker checked the craft, Bob put his ID in his wallet, and they went across Farm Lane to the open area below the Auditorium. There Jenny spread a blanket on the ground and unpacked the lunch of sandwiches and potato salad. Other blankets were in the area and at the far end were four African students kicking a soccer ball and playing keep-away.

"I don't understand why someone would just want to kick a ball like you would an old tin can. What is the purpose of the game?" Bob said.

"Not everyone plays American football, Robert. If you'd been born in Nigeria or Kenya, you would have been an All-state soccer player."

"I doubt that."

With Jim and Woody gone, there was plenty of food. The potato salad reminded him of his mother's cooking—big chunks of egg and potato and lots of onions. No one could cook like his mother or grandmothers, but having eaten several of Jenny's meals the last few months, he knew that she fit right in with the tradition of farm wives and mothers who loaded the dining table with food every day. After eating, he stretched out on the blanket and put his head in Jenny's lap. With the sun warming him and a full stomach, he was content as Jenny stoked his head. He had just about dozed off when Jenny asked, "In a few weeks we are going to graduate, and this will all be over. What are you going to do, Robert, after graduation?"

"I'm not sure. I'll get drafted some time so I might go home and wait there, or I could stay here in East Lansing. Harry has the apartment leased for next year, and I could stay with him until I get my draft notice. What are you going to do? Are you going to Bloomington and go to graduate school at Indiana University liked you talked about at Christmas time?"

"I've accepted a position in the graduate program there, but my advisor, Dr. Robinson, has just been appointed chairman of the English department at the University of Oregon, and she wants me to go out there and work on a PhD. With my GRE scores and grade point average, she says she can get me a teaching position that would pay for most of my expenses."

Jenny gazed across the Red Cedar and continued to gently twist his hair. She hesitated as she glanced at the canoes in the river and students walking on the sidewalk across the river. Bob looked up at the brown eyes with long eye lashes that blinked as she thought. He liked looking at her from this angle—he was still infatuated with her beauty, but she looked different from below.

"If I went to Oregon, maybe you could come and visit me, or perhaps you could stay out there for awhile?"

"Sure."

"Sure you will visit—or sure you will come out and stay?" Her voice was questioning.

"I'll come out and stay."

"Oh would you, Robert?"

Jenny sat up in excitement and folded her legs underneath herself. Because he had lost his pillow, Bob was forced to sit up also. He could not resist the temptation to tease her—as he had done for years.

"I could get a room at the Holiday Inn."

"Don't be silly. We can live together. We can get an apartment out there. Pop says that I can have Tommy's old Falcon. He is fixing it up for me to drive after graduation, and I have all the dishes and everything for the apartment. Would you really come?"

"Why Miss McKnight, are you taking me across state lines for immoral purposes? Boys from Lawsonville have high morals. I'll need to get a room at the YMCA or a local monastery."

"You'll stay with me. I want to study with Professor Robinson, but I don't want to leave you. It will be wonderful if you'll go with me." She bent over and hugged him tightly. When she sat back up tears were running down her cheeks. The mascara was also.

"I actually have enough money to get us out there and established, so that shouldn't be a problem," Bob said. "If you've a car, we should be all set. After what Tommy and I put that old Falcon through, the Rocky Mountains won't be any problem."

"Oh, let's do it. You can get a job with your math degree, or maybe you can go to graduate school also. You do have very good grades."

"Or maybe I can get drafted there?"

"We'll worry about that later." She grabbed and hugged him again.

Bob hugged her back as he watched cars cross the bridge. He had already decided that he was going to move to Bloomington to be near her in the fall. He just could not bring himself to say how important she was to him, and how he was prepared to move anywhere just so that he could see her every day.

"Robert, I love you," Jenny said softly as she clung to him. "You make me so happy."

Two cars crossed the bridge, as he continued to hold her. He kissed her hair. He wanted to tell her the same thing back, but just could not get the words to come. A large truck bridged the Red Cedar, and he thought about the approaching draft as Jenny clung to him. He was prepared to follow Jenny anywhere—just as the Selective Service was prepared to follow him anywhere. Oregon would be a good place to decide what he would do about the draft.

CHAPTER 25

A fly landed on Bob's cheek and rested there before moving toward his lips. A puff of air sent it off to another place of annoyance. It buzzed and landed somewhere in the bedroom to wait and return—as it had done twice before.

He had not attacked the trespassing fly because Jenny lay asleep next to him. His arm was pinned with brown hair that spread chaotically on the pillow next to him. He glanced down at the feet that stuck out from the sheets. He wiggled his toes and rotated his ankles to stretch, but the toes with red nail polish did not move. They were attached to an ankle that led his eyes to a shin, and then a knee, and then a thigh and then—the sheet stopped his eyes from going further.

On the left was a muscular leg covered with dark hair; to the right was a smaller leg that was hairless and shapelier. It was that leg on the right that he wanted to touch as he waited for the fly to return. If he moved to his right he could place his left hand on the thigh connected to those red toe nails. But the fingers would not want to stay there.

Jenny made a small sound in her throat and rolled closer to him. She threw her arm across his chest and he could feel her breath. Farther down his rib cage a soft breast grazed him. He wanted to touch her, but the guilt from last evening still remained.

The fly landed again. This time it lit on his eyebrow, but a quick wrinkling of his forehead sent the trespasser off again. He had been lying there thinking for over an hour as the bedroom became more illuminated and the sounds of birds filtered in from an open window. Early shadows were being chased by a rising sun as he heard a car start on the street below, along with several slamming doors, and a persistent barking dog. East Lansing was going to work, but he was with Jenny on this May morning.

Jenny rolled away from him and pulled the sheets over her. She still lay on his forearm, but the circulation was returning to his upper arm. Still he did not want to disturb her because he liked having her near him, and she might bring up the fight from last night. He raised his left leg and stretched it as light reflected off of the mirror across the room. He thought about graduation in another week and the end of his student deferment. It was all that he had been able to think about for two weeks. Graduation had already caused problems at home when he informed his parents that they did not need to come because he wasn't going to attend the ceremonies. The University would mail him his diploma.

"But Robert, don't you want to march in the ceremonies?" his mother asked.

"No."

"But you would look so handsome in a new suit, and you can march with all of your classmates."

"Mom, this isn't Lawsonville High School. I don't know any of my classmates."

"But Robert, you're the first one from our family to receive a college education, and you've done so well. Your father and I want to come to the college and see you graduate."

"I'm not walking."

"Sam, will you talk to Robert and tell him how important this is. He'll regret it later if he doesn't walk in the ceremonies."

"Helen, you might as well leave him alone if his mind is made up. You're not going to change it. You're just talking to the side of the barn." Sam moved through the kitchen and to the barn.

Bob knew that his father was disappointed, and so he ordered the gown for graduation, but still did not plan to attend the ceremonies. He could still change his mind at the last minute and appease his parents. The graduation ceremony didn't bother him as much as the loss of his student deferment. With the termination of his enrollment at Michigan State, he would receive an induction notice, and he knew that he would pass the physical examination. He was convinced now that the war in Vietnam was wrong, and that he should have no part in it. But the alternatives to the draft were heinous—yet he could think of nothing else.

In the last few weeks Bob had several times discussed with Harry his views on the war and how he was becoming more opposed to American involvement there. Just as at the Draft Counseling Center, Harry did not urge the defiant role of refusal that he himself had chosen, but listened and suggested.

"Bob, if you aren't certain that you can participate in the military, and you don't want to emigrate to Canada, you might consider filing as a conscientious objector status."

"Don't you have to be real religious and belong to some church?"

"The term 'religious training' is open to interpretation. But it's an effective stalling techniques to give you time to decide what you really want to do.

The local draft board by law has to allow you to apply, and if they deny your application, there is the appeal process. It would probably postpone the draft notice for at least a year or two. And perhaps you might even be granted CO status, and then you don't have to serve in the military."

"Damn fly," he thought as it landed on his other cheek. The pest had returned. He shook his head slightly, but the fly remained, and then began to walk toward his eye. He shook his head again and this time the irritant left. Jenny rolled back toward him, and a leg with red toe nails penned both his legs. Now the red toe nails disappeared as a heel pointed to the ceiling, but the thigh now exposed a hamstring that ran up to a beautiful soft bottom. He wanted to touch it, but again guilt stopped him.

Yesterday had been one of those days when everything went wrong. In the morning after walking in the rain to his math class, the instructor did not show. He had forgotten to cash a check, so he had no money for lunch, and then in the afternoon he turned his ankle in a pick-up basketball game at the Intramural Building. He had to limp home with a sore ankle and then ran into Woody at the apartment.

"Let's go to Emma's tonight. Lucille has been wondering where you've been?"

"I can't. I promised Jenny I would go to a movie with her."

"Jesus, Bobby, you're like married. One night at Emma's can't hurt."

"I can't go." He slammed the door and left the apartment. His ankle hurt the first few steps, but as he walked to Jenny's, it began to feel better. He remembered several sprains in high school and knew that once he began walking the ankle would loosen up and not feel so bad.

He arrived at Jenny's not happy about the choice of films; it was a Fellini movie. He had already seen two of them, and he did not understand either of them. Jenny enjoyed foreign films, and he hated them but went to please her. Why did they have to have subtitles and not speak in English? If they were going to go to a movie why couldn't they see a Steve McQueen or Clint Eastwood one? At least in those movies things happened instead of just a lot of talking.

"If you don't want to go, Robert, we could stay here this evening. I could help you with your conscientious objector application. Don't you have to get it in soon?"

"Yes, I should have it done by June and I need to submit it by July," he paused. "I guess that I'm going to send it in. Harry says it's an option that I should consider. Would you read it and check the spelling?"

"Sure, I can do that. Do you have it with you?"

Bob pulled two wrinkled sheets of paper from his pile of books and gave them to her along with the government form. He limped to the refrigerator for a Coke, while Jenny glanced at the paper. She sat down at the kitchen table and took a pen and circled several words. He sat down at the table, rubbing his sore ankle, frustrated and embarrassed each time she made a mark on his paper.

"I should have gone to Emma's with Woody," he thought. "A couple shots of Jack Daniels would take care of this pain."

"Well, there are a few spelling errors, and several points where the meaning is unclear," she looked at him and smiled. "But I think that we can fix those. You have confused 'there' and 'their', which is a common mistake, and a few contractions that should not be there—since this is a formal essay."

Bob felt like he was in Mrs. Scott's eighth grade English, and told to rewrite his theme. He knew that everyone was silently laughing at the farm boy who couldn't spell—especially the cute girls that he was too shy to speak to.

"Jesus Christ, Jenny—it's just a letter." The profanity burst out from a place he did not know about. Jenny had a startled look on her face as she sat across the kitchen table.

"Don't you want to do it correctly?" Again he heard his junior high teacher scold him. "Spell the words correctly, Robert—make the verb tenses agree, Robert—don't you want to do it correctly, Robert?"

No! He didn't want to do it correctly. All he wanted to do was play football, basketball, and baseball. "i before e", "e before i", or "z before k"—he didn't care!

"Aw hell, let it go. It isn't that important."

"It is important, Robert. All we need is a few minutes, and we'll have this in order."

"Screw it. I'll just get drafted."

He stood up quickly from the table and put too much weight on his ankle. He winced with pain and was mad at himself for not going with Woody.

"We really need to fix this, Robert," Jenny said as he limped away from the table. Her voice was changing from authoritarian to conciliatory.

"WE! Where the hell do you get 'WE'? Six months from now you'll be in Oregon, and I'll be headed for Vietnam." His voice grew louder. "Maybe you can find another guy in Oregon while I'm in a rice paddy in Vietnam. Maybe you can find someone who can spell. Your damn graduate school buddies should know how to spell!"

"Robert, that's not fair. That isn't what I want. I want you. And you're a good speller," Jenny pleaded. But Bob did not hear her. All he was aware of was the frustration and anger that was choking him. The question about the draft and his future was so constricting that he couldn't breathe or think. All he wanted to do was punch something or run until his aching muscles overtook his draft-filled brain, and he was drenched in perspiration. If only his ankle didn't hurt so much.

"Wouldn't it be great with me in Vietnam?" He forgot about his bad ankle and used that foot to kick his books on the floor. Now it really hurt, but the anger continued.

"And maybe I'll get shot, and they can send me home in a box to Andrews Air Force Base, and we could have a wonderful funeral in Lawsonville again. And they could bury me like they did Tommy—hell, why not bury me right next to him? And the American Legion can put a little flag on my tombstone also. And every one can meet and have a good cry over me. You can fly home from Oregon with your English major boyfriend who can spell, and you can join the crying party." His anger and sarcasm filled the room. "Maybe there'll be a God-damn American flag on the casket to go along with the one from Tommy."

Something flew by his head and crashed against the wall. He turned back to the table and put his arm to his face as another object from the table hit him in the wrist.

"You bastard! Don't you dare talk about Tommy that way, and don't even try to think that you know what's good for me. And don't try and send me off to Oregon so you can feel sorry for yourself, you selfish bastard." This time a plastic glass was thrown at him, Jenny left the table and came towards him. She swung hard with her right hand. He caught it easily and held her at arms length.

"Jenny . . ."

"You prick."

She kicked him hard in the shin, and when he pulled her close for self-protection, she stomped on his foot. Now an ankle, a shin, and a foot all hurt as he did a strange defensive dance with her in the living room. He was trying to calm her and protect himself from further injury. He had never heard her swear and now the profanity and tears flowed—all directed toward "the bastard."

"Turn me loose, Robert. You can't hold me."

"I'm sorry. I really am."

He released his hold and stepped away. A left hook came at his head that he easily ducked. It was sent with such force that Jenny spun around and fell back into him when her blow didn't connect. Her anger seeped away, and she began to quiver slightly as she cried. He held her tightly wondering how he could patch the damage that he had done. The smell of her hair and the softness of her body mixed with his feelings of guilt as she leaned on him. Finally he loosened his hold and stepped back. She stood in the center of the room then finally turned to face him. The brown eyes held tears but the anger was no longer there. He bent forward to kiss her.

She kissed back but bit his lip. Bob grabbed her with both arms. She did not resist, but exhaled and put her head on his shoulder as he squeezed. Putting his hand on her bottom, he pulled her even closer. Her arms were around him and he could feel the fingernails digging into his back as he kissed her again. They slowly knelt on the carpet. As he pushed her back, shoes were kicked off. He forgot about his sore ankle

The damn fly was back on his forehead. He wrinkled it a couple of times, but it still explored his face. He reached toward his face and the trespasser left. He turned to his right and two big brown eyes were staring at him. They blinked a few times, and then the lips and cheeks moved to a smile.

"Good morning."

"Good morning to you." He leaned over and kissed her.

"Quite an evening," she said.

"Jenny, I'm really sorry."

"Are you sorry for the rug burn on my hip?" She smiled again.

"I'm sorry for what I said." He did not mention the scratches on his back or the bite marks on his shoulder.

"I'm really . . ."

"Shh—I have been thinking as I lay here watching you." She put her finger on his lips. "I need to get dressed. I talk better when I'm clothed."

She moved away from him, sitting on the edge, and then stood. She stretched and walked across the room to the closet. Bob watched her naked back, bottom, and legs as she put on an old green bathrobe and. Turning, she pulled her hair back into a ponytail and tied it with a ribbon from the dresser. When she came back to the bed, Bob was leaning against the headboard with a sheet covering his lap. Jenny sat on the bed, took his hand and then touched his face.

"You look almost as bad as when you came in from that fight at Emma's a few weeks ago." She traced her hand over his lips, and he could feel a small cut there.

"I deserve it. Look at my back," He twisted to show her.

"Oh, Robert, I'm sorry."

"No, Jenny, I'm the one who should be sorry. I said things last night that were hurtful to you. I just don't know what I was thinking. I didn't have any right to say those things, and if I could, I would take every word back. I hope that you know how I feel about Tommy. And I don't want to tell you how you feel or what you want."

"I know. You are worrying about what comes after graduation. And you're right. They won't draft me, but they'll draft you. But this problem is a 'we' problem and not an 'I' problem. I want you to understand that for me this is our problem. I'm a part of it and I want to be a part of it. There isn't me and you—for me at least—there's only us. Do you understand?"

"Yes"

"I love you, Robert, and I want us to be together."

"I like you. I . . ." Bob hesitated as he stumbled over the words. Jenny smiled and touched his lips.

"You don't have to say it. I know that it is there. I see it in your face, and I feel it in your touch. You're like my father, and probably your father—you can't express your feelings. They get all tied up in you when you try and say them, but I feel 'I love you' every time that you touch me," she said. "The love is there, even if you can't say it. I know that."

He kissed her hand and held it with both of his. The dog which had been silent began to bark again.

"Jenny, I'm . . ."

"Shh . . . Let me finish, Robert."

"OK."

"I want us to go to Oregon. I want to see Oregon, and I want to continue to study with Dr. Robinson. Everyone tells me it is a great opportunity. But if you don't want to go, I'm not going. I do not want to go by myself."

"Let's go to Oregon."

"Good. Let's go, and we'll worry about the draft when we are out there—notice I said 'we.'"

"I heard the 'we,' but it should not be your problem. It's mine."

"If it affects you, then it's my problem, which is the way that I want it." Jenny again kissed his hand and looked up. "If you feel that you need to go into the military, I will support your decision, but I hope that you don't. I hate this war. I think that it's stupid and wrong. And I don't want Americans to die there—especially you."

"At first I thought there was some purpose to Tommy dying, but now I don't know. Maybe I just wanted to believe that the brother I loved and looked up to so much had died for some reason. I do know that Tommy was happy and proud to be a Marine and excited about going to Vietnam. I guess that back in those days it all made sense to me. Now it doesn't. I do know that I don't want to lose someone else that I love. The war just continues on and on, and I can't see any end to it."

"If I apply for CO status, it'll give me some time to decide what to do. And I do want to go to Oregon with you."

"If when the time comes and you have to make a decision, I want to be there with you. I will support whatever you decide to do. If you want to leave the country, I will go with you. I can go to graduate school in Canada, or I can get a teaching job. Or if I have to, I could waitress like I have done every summer at home. Somehow we can get by, just as long as I am with you. Whatever you decide will be right because I know you will have thought about it a great deal and will believe in that decision with you whole heart. I know that is the way that you are. But most important I want us to be together."

"I want that too."

She stared at him for a moment and then took her index finger and lightly traced a path similar to the one the fly had taken earlier. This path did not irritate but excited. She stopped when her finger rested on his lips.

"Now that we have settled that issue, what are we going to do about this, Mr. Hartman?"

Jenny stood up and her robe opened. She placed a foot on the bed next to him and pointed to a red scrape on her knee—an obvious rug burn.

"I don't understand how a big strong man like you can pick on a poor defenseless girl like me. How am I ever going to wear a dress to graduation with a burn like this on my leg?"

A large grin spread across her face that fit well with the sunlight that was bathing her back. She took the tie from her hair and shook it, and hair flowed over her shoulders and glistened in the morning sunlight. She continued to stand with her leg on the bed and the robe open. Her perfect naked body stood in sharp contrast to the worn green robe.

The feelings of guilt from the night before and the uncertainty about the future were chased away just as the sun had removed the shadows from the room this morning. All that remained now in Jenny's sunshine was passion and love.

CHAPTER 26

"We should throw blood."

"Where are you going to get the blood, and what good would that do?"

"We can get it from the Vet Clinic. Maybe if the trustees or some fat cat alumni got blood on their clean shirts they might think about what is going on in Vietnam—at least it would make the news."

Bob sat next to Harry in a room on the second floor of the Union listening as students argued about what action to take the next day at graduation. Harry had been one of the organizers of the *Coalition to Stop the War,* and this meeting had been called to develop a plan of action. Different student groups were present but so far nothing had been accomplished—only arguing and indecision.

"You White Honkies can't think of anything original. The Berrigan Brothers already did the blood thing."

A Black student with a large Afro haircut, wearing a T-shirt that supported "Black Power" hurled a challenge to the plan. His few supporters around him clapped in support. Harry had told Bob that he was not even sure if anyone from the Black community would attend; they were few in numbers and so far had said very little. A young man with white shirt and tie, wearing a "Bobby in '68" button took the microphone and finally quieted everyone down.

"As our colored friends . . ."

"Black . . . Black," shouted the group.

"Excuse me—Black Afro-American. As our Black friends indicate we needn't be copycats. We need to do something that's unique to Michigan State. We need a demonstration that's organized and peaceful so that faculty, administration, and alumni can see how we feel. We should have petitions to sign to send to Congress to show that we don't support the war."

"Bullshit!" someone yelled from the back. "Congress won't listen to you. They won't listen to anyone. Petitions won't stop this war!"

From the far side came, "Petitions are for flunky liberals who still believe that the system gives a shit about anyone except corporate America. What you need is more action and less writing."

There was a cheer from many while some sat quietly. The Kennedy supporter tried to quiet the crowd and have only one person speak at a time. Every time order was restored a comment or suggestion created chaos again. Bob leaned over to Harry.

"Harry, I've got to go. I have to meet Jenny in fifteen minutes."

"Wait outside for me."

Bob worked his way to the door. The room was packed, and it was difficult to exit. He crossed the hall and got a drink, and when he turned back to the door, Harry was just leaving the room.

"Jesus, what a mess," Harry said. "Right before you came we tried to agree on a policy statement about Vietnam, and someone said that women shouldn't have a say in the statement since they wouldn't be drafted. As you might expect, that got a lot of women pissed off. And then we have the McCarthy and Kennedy people who are fighting against each other. I'll be glad when the California primary is over."

"Does anyone listen at all in there? It seems to me it's who is able to shout the loudest," Bob said. "A political science major should have a field day in there."

"I could write a PhD thesis just on group dynamics," Harry said as he shook his head. "Putting that mess aside for a moment, what I'm wondering is how long are you going to be in East Lansing.?"

"I'll be here a couple more days. I'm not going to graduation, but Jenny is. We'll probably go home the day after graduation."

"Are you sure that you want to skip graduation?"

"Yes. They can send me my diploma," Bob said. "I already told my folks that I wasn't going to the ceremony, so now I can't go with them not there. I probably should have done it, but what the hell. I'll be back one more time in about a week. Jenny and I are going to Oregon through the Upper Peninsula, and I'll give you a call before we leave. I want to see Woody, Jim, and you one last time before we head west. Do you have someone for the apartment for the summer?"

"Yes I'm all set with that. I just wanted to make sure that you didn't take off before I got a chance to see you." Harry stopped and put his hand on Bob's shoulder. "Well, Rooms, it was a long time ago that we first became roommates. Remember how you couldn't find anything on campus the first week of classes?"

"Now you're not going to get all misty-eyed on me are you, Harry? I'm planning on leaving several pairs of dirty socks and underwear lying in the apartment when I leave so you can remember me. I don't want you to forget."

"No such luck forgetting you," Harry laughed and poked his shoulder. "I need to get back to that meeting before there is some real human blood on the floor. I'll see you next week."

"I'll leave a couple of glasses on the end tables without coasters," Bob said. Harry smiled and waved as he returned to the meeting.

Bob walked down the flight of stairs to the first floor to the grill, to wait for Jenny. He was a few minutes early so he ordered food knowing that Jenny would be eating later at her meeting. She was to attend a meeting with the President at Cowles House for *magna cum laude* graduates. Seeing her enter the grill, he was struck by how beautiful and sophisticated she was as she stood looking for him. Seeing him across the room, she waved and came to him in high heels, a red dress with a strand of pearls, and her hair up. She was stunning! Jenny kissed him on the cheek and then sat down.

"Oops, I'm afraid I left a mark on you. I'm not used to wearing lipstick."

"That's OK. I am lucky that I have such a beautiful girl to smooch me. You look very nice."

"Thank you, Robert."

"Do you want anything to eat or drink?"

"No, we'll have a meal at Cowles House," she said smiling at him. "I had such a wonderful day. Mother came up, and we went shopping. She and Pop are so excited about graduation because I am the first McKnight to graduate from college, just as you're the first Hartman. I wish that you were going to graduation with me."

"We're in different colleges, so we couldn't sit together. Besides, I can't go now that I told my folks that I wouldn't walk." Bob looked down at his French fries and shrugged. "I probably should have gone, but I can't now."

"Anyway, in another week we will be headed for Oregon," Jenny injected. "Pop has Tommy's car ready, and I just can't wait to head west. This will be really fun. I have already starting packing, and there are more things that I need to get from home."

Bob smiled as Jenny began a long list of things that she was packing and how some items would be placed in the trunk and some which would be placed in the back seat. Bob heard none of the monologue but was enjoying the sparkle in her eyes and the animation of her hands. He thought about teasing her and telling her that he was not going with her. When they were kids he would tell her outlandish lies about creatures or crimes in the area. He spun tales and she would sit wide-eyed and ask for details and explanations how "Mrs. Brown had been ax murdered," or "a combination lion-hyena that had escaped from a traveling circus." Finally, Tommy would laugh and interrupt.

"Come on Sis, Bobby's just making that up."

Then he couldn't help but laugh and she would go off mad—for a few hours. But at the next wild tale she would readily believe a story about a two-headed goat or that Mrs. Jones, their third grade teacher, had murdered three children in California and was now wanted by the FBI. Teasing her had always been so much fun, but now he knew that she was so excited about the trip that to hint that he wasn't going with her would be crushing. Besides, he was equally excited about the approaching journey. When Jenny stopped, he asked, "Does your mother know that I'm going to Oregon with you?"

"Yes, she knows. We talked about it."

"And your parents are OK with it. Or did you say that I would be staying someplace else in Oregon and not living with you."

"She knows that we are living together out there, and she's fine with it," Jenny laughed and reached across the table, patting his hand next to the French fries. "As long as I'm happy, that's all that she cares about. And you don't have to worry about Pop, either. You're Sam Hartman's son and that makes you okay in Pop's book. He always laughed at all of the things you and Tommy used to do—when Mother wasn't around. A better question is what will your parents say?"

"I haven't told them."

"Oh, Robert, you're going, aren't you?"

"If you don't take me, I'll hitchhike out. I don't want to be replaced by someone who knows how to spell and likes foreign films."

"Not much chance of that." Jenny blushed. "What do you think that they'll say?"

"I don't know. I think that they'll want me to get a job—probably their biggest concern is that we'll be going out there without a secure job for me," he said. "And not being married will be a big thing for my mother. I don't think that it'll bother my dad that much."

"I don't want to cause problems with you and your family."

"There won't be any problem. My mom has been upset with me ever since I refused to attend church after my freshman year. This will give her something to pray about and more evidence that the devil has a hold of me. She may have the whole Methodist Church praying for me. But it's me that needs the prayer, not you. She likes you and will be convinced that I'm the one leading you down the path to sin."

For a moment both were quiet and Bob saw that the excitement had suddenly vanished from her face replenished by worry. A change of topic was needed.

"I'm going to Oregon whether you let me ride in Tommy's Falcon or not. I'm not going to be left behind." Bob leaned back and grinned. "Besides I just realized that old Falcon is probably worth a hundred bucks, so I'm not only going west with a beautiful women, but also a rich one. How can you beat brains, beauty and money?" He reached across the table and touched her hand. "Jenny, you are 'exquisitely stunning,' tonight. How do you like the number of syllables in that compliment—not bad for a math major?"

"Robert, you make me so happy." A tear ran down her cheek, picking his hand up, she gently kissed it. "I love you," she said softly. She brushed the tear away.

"You got me crying and my mascara will run, and I have to meet the President in a few minutes. What are you going to do tonight?"

"There's some type of folk concert in Erickson Kiva tonight that I might check out. After that I'll just go back to the apartment. I imagine that Woody and Jim will be gone, and Harry will be all night at the Union trying to get that mess straightened out. I might pack a few things tonight. I'll load the pick-up with my stuff in the morning and probably go home tomorrow night. I'd like to stop and see you in the morning before graduation, if you don't mind?"

"That would be great. Let me put some lipstick on your other cheek and that way all of the coeds here will know that you are a branded cowboy." She kissed him on the other cheek and left the grill. She stopped in the door to turn and wav at him. He waved back and was certain that every eye in the grill was looking at her—at least the male eyes were. He thought how lucky he was going to be spending the next few months with someone as beautiful as Jenny—until the draft issue was resolved one way or the other.

Bob walked by Beaumont Tower and sat on the warm steps of the library. Traffic on the circle in front of him was heavy because of graduation tomorrow. He watched two parents taking pictures of their senior son in front of the library at the fountain and made a mental list of everything that he needed to take home. There wasn't much. He made another list of what he would take to Oregon. He would fit everything in an old suitcase and maybe a couple of boxes. He knew that Jenny would have more. Last week she had talked about dishes, a toaster, an ironing board and iron. The list had grown much longer, but he didn't listen as Jenny talked and wrote everything down. Finally he got up from the steps and crossed the Red Cedar and went to Erickson Kiva.

He really did not know anything about Doc Watson, who was the performer at Erickson, but he was quite an accomplished guitar player. He was blind and the way that his fingers moved on the neck and the speed with which the flat pick struck the strings was amazing. Although he was billed as a folk singer, Bob thought how his father would have enjoyed the music. Much of it reminded him of the twangy country music that they had good-naturedly fought over in the milk house for years. Bob was getting so he kind of enjoyed some of it, but he would never tell his father. It was too much fun to argue about the music—a battle he was certain his father also enjoyed. After the concert he had an ice cream sundae and then began the long trek back to the apartment. He day-dreamed as he walked back to the apartment.

He thought how he had changed from his freshman year at State. Maybe he was still that farm boy from Lawsonville who did not have a clue about his future, but at least he had a college degree and close friends in Harry, Jim, and Woody. And there was a beautiful and intelligent woman who was madly in love with him—and he with her. He must have done something right in the four years he had been in East Lansing. The draft loomed ahead of him, but whatever he did, he was certain that at least one person would be there supporting his decision—Jennifer Mc Knight. And this thought comforted him.

"Oregon, here we come," he said under his breath.

Bob walked into the apartment complex for the last time. He stood by a car that parked on the grass and listened to the sounds. They were the same ones he had heard for the last two years here, but now louder, as one last "heading home for summer" fling was enjoyed, and graduating seniors were preparing their headaches for tomorrow's commencement speaker. Several parties on the balconies spread before him, and directly in front were students on the second floor crowded around a keg as the Mamas and Papas sang "California Dreaming." Ought to be "Oregon Dreaming," he thought.

Instead of walking up to his apartment, Bob went down to the Sin Den because Harry would still be at the Union. Woody would be out at some bar in the Lansing area, but Jim might be home and available for conversation—if he wasn't too stoned. As always, he walked into the apartment without knocking.

"What are doing, Jimbo?" Bob said as Jim looked up from the couch where he was sitting.

"Oh, shit!" Jim said and yelled to the bedroom, never leaving the couch. "Woody, he's here."

"What's wrong with you? You look strange. Did you get some bad dope?"

"Woody, he's here," Jim yelled again louder as he rocked back and repeat. "Oh shit—oh shit—oh shit."

Woody came out of the bathroom tucking his shirt in. "Where the hell have you been?"

"I was on campus listening to a guy play guitar at Erickson. Then I wandered around for a while. What's up?"

"Did Harry get a hold of you?" Woody asked as Jim continued to rock with softer, "Oh shit, oh shit."

"No, I saw him at the Union earlier. That was around five or six. Then I saw Jenny for awhile before she went to Cowles House." Bob had a strange sense that something wasn't being said. "What's going on with you two?"

"You haven't heard then."

"What the hell are you talking about?"

Woody's mouth was open as he gaped at Bob. On the couch Jim had stopped rocking and stared. An eerie quiet wrapped everyone.

"I don't know how to say this," Woody said.

"You guys are weirding me out. Are you smoking dope now, Woody?" Bob gave a nervous laugh, but he already had a sense that there was nothing funny here, just a sense of doom about to fall.

"Bobby, I don't know how to tell you this, but Jenny was killed this evening."

"What?"

"She was crossing Grand River Avenue and was hit by a car. She died instantly."

"What?"

"The cops came to your apartment because they found your name. They came down here just as I was heading for Emma's because no one was at home at your place. We didn't know where you were, but Jim knew that Harry was at the Union organizing the demonstration. The cops got a hold of him, and he came right home. He's out trying to find you." Woody said. "Whoever hit her didn't stop, but they have a license number. The cop said that they think it was a drunk driver. They were going to notify her parents."

"What'd you say?" Bob looked at Woody and Jim. They looked strange. He couldn't figure out what was different about Woody—was it his clothes or something else? It was his entire face that looked different. Woody was trying to tell him something, but he just couldn't hear it. He would have to listen closer. "What did you say?"

"Jenny's dead. She was hit by a car on Grand River."

Finally the words were moving from his ears to his brain. He was beginning to hear what Woody was saying. But why did Woody's skin look so strange? It had a yellowish tint, and his face was distorted and distant. Why?

"I think I'll sit down now." Bob took two steps backward to a kitchen chair and sat facing the living room.

"I'm sorry, Bobby. Can I do anything for you?"

He needed to sit because his legs were going to give out. He felt a rush go through his body. He was hot, and then it went away—and then the rush came again. He placed a hand on each knee and looked at Woody and Jim. They were staring at him, and he wondered why. Someplace in the background he could hear music playing, but when his ears came to this apartment, there was only silence. He really needed to get to the barn and start the milking and turn on the radio before his father arrived.

"Do you want a glass of water?" Woody took a couple of steps toward him.

"No."

"Are you OK?" He rested his hand lightly on Bob's shoulder. Across the room Jim began to rock again.

"Yes, I'm OK."

"What can I do, Bobby? Is there anything that I can get you?"

"No, I'm fine. Just let me sit here for a minute."

Bob stared beyond the room to the sliding glass door that was half open on the warm June night. It seemed like it was a mile away, and he wondered about the three strange reflections that he saw in the glass. There was a strange eerie glow in the room. Jim or Woody must have changed all of the light bulbs in this apartment. He had never seen lights like this; he should ask them where they got the strange bulbs. And he wasn't certain if he had ever been in this apartment before. It was certainly very different from his own apartment. And where was his apartment?

Slowly the message that Jenny was dead was leaving his brain and heading to other parts of his body. The hot rushes had stopped, and now he felt a chill. He took a couple of deep breaths focusing on Woody. He knew he would be okay in just a minute, as soon as he caught his breath.

Bob leaned forward, put his head between his legs, and threw up.

CHAPTER 27

"Leave the boy alone!"

"But, Sam."

"I said leave him alone, Helen."

"But he just wanders around. He doesn't eat, and I don't think he sleeps very much—he looks awful. I tried to get him to talk with Pastor Floyd, but he won't do that. He won't go over to see the Mc Knights. He didn't say anything to them at the funeral or at the graveside, and he wouldn't go to the dinner at the church after the service."

"I know."

"Yesterday Florence Richter said she saw him way over on the County Line Road walking. I think he walks to town every day, and then he's back in those woods. Every time I try to talk with him he storms out of the house. I'm just worried sick about him."

"I know he's having a hard time, but he's going to have to work it out by himself. For now, leave him alone."

Sam Hartman walked out on the porch and the screen door slammed behind him. He had his foot on the steps headed for the barn when he saw Bob sitting on the porch swing. He stepped back and leaned against the post.

"Morning," he said. "It looks like it is going to be clear today."

"Yup," Bob replied. "The dew was heavy this morning, but it has dried off now."

He moved the swing a few inches with his feet planted on the porch. Any more movement than a small rocking motion would create a squeak that had been there for years. Repeated application of 10 WD 40 never got rid of it. Sam Hartman gazed out on the yard toward the barn for several minutes while Bob rocked.

"Well, I got to go to town and get a gear for the hay rake. That damn brother of yours ran over some old fencing in the McKnight's hay field and wrapped the wire into the tines. I don't know how he could miss that fencing; a blind man could see it with his cane. I wish that kid would use his head for something other than to hang his hat on and to keep his ears apart." Sam turned to his son in the swing.

"We're going to bale the McKnight's hay tomorrow. The Ferguson boys have been doing the milking in the morning, and Walkers do it at night. George is having a rough time right now. It's good that he had his crops in before the accident. His corn is in good shape, and I can take the wheat off for him in another month. If you get a chance, Bobby, you might stop over and see them. I'm certain that Phyllis and George would appreciate it." He took a red handkerchief from his pocket and blew his nose. Putting it back in his pocket, he stepped off of the porch and whistled. Roscoe came out from under the porch, gave a quick shake, and started bounding around.

Sam Hartman took a couple of steps to the barn and stopped. He bent down and pulled a clump of burrs from Roscoe's coat. Throwing them to the edge of the porch, he said, "If you get a chance today, Bobby, and don't have anything to do, you might put some paint on the tool shed and the chicken coop. The paint is in the shop stacked by the arc welder. That is if you don't have anything better to do. Joe was supposed to do that, but he's at basketball practice, and then he has a baseball game tonight. I can't get any work out that boy. He has more ballgames and practices than six people should."

Sam Hartman went to his truck with Roscoe leading the way. Bob watched his father go down the drive, turn on to the gravel road, and drive toward town. Roscoe was in back, barking.

Bob had been up before daylight and made his usual trip through the woods and around the Schmidt farm. His mother was right. He did not eat very much and had a difficult time sleeping. He left the house early and returned late at night after dark. Each day he hoped that he would be so tired that he could sleep, but each night he would dream of Jenny. They would be laughing and chasing each other, and when he went to touch her, she would disappear. Two or three of these dreams and he was ready for the morning sun.

As he rocked he thought of the last few days—the accident, the funeral, and the last couple of weeks as he walked and tried to make sense of everything. He could not recall the ride home from East Lansing, but he did remember the funeral service—at least parts of it. He remembered nothing of the burial. He had been to her grave several times. It was next to Tommy's, but only Tommy's grave had a gravestone. For now only a mound of dirt with dead flowers marked her grave site. He didn't know what day it was or how long ago the accident had occurred. He just couldn't remember. His mother had told him an arrest had been made, and there were charges of drunk driving. Helen Hartman had been providing more details when Bob walked out the door.

"What does it matter, and who cares?" he thought. "Jenny's gone."

His mother was right—he did walk, and it did seem to help, but he did not know where to go. He walked into town and around the high school; he walked down a gravel road where he and Jenny had parked several times during Christmas vacation; he walked through the woods; and everyday he walked around the Schmidt Farm. He never went near the McKnight farm—he did not want to see George or Phyllis McKnight or any of their children.

Finally, Bob moved from the swing to the tool shed. He surveyed the old building that housed two generations of farming equipment. When each of his grandfathers had died, anything that was metal and might be useable was brought here to the Hartman farm. He decided the building could use some repair before he began to paint it. He retrieved a hammer and nails from the shed then spent most of the morning nailing loose boards and replacing a few. The glass in one window was broken, so he cut a new piece and glazed it into place. Around noon he went up on the roof and began nailing loose sheets of tin. It was so hot, he took his shirt off. When he turned to throw it on the ground, his mother was standing by the ladder.

"Robert, would you like some lunch? I baked a cherry pie this morning."

"No, thanks anyway."

"There's fried chicken from last night, or I could make you a sandwich. I baked bread this morning—there's homemade bread, and I've a batch of strawberry preserves going."

"No thanks, Mom."

Bob began nailing. On the ground Helen Hartman looked up absent-mindedly folding the corners of her apron. She stood for a moment with the sun over her shoulder while Bob moved further up the roof, hammering. Finally, she dropped her apron and returned to the house. Later in the afternoon he spread the four gallons of paint that were in the shop. There was still more shed—but no paint so he took his usual walk back to the woods. That night his sunburned back kept him from sleeping well—along with thoughts of Jenny.

In the morning when he came back from walking, new cans of paint were piled next to the tool shed. For two more days he worked on the tool shed and chicken coop. As he was finishing up on the third evening, his father strolled by while he was on the ladder.

"Nice job, Bobby. If you want, and you don't have anything else to do, you might fix the fence that goes on the west and north side of the woods. I was going to do it this fall, but you could get started on it—if you don't have anything else to do. The fence stretchers are in the shop, and there's new barb wire that should go on top. If you replace any posts, make sure you set them thirty inches in the ground. I'd load everything on the old hay wagon that you need. Check that wagon, before you go. I think one of the tires is flat."

Sam Hartman went into the barn. Bob finished painting, cleaned the brushes, and put everything away. In the morning, after fixing the tire, he loaded everything on the wagon, hooked it to the tractor and drove to the woods. It took him two days to replace the posts that were rotten. He then restretched the fence and added a strand of barb to the top. On the fourth day he was nearly finished with only the last two brace poles to secure. He took care of one and went diagonally through the woods to secure the last one.

It was late afternoon as he moved through the woods and into a small clearing. On the opposite side of the meadow was the brace pole that had to be fixed to complete the fencing. He was feeling better and sleeping a little more at night. His sunburn was not sore anymore, and his hands had hardened so that his gloves lay on the seat of the tractor. He still avoided most of the family, except his father who he talked with briefly each morning, but only about the days work to be done or the weather. He had stopped his long walks to town, and had not been to the graveyard since he began working for his father.

Bob was walking across the meadow with his head down thinking about the time in October when he had first seen Jenny in these woods, and then the next day there had been the apple fight. He stopped!

Six inches next to his foot was a late fawn lying in the tall grass. It had been hidden by its mother and lay perfectly still with its head erect. If he had been three feet either side, or had been looking up, he would not have seen it. He wanted to reach down and pick it up. The fur looked so soft and there was a calm peaceful expression on its face as the eyes continued to blink. But he remembered not to touch it. Once he and Tommy had caught a new born fawn in these woods, took it home and showed his dad.

"You boys shouldn't have caught this little fella," Sam Hartman said. "You'll never be able to feed it, and its mama may abandon it once she smells humans on her baby. You had better put it back in the woods and hope she takes it back so the little fellow can get something to eat." Two day later they found the fawn dead.

Bob watched the long eye lashes blink across big brown eyes; they were "cow eyes"—big brown cow eyes. The fawn remained motionless and calm showing no fear.

Blink . . . Blink . . . Blink . . . Blink

"Whuff!" A deer snorted from the woods, and the fawn turned its head in that direction.

"Whuff!" The fawn got up and ran into the woods.

Bob watched it enter into the brush under the trees. He could not see anything, but he knew that its mother was calling it to safety. She would take care of her baby. He thought again of those huge brown eyes. He thought of the soft skin of the fawn that he had not been able to touch, and he remembered how when he had laid in bed with Jenny, he would love to feel the softness of her leg as she threw it over his. Jenny's leg—the skin of the fawn—he wanted to touch each, but could not.

Tommy always called her "Jenny Cow Eyes."

He felt a lump in his throat and a single tear escaped.

"Jesus Christ, you big baby."

Another tear went down the other cheek, and he wiped both eyes with his hand. He sat down next to the fawn's indentation and coughed to clear the lump in his throat. He gave up wiping his eyes because he could not keep up with the tears running down his cheeks. A bobwhite whistled in the distance and then one answered back. He thought about what Jenny had said.

"When I could finally cry, I began to get better."

The fawn's impression disappeared as a larger body was laid on top of it. Bob spread both of his arms out wide and looked up at the sky where a few clouds floated. Now the tears no longer ran down his cheek, but straight from his eyes, across his temples, and then watered the ground. He heard the bobwhite call again and the answer.

"Probably they are mates and have been separated," he thought.

"Jenny—Jenny—Jenny."

CHAPTER 28

"Mom, can I use the car this morning."

"Sure, honey. What do you need it for?" Helen smiled as Bob polished off his breakfast of eggs, sausage, homemade toast, and finally pancakes drenched in butter and maple syrup.

"I need to go to the bank and get a few things in town," he said. "I might stop and see Mr. and Mrs. McKnight this afternoon."

"That would be nice. If you don't mind, I have a pie and a loaf of fresh bread that you could drop off for them."

"Sure."

Bob left quickly after he finished his breakfast. If he stayed too long, his mother would start quizzing him about what he was doing or how he was feeling. He could see the happiness on her face when he came downstairs and ate the first large meal in over three weeks. He had trouble falling asleep, but then slept until way past daylight. It seemed strange to be at home and not to be up early. Everyone was gone from the house except his mother and Sarah, who was watching Captain Kangaroo.

He drove to the bank and then stopped at a local sporting goods store to buy a backpack. He had a few other items to purchase, and he spent a couple extra hours in town wasting time because he did not want to drive to the McKnights', but he knew that he must.

In the afternoon he drove in the yard of the McKnight farm where he had walked Jenny home last October. He had been here thousands of times and probably knew the barns and the house as well as anyone. And yet the place looked different. He got out of the car, taking the pie and bread with him. Phyllis and George McKnight were sitting on the front porch. Although the rockers had been there for as long as he could remember, he had never seen George McKnight sit in one. He usually was in the barn or working in the field. As he approached, Mrs. McKnight got out of her chair and put the pan that had been in her lap on the floor. Mr. McKnight continued to rock but now had a grin on his face.

"Mrs. McKnight, my mom sent this pie and bread over to you."

Phyllis McKnight came down the steps. Bob stood holding a pie in one hand and a loaf of bread in the other as she put her arms around his chest and squeezed. He stood in the yard a few feet from the front porch as the sounds and smells of the farm surrounded him, and she clung to him with her head on his chest. He didn't know what to say or do—so he did nothing. Finally, Phyllis McKnight sighed and stepped back.

"Robert, Robert." She brushed the tears from her eyes. They were Jenny's brown eyes surrounded by many wrinkles and holding a deep sadness. He could feel a lump in his throat as George Mc Knight took a blue handkerchief from his bib overalls and blew his nose.

"Come sit a spell." She took him by the arm and led him to a chair on the porch.

"Do you need something to drink?" George McKnight asked.

"Some ice tea or water would be fine."

George McKnight shuffled to the kitchen door. Although he was wearing his familiar bib overalls, Bob had never seen him in bedroom slippers. He seemed old and weak. Most men picked up a hay bale with both hands; George McKnight moved hay with a bale in each hand. Now, Bob wondered if a glass of tea might be too heavy for him.

"How is Mr. McKnight doing?"

"Not well, not well at all." Phyllis McKnight picked up the pan next to her rocker and began shelling peas. "Most people around here probably think George cares more for his cattle than he does for his children. But that ain't so—you don't live with a man for almost thirty years and not get to know him. He loves his children—all of them deeply. He just doesn't say it out loud." She dumped the peas into the pan on her lap and rocked as her fingers opened shells quickly and effortlessly. "Bobby, hand me that other pan of peas, please."

"When Tommy was killed, George just disappeared into the barn, like he always does when he has something on his mind. But Jenny's death has taken the wind right out of his sails. I don't know if it was because it was the second death or it was Jenny. Most everyone knew that Jenny was the apple of his eye and could do no wrong."

"I just wish that the old George would come back. I'd like to have him storm out of the house mad about something, or hear him yelling and swearing because the hogs are out. Or have him laugh after you and Tommy had done some of your foolishness. You know, I'd always get mad at the tomfoolery you boys did, but George would just hug me and say: 'Ah, they're just boys, Phyllis,' and then he would go off to the barn whistling and laughing."

"And how are you doing, Mrs. McKnight?"

"Well, someone has to hold the family together. I guess you only have so many tears to cry for someone. I just haven't reached that number yet. But we are getting by. I know your mom and dad have really helped with everything around here. Between them and the neighbors, the work on the farm is getting done."

George Mc Knight came out with glasses of tea. He sat down and began to rock as Mrs. McKnight continued to shell peas and chat. Bob commented on what good weather they had been having and how the corn was growing well. Then he told them how he had fenced in the old wood lot that was between the Hartman and McKnight farms that Tommy and he had played in so much when they were younger. Seeing that both McKnights enjoyed the stories, he began to recount stories about their activities there.

"One time a bunch of us was having a corn cob fight at the Schmidt's farm and Jenny was hit in the head and got a small cut over her eye. Tommy was really mad because you weren't supposed to aim at anything above the shoulders. When George Whitefield said that it didn't really matter because Jenny was a girl and shouldn't be playing anyway—well, he and Tommy got in a pushing match and Tommy gave him a bloody nose. That ended the corn cob fight for that day."

"Tommy was a good boy," George McKnight said as he rocked. "He always looked out for his sister."

Bob told stories about green apples, hay forts, throwing tomatoes at passing cars in the night, and other exploits that he had had before he went to college. All of his tales included Tommy and Jenny, and both parents enjoyed these reminiscences. Phyllis McKnight continued to work quietly as she listened. She had finished shelling one pan of peas and then began another. When there was a pause, Mr. Mc Knight leaned forward and asked, "Say Bobby, there is one thing I always wanted to know. Did you and Tommy put that pig in the high school when Tommy was a senior?" Bob froze as a quick burst of panic swept through him. Should he use truth or avoidance?

"Yes, we did."

"I knowed it! I knowed that you two rascals did it, soon as I heard about that hog running in the hall," George leaned back, slapped his knee and gave a large and long laugh. Encouraged, Bob related the story of the pig in high school. He and Tommy had stolen a feeder pig from a neighboring farm, and with the legs and snout tied, they had transported it to the school just after midnight on a Saturday. Earlier they had taped the latch on an outside door and had been able to enter the school at night, then had freed the pig into the school hallway by the principal's office. Early Sunday morning a custodian had discovered the pig wandering the halls and had called the principal, who was furious and threatened to expel whoever had done the trick.

"The funniest part was that later we heard that the principal had been teaching a Sunday School class when the janitor called him to school, and in the process of trying to catch the pig, he slipped in some pig manure and got it on his suit and in his hair. On Monday he had an assembly for all of the boys and he was really mad. I made sure that I didn't set next to Tommy because I knew that I would get laughing."

"I knowed that you son-of-a guns had did it when I heard about it from the boys at the co-op," George McKnight said. "I heard that on top of all that, that old Sunday school teacher got to swearing quite a bit. That must have been a sight to see that old Sunday school teacher cussin' just like he was a regular old farm boy, like you and me." Bob found himself wiping tears from his eyes as George did with his handkerchief. Phyllis shelled peas and seemed more interested in her husband's laughter than the story.

The Ferguson twins drove into the yard and parked by the milk house. They waved as they got out of the truck and went into the barn to milk. Bob looked at his watch and realized that he had been sitting there for over two hours.

"I'd better be going," he said as he stood up. "I've got some chores to do at home."

George McKnight stood by his rocker. Bob's hand disappeared into a calloused paw. The other went on Bob's shoulder as George vigorously shook his hand. There was a big grin on George McKnight's face, and Bob sensed that there had not been one there for several weeks.

"You take care now."

"I'll walk you to your car," Mrs. McKnight said as she again took his arm and stepped off of the porch with him. Bob remembered the many times on campus that Jenny had walked holding his arm in the same manner. He felt that lump rise again in his throat. When they stopped at the car, she hugged him. Tears filled her eyes as she continued to hold his hand.

"Robert, I want to tell you that you were so good for Jenny. After Tommy was killed in Vietnam, she changed. There was a sadness and gloom around her. It was more than Tommy's death; something happened and she went into this shell, but she wouldn't tell me what it was. But I know she'd changed. In October when you walked her home, the next day all she could talk about was you. I think that she always had a little crush on you, and these last months she would jabber on and on about what you two were doing. I know that she was really looking forward to Oregon." Phyllis Mc Knight paused still holding his hand. "I guess what I'm saying is that you really made her happy."

"She really made me happy. I miss her very much."

"I know. We all do."

Bob turned quickly and got into his mother's car as the lump got bigger. George McKnight called from the porch, "Don't be a stranger around here."

Bob used the circle driveway and drove around by the barn and past the Ferguson's truck as he pulled onto the gravel road. He went on home regretting that he could not have said how he really felt about Jenny, but could only tell funny stories about Tommy and himself. Parking the car, he noticed that his father's pick-up was gone and he was sure that the milking was done.

He did not want to talk with his mother, so he went to the shop to take care of the tools he had used building the fence. He hung the fence chains up, straightened the stretchers, and put the hand tools away. There were several pieces of scrap metal lying around the shop and he sorted it into bins of IRON, STEEL, COPPER, ALUMINUM, and BRASS. Next he grabbed a broom and began sweeping the floor. He had been at it for about ten minutes and was just pushing the last of the dirt out the open sliding door, when Elwood Rademaker stepped into the shop with two brown paper sacks.

"Woody! What the heck are you doing here?"

"I drove down to see you." He held up two brown bags. "I stopped in town and bought us a couple of quarts to drink. I was afraid that you might have joined the church out here on the farm."

"I don't want any."

"I didn't ask you if you wanted any. I asked you to drink one. You know what I always say: You can't trust anyone . . . ."

"Who doesn't like beer." Bob completed the saying with him, and took the open quart.

"Well, now that I'm here, how are you?"

"I'm OK."

"You're lying aren't you?"

"No."

"You're lying like hell. You looked better after the fight we had with the frat boys in the spring." Bob took a short drink as Woody watched.

After an awkward silence, Bob said. "I appreciated you and Jim and Harry coming down for the funeral. I know I didn't say anything at the time, but I knew that you were there."

"That's OK, Bobby. She was a special lady," said Woody. "Friends always stick with friends."

"What are Harry and Jim up to these days?"

"Harry has a new roommate. I think he's somehow connected with the same anti-war effort that Harry is. Jim is home with his parents in Grand Ledge. They are making him see some kind of shrink. He failed most of his Spring Term classes, so I think they kicked him out of State. He's going to take classes at Central in the fall, but who knows what will happen with old Jimbo. He bought a guitar and is teaching himself to play it. Says he is going to be a folk singer and write protest songs."

"Well, who moved in with you, if Jim moved home?"

"Oh I gave up the apartment and moved in with Lucille a couple of weeks ago," Woody said as a grin spread across his face. "I do have this feeling that she moved in with me; we just happen to live at her place."

"You're kiddin' aren't you?"

"Nope, swear to God, Bobby, it was her idea to live together. She wanted to come down here with me today and see you, but she has a new job and couldn't get the time off of work. She always liked you a lot—she thinks you're cute and a real gentleman." Woody took another swig of beer and then added, "But what the hell does she know. She let me move in with her."

Bob laughed and felt beer go up his nose.

"It's good to see you laugh. You use to do a lot of that."

"I haven't found much to laugh at the few weeks."

"I know you got kind of the nasty end of the stick."

"Yah, I sure did."

They both stood in the doorway of the shop without saying anything. The afternoon breeze had died down. Occasionally the sound of cattle in the barn lot could be heard or of a car traveling by the house. Other than the noises of approaching night, it was still. Woody finished his quart, dropped the empty into a trash can by the door, and leaned against the door jam.

"Are you nursing that beer or are you going to drink it?" Woody asked, and then added with a grin. "You're probably pissed that I didn't bring Jack along for the ride from Lansing?"

"No, that's OK. I just as soon not have any Jack Daniels today. Save it for yourself." Bob took another sip of beer. Woody chatted for awhile about what Lucille and he had been doing for the last few weeks. Bob finished the quart and dropped it in the trash can.

"I need to get back to Lansing," Woody said. "If I'm not home by eleven when she gets out of work, she thinks I'm out whoring around." Woody put his hand on Bob's shoulder and looked him in the face.

"Look Bobby, I'm not smart like you, Harry, and Jim. I didn't even graduate from high school. When I was a senior I had a choice between a juvenile detention home or the army. I took the army and ended up in Vietnam. And I was scared shitless all the time I was in Nam. I saw shit and did shit that I hope I can forget some day."

"But if I learned one thing in Nam, it was to enjoy and appreciate the good things that happen to you—whether it is for one hour or one day. Jenny was a very special lady and I envy you for the time you had with her. I wish that it could have been longer—you deserved it. But don't loose sight of the moments you had. You and Jenny really had something special. I hope that Lucille and I can find that same thing."

"Thanks Woody. I appreciate that."

"Well, I'd better head home. Take it easy, and if you ever need anything, you give the old woodpecker a call. Remember friends are always there for each other, and I'm there if you need anything. I expect that I'll see your name in the paper or on TV someday for something famous, and I don't mean kicking the shit out of some stupid frat boys."

"You're name will be there before mine," Bob laughed. "—DUI, or indecent exposure."

"You are probably right,"

Woody laughed, gave Bob a shove on the shoulder, and went out the door. Bob walked with him to his car then watched him leave and drive toward Lawsonville. He smiled as he saw Woody in five years driving a station wagon with two kids in the back and Lucille bottle-feeding a baby in the front.

CHAPTER 29

"Mom, I'm going to Oregon."

Helen Hartman set the apple she was peeling in the bowl on her lap as she sat across from her son. After Woody left for Lansing, Bob went to the house for supper. He helped himself to a second plate of meat and potatoes.

"When are you going?" she said, putting her knife on the table and pushing a bowl of fresh cooked peas toward him

"I'm going to leave in the morning."

"How are you going to get there?"

"I'll hitchhike."

She put the bowl with apples on the table and wiped her hands on her apron. She looked at her son.

"Are you sure that it's safe to hitchhike all the way across the country?" she said as Bob put a large bite of steak in his mouth. "Wasn't that where you and Jenny were planning to live?"

Bob stopped and looked at his mother who sat across from him with both hands resting on the kitchen table. He swallowed the piece of meat and put his fork down.

"How did you know?"

"Phyllis told me several weeks ago about your plans. You never fooled anyone about you and Jenny—especially me." Helen Hartman paused and added softly, "I knew how you felt about her. Remember, I'm still your mother and you never have been able to hide anything. If you couldn't tell from your face, all you had to do was to look at Jenny's—her feelings were all over her face. I think that she was always sweet on you, especially after you bloodied the nose of that Winston boy in school."

Bob thought back to freshman year in high school in study hall when Jamie Winston, who was in tenth grade, said something nasty about Jenny. A pushing match ensued, ending with Jamie's nose bloodied and both boys in the principal's office. His mother had to come to school to pick him up, and she lectured him all the way home about fighting. He was suspended for three days. The worst part was that he had to go to the barn and tell his father who was there loading corn. Sam Hartman listened and said, "Was it worth it?"

"Yes, Sir."

"You'd better pick up a shovel and help me load this corn." Sam turned and began shoveling.

Helen Hartman straightened the two bowls—one with peeled apples and the other with peelings and cores. "Do you want some more meat or potatoes, dear?"

"No thanks, Mom."

"Have you talked to your father about what you are planning on doing?"

"No. I looked for him this evening, but he's gone somewhere."

"He's at a Farm Bureau meeting in town," Helen said. "There is some problem about the county ditches, and several of the farmers are upset about what the Drain Commission is proposing. Your father is not happy either, but at least, he'll be one of the reasonable voices."

"I'll see him in the morning before I leave."

Bob pushed his plate aside and finished his milk. He had known it would be difficult to tell his parents of his plans to leave, and he knew that his mother especially would argue with him and give him all kinds of reasons why this was "a dumb idea." He wished that she would start yelling at him, so he could get mad and yell back and then leave the room. But she just sat quietly, looking very small and old.

"I'm not going to try and stop you," she said. "You wouldn't listen to me anyway. You're so much like your father. When he doesn't like my suggestions, he just goes to the barn and does what he wants to do. You're just the same. I love you both very much, but I've come to realize that I'm not going to change either one of you."

She got up from the table and went to the cupboard. She took down an old Maxwell House coffee tin hidden behind the baking supplies. She took the lid off, removed a wad of dollar bills, brought it over to the table, and laid it in front of Bob.

"Take this with you. It's not much, but it may help. It's a little that I have saved from the egg money."

"Mom, I don't need this. I have plenty." He slid the money back.

"Take it, Robert. It is such a small thing I have to give." She slid the money back to him. It sat there as both were silent.

"I know that Jenny's death has been hard for you, and I wish that I had an explanation. My faith tells me that it's all in God's plan, but I don't think that will work for you—at this time. God has blessed me with five wonderful children, and I love them all the same. But the first one is always special—or maybe it is just hard to let the first one go. Your father says that I need to 'let you be,' but I just can't. I will always worry about you and keep you in my prayers."

Bob stood up and hugged his mother as she squeezed him tightly.

"Robert, you are so big and tall now. It seems just the other day you would run across my kitchen floor with your dirty boots yelling, 'Mom, can I have one cookie?' And one cookie would be in your hand and three others would go in your pocket. And then 'BANG' you were out the door." She pushed herself back but still held on to his hips. "You are so handsome—just like your father when I first saw him after the War."

Helen Hartman kissed her son on the cheek and then went out on the porch. Bob looked at the pile of dollar bills on the table as he listened to the rhythmic squeak of the swing on the porch. Except for a single calf bawling for its mother in the barn, stillness surrounded him. He went upstairs to his bedroom.

He loaded the things that he would be taking with him into the backpack that he had purchased in town. A light sleeping bag went in the bottom and into a pocket on the side he put his toiletries. Deep in the pack, carefully wrapped, were a few pictures of Jenny and some letters and notes from her. The only book he took was the *Oxford Book of English Verse*. Jenny had left it in his apartment, and although he did not like or understand poetry, someday he might. He put three hundred dollars in cash in an envelope and pushed it to the bottom, and then put his clothes in on top. He had a hundred dollars in his billfold and another hundred would be in his shoe. Woody had said that was where he always kept his extra money when he was in the army. Two side pockets were left empty which he was certain would be filled with food in the morning by his mother.

It was dark as he lay on the bed looking up at the ceiling. He didn't know if he would ever see it again. Although it was the smallest of the upstairs bedrooms, he had always had a room by himself. Joe would probably move in here after he left. He heard the sounds of summer out the open window as the breeze moved the curtains in the soft glow of the yard light. His father's truck pulled into the drive, and he heard the door slam and Roscoe bark twice. He drifted off to sleep.

He woke in the morning with the sound of cattle from the barn. He saw that it was after seven which was later than he usually slept. But it had been a restful sleep—something he had not enjoyed for some time. He dressed, grabbed his backpack, and went down stairs.

"Would you like some breakfast? I packed a couple of things for lunch for you to take."

"No thanks, Mom. I'll just get going." He hated all good-bys and this one in particular.

She sat at the kitchen table with reddened eyes, her hands folded in front of herself. As usual her hair was neatly tied in a bun and her clothes clean and pressed, but she looked tired. On the table were two sacks with the tops closed. As he put them in the pockets of his knapsack his mother stood. From the pocket of her apron she took a book.

"Take this, Robert. Here's your Grandma Clark's Bible. It has the Old and New Testament, but the print is too fine for my eyes to read any more. You may not have any use of it now, but maybe in the future."

The worn Bible had several dollar bills sticking out from its edges. He placed it in one of the side pockets with a sack lunch. He hugged his mother, surprised how small she seemed. She disappeared in his arms as she embraced him. She reached up and kissed him on the cheek.

"Good-by, dear."

Bob walked out the door and toward the barn where he knew his father would be. Instead, his father was leaning on the tailgate of the truck next to the tool shed. He stood smoking a cigarette, a couple of butts already on the ground beside him. Roscoe, lying in the bed of the truck, got up and barked in greeting as Bob approached.

"You ready?" His father asked.

"I can walk to the highway, Dad. It's not far."

"I'll drive you."

"We can wait a few minutes, if you need me to help you with the milking." The cows were bellowing from the barn yard, and Bob knew that they had not been milked this morning.

"They'll be OK."

Sam Hartman and his son drove out of the drive with Roscoe barking in the back. In silence his father looked straight ahead with both hands on the steering wheel saying nothing. There were so many things that Bob wanted to say to his father, but he didn't know where to start. Finally he said, "It looks like it will be warm today."

"Yes, I believe it will. Dew was a little heavy this morning, but it'll dry off fine by the afternoon."

"Are you baling today?"

"Yes. All I have to do is get your brother's butt out of bed, and he can rake that alfalfa that I cut yesterday. We can probably bale a few loads this afternoon." They were at the highway. Stopping the truck, Sam Hartman continued to look straight ahead. Bob could not make himself put his hand on the door handle. Finally, Sam turned to his son.

"There is a Prince Edward can in the glove box. Get it."

Bob took it out and opened the old tobacco can. Inside were tens and fives stuffed together. There must have been a couple of hundred dollars there.

"Dad, I have money. Mom gave me some last night, and I still have some in my savings account."

"Was it from that old coffee can on the top shelf that no one is supposed to know about?" For the first time there was a slight smile on Sam Hartman's face.

"Yes."

"Well, you take that money. A man can always use a little folding money in his pocket. If you don't need it, then send it back. I was going to try and replace that old John Deere in a year or two, but hell." And now there was a nervous laugh. "If I didn't have that old son-of-a bitch to swear at and hit with a hammer, what would I do?"

"Thanks." He stuffed the money in his shirt pocket knowing that to refuse it would be an insult to his father.

Sam Hartman paused and placed his right hand on Bob's shoulder. Bob was bigger than his father now, but that hand seemed to cover his entire shoulder and weigh more than he did.

"You take care, Bobby." The hand squeezed. "I've always been real proud of you and still am. You're a good person. You're honest, and you know how to work. You've been raised right, and if you follow your heart, it'll always tell you what to do—and what is right." There was another squeeze that would have been painful in any other situation.

"You let us know when you get settled somewhere, or if you need something. And don't forget to call your mother. She worries about you."

"I will."

Bob got out, took his backpack from the bed of the truck, and gave a last pat to Roscoe's head.

"You chase those rabbits and leave the skunks alone, you old hound dog."

When he stepped away from the truck, Sam Hartman drove across the highway and up a hill where he turned around and came back. He stopped at the intersection and then drove by Bob down the gravel road. Both hands were on the wheel and he looked straight ahead as he passed. In the back, Roscoe barked and jumped. He was still barking as the truck raised dust on the road on its way back to the farm.

Bob picked up his backpack and walked west, sticking his thumb out to each passing vehicle. He could still feel the weight of his father's hand on his shoulder, and he was swept along in a rush of uncertainty. But each step took him from his past to his future, and each step took away a small amount of hesitancy and uncertainty. The weather was warming. This would be a hot July day. He could smell the fresh cut alfalfa in the field that he walked besides.

"It would take two days to bale the alfalfa in that field—unless you had two balers going at the same time," he thought. "This was a good day to make hay."

A car pulled over on the shoulder ahead of him. Bob ran to it, opened the door, and looked in. The man behind the wheel in a suit and tie leaned over.

"I'm going to the other side of Chicago. Do you need a lift?"

"Yes," and he threw his pack in the back seat.

LaVergne, TN USA
28 January 2010
171408LV00002B/14/P